ALL AT ONCE IT'S YOU

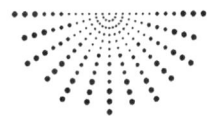

ROSIE CHAPEL

All At Once It's You

Rosie Chapel

First printing 2018
ISBN: 978-0-6482797-0-9 (e-book)
ISBN: 978-0-6488365-7-5 (paperback)

Ulfire Pty. Ltd.
P.O. Box 1481
South Perth
WA 6951
Australia

www.rosiechapel.com

Cover Designed by Lisa Miller with Got You Covered

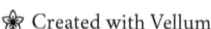 Created with Vellum

For my husband, who is my evermore!

ACKNOWLEDGMENTS

To Amy, Julie, Lilly, and Melody ~ for your friendship,
tolerance, and support ~ I love you!
My abiding gratitude to JL for her editing patience
Sincere appreciation to Graham of A Fading Street
Publishing.
Heartfelt thanks to Lisa for the gorgeous cover.

I recently updated the cover for this book, but remain
forever grateful to Bella Emy, who created the original.

All At Once It's You

CHAPTER ONE

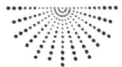

It had been a very long and uncomfortably warm day, to say it was only April. Even now, as the sun began to dip towards the horizon, mirages continued to form and vanish on the hot tarmac. All around her, as far as the eye could see, flowed an unbroken expanse of undulating moorland. Alexandra Mallory squinted against the glare, wondering how much further it was to her destination.

She had been driving for hours and this, supposedly final, section of road felt lonely. She was beginning to think the whole thing was a cruel joke, and the village she was heading for would turn out to be a figment of someone's tormented imagination. *Didn't horror movies start this way?* There was nothing to indicate any habitation. No signposts, no hint of rooftops, not even a sheep.

Pulling onto the grassy verge and switching on her hazard lights, Alex — to her friends — studied the map again. She had a GPS app in her phone, but it was distracting to drive with it yelling instructions at her, and she always struggled to judge given distances. This usually resulted in her turning either too soon or way beyond the intended route.

As far as she could tell, she was where she was supposed to be. Using her thumb to measure the distance, Alex guessed she should be no more than four, probably closer to three miles from the small village of Rosedale Abbey where her new employer lived.

Setting off before dawn that morning, driving up from her home in Boxgrove, a village just outside Chichester, Alex had hoped — breaks permitting, to arrive well before dusk. Unfortunately, a pile up on the motorway had caused traffic to be diverted along slow-moving, country roads.

On any other occasion she would prefer the less hectic route, passing through villages and towns far from the busy arterial roads, but not today. Today it frustrated her, because she was due to begin a new job. A job she did not expect to be interviewed for, never mind awarded, and she didn't want to turn up in the middle of the night.

Deciding she might as well stretch her legs, Alex switched off the ignition, got out of the car and propped herself against the door. At first glance, the landscape in front of her didn't seem much different from where she grew up, but even though the golden light of the late afternoon softened the horizon, there was a wildness about it. The feeling that no matter how long you lived here you would never own it, more it would own you.

Maybe it was the isolation, maybe it was the vast emptiness — whatever it was, Alex was captivated. She drank in the view, inhaled the heady air deep into her lungs, and for a brief moment a sense of reckless abandon seized her, urging her to open her arms wide and spin around.

This was the North Yorkshire Moors!

She had made it.

꙳

Three months earlier, Alex — who had long been a volunteer both for the education workshops and any ongoing archaeological research at Fishbourne Roman Palace — had seen an internal memo requesting expressions of interest for a medium-term contract, assisting an eminent archaeologist with a new book he was writing.

Initially, the contract was for a year, with the possibility to extend by mutual agreement should it prove necessary. The position involved research, knowledge and possible translation of ancient texts, as well as the expected proficiency with computers, online databases, typing skills, and so forth.

Alex had vacillated for a few days, before emailing her best friend, Kassie, to ask whether her husband would be able to shed any light on this Professor Reuben Faulkner, and whether the job was legit. Alex had only a vague recollection of Faulkner's work. An odd journal article here and there, she had come across while studying for her degree. Her area of expertise, if one could call it that, was in a different period, much earlier than Faulkner's but she was conversant with most ancient texts, and Roman history was as much a part of her as breathing.

After uni ended, Kassie had landed an enviable job at one of the International Schools in Rome, and later became a part-time tour guide. It was during one of these tours Kassie had met her future husband Gabriel St Germain, who also happened to be an archaeologist. Alex hoped, correctly as it turned out, Gabriel might know Professor Faulkner.

Kassie's reply stated the professor was renowned for his work on both the Nerva-Antonine and Severan Emperors covering a period from AD96 to AD235, and as far as Gabriel knew, Faulkner's latest research concentrated on Hadrian's reign. Adding her husband had suggested Alex 'go for it' and that he'd put in a good word for her, Kassie's email was enough to persuade Alex it was worth submitting her application.

She heard nothing for several weeks then, out of the blue, received a phone call from the professor himself. They spoke at length, and at the conclusion of their conversation, he had offered her the position. It was a dream job. Alex could not get enough of Roman history and Hadrian was one of her favourite Emperors. She harboured a lingering, and irrational, notion it was too good to be true, but within four days she had received, read, signed, and returned the detailed contract.

Putting in her notice at the mind numbingly, boring admin office where she worked three days a week was easy. Informing the team, she volunteered with at Fishbourne of her plans, less so. She loved working there. Although sorry to see her go — Alex had been assisting at the centre for so long she'd become part of the furniture — they were genuinely pleased for her.

As outlined in the original advert, the contract was for a year. It was 'live in,' and should the professor decide he needed to travel for any reason associated with his research, he would cover all expenses. There was a month's probation, offering a 'get out' clause, within that period, if either felt it wasn't going to work. Alex couldn't foresee that happening, not from her end at least.

Now all her planning was done, she had packed up, rented out her apartment, and said her goodbyes. Suddenly, she was here, on this isolated moor with what seemed like the whole world spread out in front of her.

Walking around to the front of the car so she was off the road, Alex ran her hands through her curly, shoulder length hair, then raised her arms above her head and rolled her neck, trying to ease aching muscles, allowing herself a few more minutes to admire the scenery. About to get back in the car, she heard the hum of an engine. A vehicle seemed to be coming very fast and, not wanting to impede its progress, she perched on the bonnet to wait until it had driven past, before setting off again.

The car, something dark and grey and sleek — Alex had no clue what it was except it appeared to be in stealth mode — shot along the road. Biting off a chuckle at the idea of James Bond driving by, she opened her door, only to see the red brake lights flash on. The car reversed slowly, until level with her. A tinted window slid down and a disembodied voice asked whether she was lost.

"No, thank you for asking. I was just stretching my legs." Unwilling to elaborate Alex presumed that was enough of a dismissal. Apparently not. The door opened and a tall man unfolded himself from behind the steering wheel.

"Where are you headed?"

Alex twisted her lips and contemplated him. He didn't look like an axe murderer, — *did they have a 'look'?'*

"It's okay, I'm not an axe murderer. I live hereabouts and it's easy to take the wrong turn if you're unfamiliar with the area."

Alex felt heat creep up her cheeks, *was he a mind reader too?* "I'm on my way to Rosedale Abbey. I believe it's over there." She flung her arm in what she hoped was the right direction. Her tone was cool, but not unfriendly, and she saw his mouth tighten.

"You are correct. It's a little over three miles. Be careful when you enter the village. There are often children playing, and when the sun is going down, it's harder to see them."

"I assure you, I will take the utmost care. Thank you for your concern. I must be on my way."

They were talking in a very formal manner. He seemed annoyed, yet Alex had no clue why, frowning in puzzlement. She didn't usually rub people up the wrong way; maybe he was naturally grumpy. She felt a smile curve her lips at that, bowing her head so he wouldn't notice, which was a shame, because she completely missed the spark of interest glinting in his eyes.

"Perhaps I'll see you around," Alex threw out, settling herself in the car. "'Bye for now." She turned the ignition, flipped on the lights, and drove smoothly off the grassy hard shoulder onto the tarmac.

The tall man watched her until she was a speck in the distance, his brow furrowed in thought. *Curious. Who on earth was she coming to visit?* Unable to answer his own question, he hopped in the car and sped towards Whitby, where Diana, dinner, and dancing awaited.

CHAPTER TWO

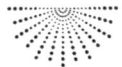

Alex drove cautiously through the little village, the evening light giving it an almost ethereal aura. Her window down, the better to breathe in the spring air, she could hear the sounds of children playing, the drone of an occasional lawnmower and the yip of at least one dog. Restful, familiar sounds, they seemed to welcome her to the neighbourhood. Oddly, it did feel as though she was coming home.

She shoved that absurd idea aside. This area of the country was new to her, so it was impossible to be anything other than mildly interested, or at the very most excited, but home? Nope, that was for dreamers. While true, she hadn't visited these moors; Alex wasn't unfamiliar with the north of England, but the area she knew was much further north. Her face stiffened as memories threatened, so she applied her concentration to finding her destination, before everything she had resolved to block out, reared up.

Grudgingly, she relied on the GPS, hoping it wouldn't direct her down a dirt track into a field, relieved when, a few minutes later, she was following a long, properly graded driveway, lined with silver birch trees. It opened out onto gravelled semi-circle, in front of a sprawling house, although the term 'house' was a misnomer. The place was huge.

Unsure where to park, Alex drew up at the far side of the drive, tucking her car against the hedge. Switching off the engine, she stepped out. Before doing anything else, Alex admired the soft, greyish stone of the building.

White-painted window frames were scattered, seemingly at random, across the façade. Light spilled from some, throwing bright patches over a garden, greying as the day waned. Several chimneys stood proudly from the moss-green, tiled roof, two of which had smoke coiling from them. The scene evoked childhood fairy tales — of cottages nestled in the woods, hiding secrets yet to be discovered; of magic and enchantment.

Shrugging at her fanciful imagination, Alex walked over to the door and grasping the wrought iron knocker, rapped three times.

"Coming!" Called a voice from the depths. Less than thirty seconds later, the door swung open to reveal a tall, shaggy-haired gentleman who, Alex estimated was some-where in his late fifties.

"Ms Mallory?"

"Yes sir... Professor Faulkner? Pleased to meet you." Unsure what to do, Alex put out a hand to shake the professor's, only to squeak with surprise as she was drawn into an avuncular hug. Then he placed a hand on each of her shoulders and studied her in the light from the hallway.

"Welcome to Moorview. I'm so glad you're here, and not looking as tired as I expected. Just seen the news. Traffic's dreadful all the way up the country, and I was wondering whether you were still stuck in one of those jams." His eyes twinkled as his face creased into a genial smile. Alex relaxed.

"It was a bit of a nightmare, but I'm here and it is so beautiful…" she swung her arm out to one side, "…you chose a glorious piece of England in which to live."

"Hah! God's own country this…" he winked. "Come on, come on let's get your luggage, and settle you in. There's a hot meal about ready. I daresay you're starving." He made it a statement, not a question, but Alex nodded anyway.

"I am actually, thank you," she said, as they crunched over the gravel to the car. Alex popped the boot lid and began to hoist her suitcase. Professor Faulkner shooed her out of the way and lifted the case as though it weighed nothing, leaving Alex to bring her overnight bag and handbag. "Is it okay left here, or should I move it?" She asked, preparing to lock the vehicle for the night.

"'It'll be fine here. I doubt my son will be back tonight. He's got a place in town and will probably stay there." The professor's voice had a flat note to it as though he disapproved. Having just met him, Alex wasn't about to question it. Instead, she clicked the remote and followed her new employer into the house.

Several nondescript dogs wagged their way over when she entered a large, brightly lit room — which turned out to be the kitchen — demanding to be petted. Two very regal cats glared at her from their positions of power on top of an old wooden cupboard in one corner. Alex glanced around. The room was furnished with an eclectic mix of modern, and what looked to be antique, fixtures and fittings.

Wedged in a nook — which might once have been a fireplace, now all bricked up — stood an old AGA, being used to store vegetables rather than for cooking. In the middle of the flagged floor, a large, well-scrubbed wooden table — already set for dinner, its six matching chairs, tucked in neatly. Above and beneath the generous number of worktops, all manner of cupboards and units filled the walls. They looked old, but Alex surmised they might well be modern just selected for their aged appearance. A Bristol-style, ceramic sink and double drainer unit was situated under the only window, alongside an impressive oven.

A delicious smell filled the room, and Alex guessed it was the contents of the huge pan bubbling away on the stove. It was one of the cosiest rooms she'd ever seen.

The professor followed her gaze. "It's rather nice isn't it?" He grinned, not giving her any chance to respond to this massive understatement, leading the way through to the opposite side of the room and along, what felt like, a wing of the house. "These will be your rooms. We converted this end of the house into a granny flat, so you've got a decent amount of privacy." He flicked on the light and waved his arm around pointing, "Bedroom, bathroom, and small sitting room."

Alex wandered through the three rooms. The walls of both the bedroom and sitting room were painted in a shade that could only be described as wheat — but pale, just before it ripens. Splashes of colour in the bedding, curtains, and cushions, gave the space a Mediterranean feel. The bathroom was decorated in a creamy hue with pale blue accents; matching towels hung over a heated rack, the colours refreshing but not cold. The whole suite was welcoming and comfortable.

Wheeling her suitcase into the bedroom, Professor Faulkner said he would leave her to get sorted out and to pop along to the kitchen when she was ready.

Thanking him, Alex waited until he had closed the door and stood in the middle of the sitting room, hands pressed to her cheeks, unable to stop a huge grin from splitting her face.

"Oh, my goodness me, Alexandra Mallory," she said to herself. "This job is going to be *awesome!*"

An hour later they were tidying up after a tasty stew with jacket potatoes. The view from the kitchen sink was remarkable. Alex asked whether the property bordered the countryside, because the grounds seemed extensive.

"There are houses either side, but they're not too close, and there's nothing behind, except the moors," the professor explained. "It's quiet here most of the time, except when the owls begin their nightly calls, or first thing in the morning with the dawn chorus. There's none of those urban sounds you're probably used to, but sometimes the silence here can be just as deafening." He paused then asked. "Cup of tea? Coffee? Hot chocolate?"

"Would you be offended if I said hot water?" Alex blushed a little, knowing her choice of hot beverage was odd. "Only, I don't sleep well if I drink anything else at night," she felt compelled to elaborate. The professor grinned and said he'd heard worse, pouring her a large mug of hot water while brewing himself a cup of tea, which looked strong enough to pull a hay cart.

Alex was about to say goodnight, presuming she would spend her evenings in her rooms, when her employer asked whether she would like to join him in the lounge. Accepting, shyly, she accompanied him through to a long room, which despite its low, open beamed ceiling was surprisingly airy.

A fire burned merrily in the grate, circled by a sofa and two large armchairs — a coffee table covered with newspapers, between them and the hearth. The alcoves at either side of the fireplace had been turned into bookshelves, and a quick glance told Alex one side was leisure, the other side, research. She recognised many of the tomes, and the history nerd in her wanted nothing more than to spend hours browsing through them.

Politeness reasserted itself, and she sat in one of the

chairs at the professor's invitation, sinking into its cushioned comfort. A small sigh escaped her lips.

"Is everything okay?" Professor Faulkner asked, mildly concerned he'd forgotten to tell her something important.

"I'm sorry, yes everything's fine. That was a happy sigh. I can't remember the last time I felt so relaxed." Then remembering where she was, and in whose company, she shot upright. "Oh dear, sorry, here I am barely arrived, and already lolling about like I've been here forever." She couldn't seem to stop apologising and bent her head, hot colour rising up her cheeks. An habitual introvert, Alex never pushed herself forward. She had learnt learned long ago it wasn't worth it. To hide in the shadows was easier, safer.

The professor chuckled. "Fret not," he said. "I'd like you to treat this as your home while you are working here. I won't always be around at regular mealtimes, so I expect you to help yourself…" they began to chat about the daily schedule, her work hours, breaks and so on.

Occasionally, it might prove necessary to go into the university at York, if so, they would make a full day of it and plan everything else accordingly. Reuben showed Alex his office. A larger than standard sized room, containing two desks and three tables, all piled with books and manuscripts and facsimiles of ancient text. The walls were open stone, decorated with tapestries, illuminated manuscripts — not originals, Alex assumed — and images of Roman ruins. It was all she could do not to dive right in.

She tried to contain her excitement, turning to her employer, beaming in delight.

"Professor, this is… I am… never could I have…" she faltered, the words catching at the back of her throat. She took a breath. "Thank you, sir, for this opportunity. You have no idea."

"Please, call me Reuben," he grinned. "Sir or Professor

makes me sound like one of the crusty old academics who taught me. I'd like to think I have a few years to go before I am quite that aged."

Alex laughed, and blushing... again, said she would be happy to. They went back to the lounge, finished their drinks. Alex was dropping off in her chair, the long day's drive catching up with her. When Reuben suggested she have an early night, she couldn't summon up a single argument to the contrary.

CHAPTER THREE

Grateful for his understanding, Alex walked along to her rooms, barely managing to use the bathroom before falling asleep, not stirring until the aforementioned dawn chorus jolted her awake around 5 a.m. Daylight was breaking. She had forgotten to close the curtains the previous night, and the soft pink sky begged to be admired from outside.

With a hasty wash and throwing on the same clothes worn the previous day, Alex unlatched the French doors in the sitting room and crept out. Standing on the patio, sniffing the cool air, she lifted her arms above her head, and arched her back, trying to loosen the kinks lurking from long hours spent in the car.

A wet nose snuffled her palm when she dropped her arms to her sides and, glancing down, Alex saw the four dogs milling around her ankles. She could not decide what their breeds were — if, in fact, they were a particular breed — they all looked rather mutt-like to her. Crouching down she patted them, and they wriggled against her, each trying to get as close as possible, making her laugh.

"Do you usually go for a walk at this time of day?" she asked them. They tilted their heads, staring at her seriously, mouths open, tails wagging, and panting slightly. Unwilling to take them out onto the moors without leashes, Alex walked around to the back door, which was ajar.

"Hello," she called quietly. No answer, but checking around the utility room, she spotted four dog leads hanging on a large hook. Clipping them on, and making sure she held them securely, she followed the way the dogs led, down the garden, through a wicket gate, and out onto a track.

The track climbed steadily for a few minutes, and when they reached the top, Alex came to a halt, spellbound. Spread out in front of her were miles and miles of gently rolling moor, green at the moment, from spring rains.

Rosedale Abbey nestled in a dip created by centuries of farming, and the mining of magnetic ironstone from the 1850's onwards. Taking the time to read up on the area, once she got the job, Alex discovered it had been inhabited continuously, for at least ten thousand years, and was amused to learn there was no rose and no abbey. Historians surmised that 'Rosedale' was probably of Viking origin, possibly from 'rhos' which meant moor, and 'Abbey' related to the remains of a Cistercian priory — inhabited by nuns rather than monks — which stood for about four hundred years from the late twelfth century until Henry VIII's Dissolution of the Monasteries in 1535.

From the peoples of Mesolithic, Neolithic, and Bronze Age, through the Brigantes, Romans, Angles, Saxons, and Jutes, to the Vikings, this land had seen them all come and go. Centuries of farming followed, until the advent of the Industrial Age, during which the area was mined. Now, a hundred and fifty years later, tourism brought most of the income to the village.

What a place to research history.

Alex walked for about an hour, returning to the house feeling invigorated, and hoping she would be able to do the same every morning. Ensuring the wicket was latched securely, she unclipped the dogs, wiped their feet on a towel, which seemed suited to the purpose, and let them into the warmth of the kitchen. She headed to her end of the house, leaving her wet shoes on the doormat. Indulging in a quick shower, she was pleased to note the heat from the water, on top of the walk, loosened the last of her tight muscles.

Aware she wouldn't be required to dress in a suit, Alex dithered over the appropriate attire of a research assistant. Eventually, she chose a pair of dark green chinos, a sage green, long sleeved T, and hip-length chunky-knit cardigan. It was cool at the moment but if the day was going to be anything like yesterday it was unlikely to stay that way.

Making her way to the kitchen, Alex pottered about, boiling the kettle, and hunting out what seemed likely prospects for breakfast. Then, she did what she most desired the previous evening — went into the lounge and made a beeline for the books.

When Reuben stuck his head around the door, half an hour or so later, she was far away in the first century AD, a book on Vespasian's rule catching her eye. It took her employer two attempts to attract her attention, waving off her stammered apologies.

"I'm always pleased when those books come off the shelves. While I'm in the middle of a new project, any I'm not using tend to get neglected," he chuckled. Replacing the one she was reading in its allocated spot, Alex joined Reuben in the kitchen where they chatted over breakfast. Alex explained she had taken the dogs for a walk, hoping he didn't mind.

"I found their leashes and didn't let them off. It was perfect, just the dogs and me. Not another soul to be seen."

"They will go for as many walks as people will take them, and they'll love you forever," Reuben assured, as the oldest one came to loll against Alex's leg while she was eating. Alex ruffled his fur. "That's Ben, he's just registering his interest aren't you, mate?" Ben fixed his huge dark eyes on the woman whom he was *positive* would fall for his doggy charms.

"Patience, Ben," she grinned. "At least give me chance to eat some of it." Ben's tail swished on the stone flags and he settled on the floor by her feet. The other three — Pip, Coco, and Gus, as introduced by Reuben — formed an orderly and ever hopeful queue behind Ben, determined not to miss out.

Once the kitchen had been set to rights, the dishwasher stacked, each of the four, not-so-patient, dogs given a tasty treat, and after Alex had finished getting ready for the day, she made her way along to the office. Reuben was already seated at one of the desks but stood to clarify what he wanted Alex to get started on.

When Alex asked, Reuben assured her, he didn't mind if she listened to music through headphones, as long as the work was done. Flicking her iPod to her favourite mix of tunes, Alex was soon absorbed in her task. Neither of them heard a car pull up, the front door slam, or the heavy footfall along the stone passage.

The door swung open.

A tall, dark-haired man came in, his eyes scanning the room. Reuben spotted him and stood, a welcoming smile warming his face. The visitor stared at the young woman seated at the opposite side, her back to him. She looked familiar somehow, but he couldn't place her.

Alex remained unaware of his scrutiny. Her hand — unconsciously swaying with the music in her head — twirled a pencil, as she concentrated.

"Jake, you're home early. Did you have a good evening?" Reuben interrupted his son's contemplation.

"Thanks, I did. Who's this now?" Jake frowned in Alex's general direction.

"This is Alex Mallory. I told you I was hiring an assistant. Don't you ever listen?"

"Of course, I listen, but you said… ahhhh, right… I get it."

"What are you blithering about, son?" Reuben looked confused; his mind already drifting back to the documents he'd been reading.

"Yeah, you told me an Alex was coming. I assumed it was a man." Jake's tones were irritated.

"Still hung up on this, Jake? She was the best applicant, what was I supposed to do? Reject her, in the hopes a bloke might eventually apply for the position, all because of what happened last time. I haven't had one single male apply, and I can't keep waiting. I have deadlines. Don't worry about me, Alex isn't like that."

"And how the hell could you possibly know that, Dad? She must have been here less than twenty-four hours, since you were alone when I left yesterday afternoon." The image of a tired young woman, perched on the bonnet of a car, at the edge of the moor flitted into his mind.

His gaze swung back to Alex, his brow creasing again. Almost as though she heard his thoughts, Alex turned her head and he was presented with the most ridiculous visage.

In the process of deciphering some text, she was wearing magnifying glasses in order to read the characters more easily. They made her eyes bug out and seem enormous, totally hiding the rest of her face, and in spite of his annoyance, Jake couldn't help himself. He burst out laughing.

Immersed in history and classical music, something prompted Alex to glance over her shoulder towards the door. The magnifying glasses made anything beyond about three inches in front of her extremely blurry, but she was pretty sure there was an extra person in the room. Then she heard a bark of laughter and, puzzled, removed the glasses, blinking as her eyes adjusted.

She felt her jaw drop. *It was him. The grumpy driver from the previous afternoon. What was he doing here? One of Reuben's colleagues perhaps?* She wasn't really sure what to do, but felt it polite, at the very least, to close her mouth and introduce herself. Taking the tiny buds out of her ears, Alex pushed back her chair and stood. He was laughing. Maybe he wasn't grumpy after all. Smiling, in what she hoped was a confident manner, she walked over to him, holding out her hand.

"Hello, I'm Alexandra Mallory, Reu... Professor Faulkner's very new assistant."

Abruptly, his laughter ceased. He ignored her outstretched hand, and his eyes bored into her, his expression becoming grim. Alex was nonplussed, wondering what she'd done to cause such displeasure. Her smile died, her hand fell awkwardly to her side, and heat washed up her cheeks.

"Well... err... pleased to meet you... whoever you are," this last muttered under her breath. Apparently unconcerned, Alex turned on her heel, and went back to her desk. Ramming her earbuds in, she shoved the glasses back on her nose and focussed on the facsimile in front of her. Careful observation might have spotted a tremor in the hand holding the pencil. She didn't want to lose this job.

. . .

"Jake," Reuben ground out in fierce undertones. "What is *wrong* with you? That was plain rude."

"You don't need an assistant, Dad, I could do what she's doing." Jake flicked his hand towards Alex. "All those hours on digs must count for something."

"When? When could you? And since when have you ever wanted to? You're an engineer, not a historian. How could you possibly put in the hours I need, to get this book finished by the due date? I can't hang around all day, hoping you might fit me in for a few paltry hours to go through texts and search databases. I need the information as I'm writing, not two weeks later."

It was the same old argument. Jake wanted to help his father, but his job often took him away for days, sometimes months, on end. He loved history, almost as much as Reuben did, but knew his limitations and, in all honesty, spending all day every day researching, would drive him batty. Regrettably, the last assistant hadn't worked out so well and Jake, who did not want a repeat, was inclined to be over-protective.

To be fair, this Alex person looked less of a problem. For a start she appeared to be working, rather than trolling through social media pages, or taking selfies, which was all the last assistant, Tricia, seemed capable of. It was difficult getting anyone to come out here.

Rosedale Abbey was miles from anywhere and most young people preferred the, relatively, lively centres of Whitby, Scarborough, or York to a sleepy little village. Tricia, her admirable computer skills aside, was one such person. The idea of working for an academic far more interesting on paper than in actuality.

There was also another reason her employment had to be terminated, but neither Reuben nor Jake was about the dredge that up. Jake's comments were enough.

Jake, unwilling to admit he was out of order, said only, "I'm going to pack a few things, I have to be in Manchester 'til the end of the week. Meetings," when Reuben raised a quizzical brow, "be careful Dad, that's all I ask."

Reuben smiled. "Don't you worry about me son, Alex will work out just fine, you'll see." Abstractedly, he patted Jake on the arm, a new train of thought distracting him, and he moseyed back to his desk, fingers soon flying across the keyboard.

Jake grinned, used to his father's absent-minded ways, and was about to leave when movement caught his eye. Alex stood to stretch across the desk, reaching for a book, her slender fingers scrabbling to catch the corner. He was about to step over to help, when she grasped it. She pulled it towards her, opening the cover, her face lighting up in a smile of delight. Fascinated, by what seemed almost a ritual, he watched her lifted the old volume to her nose and inhale, stroking the page when she set it down. *Maybe she would work out after all.*

Shaking his head to rid it of the image, Jake walked out, letting the door swing quietly closed behind him.

CHAPTER FOUR

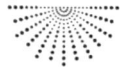

Alex soon forgot the unsettling interruption, the rest of the day — the rest of the week for that matter, passing uneventfully. Every morning, she got up with the dawn, walked the dogs over the moor, and worked hard, often repeating her walk in the evening, and slept like a log.

The combination of fresh air, hours of concentration, and the silence that descended after dark, served to make Alex feel more content than for as long as she could recall.

Reuben tried to apologise for Jake's behaviour, after clarifying who he was, but Alex waved it aside. She assured the professor it was nothing, the man was entitled to his opinion, and it was nice his son was so concerned about his father. Reuben thought he detected a flicker of something — was it hurt, wariness? — in Alex's face when she said this, but it was gone before he was certain. He let it go, but made a mental note to suggest to Jake, he apologise next time he came home.

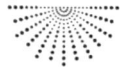

Her first week slid into the second and in the blink of an eye, Alex realised she had been at Moorview a month. Reuben and she worked well together, the project progressing steadily. A methodical person, Alex perused everything Reuben had already collated, to get a feel for how he liked to organise his research.

It wasn't long before she developed a knack for knowing exactly what type of material he needed, whether it be inscriptions, ancient texts, journal articles, or reference books. The office began to resemble a rare volume book-shop. Old tomes and papers scattered on every available surface, including the floor.

One morning, Reuben suggested a trip into York. He had a meeting with one of his former colleagues at the university and would take the opportunity to pop into the library. Preferring physical books to reading online, Alex was more than willing and offered to drive, as long as Reuben directed her once in York. She had a dread of one-way systems and navigating through unfamiliar towns.

Her tales of misadventures in such endeavours had Reuben in stitches most of the way into the city, and before Alex had a chance to get flustered, they were parking in one of the visitors' bays. Escorting Alex into the history section of the library, he told her to 'go for her life' and he'd find her when he was done.

On his return, he found Alex virtually buried under a great pile of books, making copious notes, her hand flying across the pages. He watched her for a moment, amused she was taking handwritten notes, not typing onto a laptop or tablet. Reuben wasn't particularly surprised with her, what would be considered, old-fashioned approach.

He had come to realise, during this last month, Alexandra Mallory wasn't a typical young woman. She seemed to favour the simple things in life, not all the gadgets and technology her contemporaries loved so much and usually relied on. Yes, she was competent on the computer, accessing databases, doing research, and typing up his notes — but almost everything else she did 'longhand.'

Reuben found this refreshing. Plus, she was cheerful, funny, unobtrusive, and clearly adored her new surroundings, for which he was eternally grateful. If she were to leave, it wouldn't be because she was bored out of her skull.

Alex had lost all track of time, browsing through the legion of books she pulled off the shelves, praying no one came to ask what she was doing with so many. In one, she had come across a thread, which she was trying to track to its origin, or at least to a point where she could then trace an inscription or ancient text. Her notebook was filling rapidly; references, authors, sources, as well as her own theories. It was exhilarating and much as she had loved working at Fishbourne, this — hunting down tiny pockets of information — this was her passion.

A subtle cough brought her back to the brightly lit, modern library, and she noticed Reuben standing near the table she had commandeered.

"Oh, grief, how long have you been waiting for me? I'm so sorry." She began to stack the books ready to return them to their rightful place.

"Don't panic, Alex," Reuben chuckled. "I was about to suggest lunch, but I don't want to drag you away if you're in the middle of something."

Alex bit her lip, dubiously. It might take another hour to jot down the rest of what she had unearthed but had no desire to make her employer late if he had another appointment to get to.

Reuben guessed something of her thoughts. She wasn't

very good at hiding them. "Tell you what, how about you carry on here. I'll see whether there's somewhere I can grab a couple of sandwiches. Then we'll find a nice spot by the river to eat them. Will that give you enough time?"

Alex didn't think so, but it was better than nothing, and she already had a lot to work with. "That would be great, if you don't mind. It'll probably take me half an hour..." she let that dangle as Reuben grinned.

"Okay, I'll be back shortly, coffee or cold drink?"

"Ohhh, if they have iced tea, that would be lovely. If not, water please."

Reuben nodded and was gone, leaving Alex to work as fast as she could, to collate as much as possible. Within seconds of his departure, a staff member appeared at Alex's elbow, indicating she could use the professor's log in code if she wanted to scan or print anything.

Sighing with relief, Alex scuttled over to the bank of copiers. Thankfully, they were the same model as the ones she used when at uni, and she scanned the remaining articles and references onto a thumb drive. She was replacing the last few books on their respective shelves... it didn't seem fair to dump them on the trolley... when Reuben strolled over, a bag full of goodies in one hand, a steaming hot coffee in the other.

"I can't drink the swill my colleague serves," he explained. "I need a proper cup of coffee."

"I understand completely," Alex grinned. "At my last job they only had instant... ugh." Screwing up her face in recollection. The pair walked back to the car discussing the merits of fresh beans over ready ground, and single origin over blends.

Reuben directed Alex through a maze of back roads and soon they were by the river, on the outskirts of the city.

Pointing down a long lane, Reuben said there was a carpark at the end and a few picnic benches.

It was a warm day; the sun was shining and the sky an almost cloudless blue. Alex parked the car, and they chose a bench a little way along the footpath. Conversation dwindled while they munched on the egg salad rolls.

The only sounds the muted quacking of several ducks foraging in the reeds, even the birds had fallen quiet. Sipping her iced tea, Alex tilted her body backwards slightly to stare at the sky through a leafy canopy of birch trees.

"So, Alexandra Mallory, are you settling in?" Reuben broke into her reverie.

She twisted slightly so she was facing him, then looked out over the river, the mottled light making interesting patterns on the water, mulling over his question. *Was she settling in?* She believed so, but was she doing what he wanted? *Was her work up to standard?*

Although eminently competent at both her previous job and Fishbourne, Alex had endured years of being told she was neither use nor ornament, making it hard to gauge what people expected of her.

Reuben noticed several emotions flit over her face and wondered what prompted them. He frowned, hoping she wasn't going to tell him this job wasn't for her. He didn't think he'd misread her.

"I think so," Alex started, her voice hesitant. "I love the work, I love the village, the moors, your dogs, my room, and you are so easy to work for. Oh, sorry… that's not to say… rather I meant…oh dammit…" hot colour flooded her cheeks. *Way to be too familiar Alex*, she chided herself.

Reuben laughed "Alex, stop panicking, there's nothing

wrong with being honest. I'd rather be an easy-going employer than a hard-headed stickler, always cracking the whip. I only asked because we've reached the end of the probation period. I'm pleased with your work ethic, but don't want you to feel obliged to stay on, if you feel it's too isolated or the job not what you expected.

Alex grinned, in relief. "So, my terrible taste in music hasn't had a detrimental impact then...?" alluding the odd occasion when Reuben had been privy to her penchant for soundtracks from musicals, or tunes from the 80s.

"Hahaha, even taking that into account. I think we muddle along well together. You seem to anticipate what I require with respect to my project and use your initiative more than any assistant I've employed to date. On their own, those two would be enough to sway the vote, plus my dogs love you — a sure sign you're up to par." He shoved Alex in the shoulder, "So whaddya say? You in it for the long haul?" His engaging banter made her laugh along with him, and she held out her hand.

"Absolutely." They shook on the deal.

Scrunching up the paper in which the sandwiches had been wrapped, they threw their rubbish in the bin at the edge of the path and sauntered back to the car. The drive home was comfortable, they chatted about nothing in particular, although, as ever, the conversation veered towards their favourite topic. Ancient Rome.

By the time they got out of the car at Moorview, they were embroiled in a lively debate over whether Domitian was really as bad as he was portrayed, or whether he was simply a victim of circumstance. His rule maligned by sparse surviving source material, with even less evidence to counter such assertions.

For Reuben, these discussions were a chance to see whether Alex could argue both sides of an issue, impressed with how much knowledge she had retained from her studies. The subject wasn't new, it was one historians visited with regularity, but it was fun. They were so involved, neither noticed a tall shadow propping up the doorjamb.

"Afternoon, Dad." A deep voice spoke, making Alex squawk with shock, as the shadow detached itself. It was so long since she had seen Jake, she'd almost forgotten his existence.

He had been home a handful of times since her first morning, but behaved as though she wasn't there, so she avoided him. If he spoke at all, it was in a brusque manner, and any eye contact felt like a tacit rebuke. It was uncomfortable, but she shrugged it off. Unfortunately, his attitude made her feel like an interloper — rather awkward when she got on so well with his father.

Greeting his father, Jake ignored Alex.

"Excuse me, Professor," she said quietly. "I'll pop the kettle on, then type up this morning's notes." She tried to slide past Jake, but he refused to budge forcing her to look him in the eye, pretending not to be affected by the mistrust in his expression. She lifted her palms in appeal. "Sir."

The corner of his mouth lifted in what could almost be described as a smile and, after a long moment during which he pinned her with his gaze, stood aside.

Alex shot through the door and along to the kitchen. "What have I done to rattle his cage now, I wonder?" She enquired of Pip, the smallest of the dogs, a creamy wire-haired terrier cross, who despite her diminutive stature ruled the others with an iron paw. Pip waddled over for a tickle but did not deign to answer. "Just by breathing, I guess. Ah well, nothing I can do about old grumpy pants. I've no time for his nonsense."

She pottered about the kitchen, grabbing two cups, and a tea bag for Reuben. *Ought she to make one for Jake too? Grrr,* she groused inwardly, retracing her steps to where father and son were still talking.

Hovering, she waited until there was a break in conversation. "Sorry to interrupt. Mr Faulkner, would you like a tea or a coffee?" Alexandra asked, politely, her tones bland.

"Coffee. Black no sugar," Jake said carelessly, hardly acknowledging her. Alex stomped back to the kitchen, muttering under her breath indignantly, *black coffee — that figures — black like his soul. What was it with him? Was it her or was he born rude?* She slammed drawers and banged storage jars, then slopped boiling water over the teabag in one of the three cups, deciding not to fill her own, while waiting for the coffee to brew in the stove top percolator.

She stood, palms down on the table, arms outstretched, and head bent, taking deep breaths. She was angry. It was years since she had allowed herself to be angry. Extremes of emotion were frowned upon when she was growing up, and she learnt it was better to appear calm and unflappable than let your temper fly. She had forgotten how good it felt to vent, but she needed to walk it off or she might say something she would regret.

CHAPTER FIVE

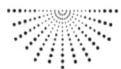

Pouring the coffee, Alex placed it, and Reuben's tea, on a tray along with a plate of biscuits, leaving her own cup on the bench. Going through to the lounge, she set the tray on the table in front of the fire and went back to the front door.

"Drinks are in the lounge. Please excuse me, I need a break. I'll take the dogs." Without waiting for comment or permission, Alex headed to her room, changed into more sensible footwear, gathered the dogs, and marched out of the gate onto the moor.

She stayed out long enough that the fresh air and beautiful scenery soothed her frayed nerves. Alex knew her anger was irrational, but she also knew it was rare she rubbed anyone up the wrong way. She didn't think she had enough personality to warrant so strong a reaction.

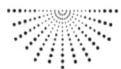

The afternoon was coming to a close when Alex returned. Before going to the office, she indulged in a long hot shower, hoping this would wash away any residual irritation. By the time she was seated at her desk, typing up her pages of notes, her temper had subsided.

She didn't stop working until Reuben called her for dinner, and even then, it was with reluctance. Fascinated by some of the information she had uncovered, Alex was loath to leave it. Resolving to do some more after the meal, she minimised her tabs and put her computer on sleep mode.

To her chagrin — although where else would he be? — Jake was in the kitchen. *Yay.*

Alex offered to help Reuben, who said it was all done and to take a seat. She was about to sit in her usual spot when Jake, all but shoving her out of the way, got there first. Flushing, Alex took the chair at the opposite end of the table, as far from him as she was able, the atmosphere becoming strained.

Aware Jake was the cause, Reuben did his best to lighten the tension, but it was a struggle. Alex tried, but couldn't find it in her to be cheerful, she felt out of place, and began to question whether she should stay. She didn't want to be the cause of friction between father and son, it wasn't fair to Reuben.

At the end of the meal, she said she would be in the office if needed.

"Not coming to pick on the crappy movie they're showing tonight?" Reuben grinned. They had taken to watching whatever movie, rubbish or otherwise the local TV channel aired. Alex's only proviso was she wouldn't watch horror. It was a fun way to wind down after a day of concentrated effort and they liked to best each other by guessing what else the actors had appeared in.

"I think I'll pass, tonight. I really want to get those notes typed up, I doubt I'll sleep until they're done, too interesting and there's several threads which keep pestering." Almost certain she heard 'suck up' from Jake's direction, Alex now totally fed up, shot him an icy glare. "Bless you, sir, I hope you're not coming down with a cold." She pushed back her chair and stood, her gaze swinging back to Reuben. "Anyway, gives you an evening with Jake, it'll make a nice change. You did say he seldom comes home." On that barbed comment, she walked out, head held high.

Reuben, swallowing a bark of laughter at Alex's jab, turned on his son. "Okay, I've had enough of this Jake. What is your problem? Alex has been here a month. Today I informed her the probation period was over and, if she's happy, I want her to stay. Don't ruin it with your prejudices and your childish nonsense. Put yourself in her shoes for five bloody minutes and see how you would feel if someone treated you the way you treat Alex. What has she ever done to deserve it?"

Jake had the grace to flush. "Sorry, Dad. I can't seem to help it. There's something about her. I can't put my finger on it. She's not secretive exactly, but..." he paused. *Why did she bother him?* It lurked the fringes of his mind, but he couldn't pinpoint it. Shrugging, all he said was, "...it's like she's hiding something.

"Don't be an idiot. You haven't known her long enough to pass such facile judgements. That's just so you can feel better about being a grump. She works hard, and under normal circumstances is a bright, friendly young woman, who just happens to love history. Give her a break," Reuben scoffed, his son's attitude towards Alex frustrating him. "If she quits because of you, I'll... I'll... well, trust me you'll suffer the consequences."

"Dad! I've said I'm sorry." Jake was becoming annoyed now.

"Well maybe it's not me you should be apologising to." Reuben got up from the table, and banged around, putting pans in the sink to soak and slotting the plates into the dish-washer. "You're nearly thirty-five, for God's sake, act it."

They continued in this vein for several more minutes, neither remembering to keep their voices down and neither realising the door was ajar. It was unusual for Reuben to get upset, and Jake knew he was being petty, but he could not, for the life of him, explain what it was about Alex. She got under his skin, and she was an irritation he didn't need. Not after Tricia.

"I'll go eat humble pie," Jake assured his father.

He turned to go to the office.

Alex coming into the kitchen stopped him.

She was pale and asked whether she might have a word with Reuben in private. Reuben flicked a loaded glance at his son.

"Of course, Alex, is everything okay?" he said solicitously, ushering her over to the sink, not fully out of Jake's hearing, but far enough.

"Reuben, I've been think—"

"Don't you dare say it."

Her eyes widened in surprise. "What?"

"That if your presence is going to cause arguments between my son and I, you should resign."

Alex gaped. "How on earth did you know that's what I was going to say?"

"Because, you may have only been here a month, but I can read you like those books you bury yourself in."

Alex held his gaze. "I don't want to be a point of contention. Not again." The last two words spoken so quietly Reuben had to strain to hear them. He frowned.

"What do you mean 'not again'?"

She shook her head. "It doesn't matter, suffice it to say, if my being here is an issue I'd rather leave now before…" She swallowed the rest of her sentence, unwilling to admit how hard it would be to leave this place, which felt like home.

For the first time in her life, Alex felt welcome and appreciated, but she absolutely would not stay if she came between Reuben and his son.

"Anyway," she instilled a bright note into her voice, "have a think, it won't take me long to pack." Straightening her shoulders, she was gone, back to the study before either of them could stop her.

She missed the look Reuben shared with Jake, both were puzzled, and one felt like a heel.

"Now look what you've done," Reuben hissed, this time keeping his voice lowered. "Fix it."

"What did she say?" Jake demanded.

Reuben gave his son the gist, adding, "...she said, 'not again' when she mentioned being a point of contention. There was something..." he didn't finish, ruminating over Alex's words and her expression. "I don't know Jake, be careful. Apologise and, for once, sound as though you mean it."

Jake inclined his head and made his way to the office. He paused for a moment in the doorway watching Alex while she worked. Earbuds in, and fingers flying across the keys, she was absorbed in her task, occasionally glancing at the papers sitting next to the computer and shuffling one out of the way when she had finished with it.

Jake found himself studying her. She was probably of average height, with — he supposed it would be described as — dark blonde hair, shoulder length and curly. Her skin was clear, and even in the soft light he could discern a smattering of freckles over pale cheeks. Oddly, he couldn't remember the colour of her eyes — but who cared? Not him. He shrugged slightly and stepped right into the room.

Her back to the door, Alex was unaware of Jake's approach until he reached the other side of her desk. A shadow fell across the computer, and she raised her head, a ready smile tilting her lips, which faded when she saw who it was. Schooling her features, she waited, refusing to speak first.

When her smile dropped, Jake was unnerved by a corresponding drop in his stomach; at the same time registering her eyes were the most incredible shade of brown, like wells of dark chocolate. *Hell, Jake get a grip, apologise, and leave.*

"Miss Mallory, I'm sorry to disturb you but I wish to apologise for my behaviour."

She waited for him to continue, no hint as to how she felt.

With a resigned huff, Jake decided to come clean. "The last couple of assistants caused problems. They weren't conversant with history, and although one of them was more capable than the other on the admin side they never seemed to grasp what Dad needed. There was also the issue of them both assuming this is a glamorous job, lots of overseas travel to ancient sites, rather than the office-based position it actually is. That my father is well known in the academic world was an added benefit. The final straw was both thought him a catch and did everything they could think of to hook him."

Alex goggled — there was no other word for it — at Jake during this little speech. She started to stutter something, then thought better of it, letting him finish.

"Anyway, he told me he'd hired someone called Alex and I assumed it was a bloke. Then you arrived, and you're... well, you're..." he stopped, confused as to where his own words were taking him. "Well, you're not a bloke, clearly. It seems as though you know your way around ancient material, and

Dad tells me you can translate texts and inscriptions. That's a first for any of his assistants," he grinned wryly, detecting a slight softening in her expression.

"At the end of the day, Dad is really pleased, but I was worried you were like the others, and over-reacted. Forgive me?"

Alex eased back in her chair, trying to get her head around what he was saying about her predecessors. She was floored anyone would apply for a job as a way to grab a husband, or at the very least a meal ticket. She understood Jake's concerns and it showed he cared for his father.

By now Jake was perched on the edge of the desk, seemingly more comfortable now he'd got that off his chest.

While Jake explained, Alex found herself admiring his physique. Even sitting, he looked exceptionally tall. Well over 6 feet she reckoned. Mind you she was lucky to scrape 5' 3" so most people were tall compared with her. His height didn't translate into bulk though — he was sparer, maybe a little lanky, a trait Alex discovered to be unexpectedly attractive.

Slightly longer than the current trend, his hair was dark, not quite black and she noticed a thread or two of grey at his temples, prompting her to wonder how old he was. His facial features were angular; a straight nose and *would that be called a chiselled jaw?* she mused, not really knowing enough about men to describe them adequately. His eyes were grey and, although until about five minutes ago they had resembled cold steel, now they were warm, like slate.

Was he handsome? She couldn't decide. Tilting her head, Alex pondered this. No not handsome, not in the classic sense. He was too austere for that, but there was something, something underneath his confident and way too charismatic façade. Something that appealed to her. Appalled by her train of thought, Alex dragged her attention back to the conversation at hand.

The room was silent. Jake had finished speaking and was watching her quizzically.

Dammit, had she been so caught up in daydreaming, she'd missed something significant?

CHAPTER SIX

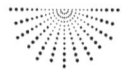

"Sorry, I was listening and yes, I get it. I suppose I would react the same way if I thought someone I loved was being manipulated." Alex was relieved when her reply seemed to satisfy him.

"Jake, whether you believe me or not, I had no real idea who your father was when I applied for this job. I am far more familiar with Roman history circa first century or so AD, than I am with the era your father is expert in. I only had the vaguest notion of who he is. I had to check with my friend to see whether her husband knew anything about Reuben and whether it was prudent to apply for the position." She smiled sheepishly. "When Gabe said it was leg—"

"Hang on, you don't by any chance mean Gabe St Germain?" Jake interrupted.

Alex nodded. "Kassie's my best friend, we grew up together. I met Gabe at their wedding last year. I was lucky enough to do a couple of lectures for the tour they took to Hadrian's Wall over the Easter holidays," she said, referring to a series of intensive university courses recently introduced by Professor St Germain and his wife, each of which were conducted on an ancient site somewhere around the world.

"It was amazing. Anyway, Gabe told me Reuben was on the up and up, so I took a chance. I love it here. I love the peace and the moors and the work, and your dad is such a gentleman. I don't want to leave but I'll be gone in a heart-beat if my presence is going to cause problems." She wound up, rubbing her forehead distractedly. *Had she persuaded him she was capable and more importantly, that she didn't fancy his dad?* Alex couldn't be sure, but she'd run out of explanations. It was up to him.

It was Alex's face when she talked about her love of the area, which banished the last of Jake's scepticism, that and the fact Gabe St Germain knew her. Gabe and Jake had been friends since their uni days and, occasionally, Gabe worked with Reuben. Jake knew his friend would not have recommended Alex apply for the job if he didn't think her eminently suitable, trustworthy, and discreet.

"How about we start again."

Alex looked confused, when he stood and held out his hand.

"Good evening, Miss Mallory. I'm Jake Faulkner, and I'm pleased to meet you."

In quick understanding, she grinned, and pushing back her chair, stood also. "Good evening, Mr Faulkner. I'm Alexandra Mallory, and the feeling is mutual." The shook hands, and a frisson of something indefinable snaked up Alex's arm. She glanced up at Jake, startled. He smiled, but his eyes gave nothing away, so presuming it was in her imag-ination, she ignored it.

But Jake had felt it — it had sparked up his arm like the sting of static. He nearly snatched his hand away, except he rather liked the feel of her slender fingers in his. *No, Jake, don't even... you have Diana.* Deliberately shoving it aside, he resumed his perch, and asked Alex a few pertinent questions. The pair chatted about Reuben's project, discovering how much they had in common, at least where history was concerned.

⚓

At some point, Reuben appeared with a tray of hot drinks and a dish of chocolates, and joined in. Each of the three brought a different perspective to the table. Before long, their conversation became a serious discussion, as they tried to come up with a solution for one or two pieces of source material, which were niggling at Reuben. Alex took notes here and there as warranted, marking things to look up the following day.

It was well after midnight when they said goodnight, but as Alex crawled into bed, staring at the stars through the roof light, she was glad they had cleared the air. Curiously, Jake's face was the last thing that flittered through her mind as she slipped into sleep.

Jake stayed the next day and the next, then for the weekend, and then didn't seem inclined to leave at all. Alex, who had convinced herself she didn't care one way or another, was glad his continued presence pleased Reuben, who was like a kid at Christmas. Seemingly it was years since Jake had spent so long in his childhood home.

⚓

May became June, the days, hazy with heat, lengthened, and the evenings drew out, encouraging people into their gardens or maybe drive to the coast or, in Alex's case, another walk. At this time of year, the moor was alive with birds, intent on chasing down the variety of insects which zipped about. Their cheerful song a melodious accompaniment to every stroll.

Jake had asked whether Alex had any objection to him joining her on her morning sojourns, and although surprised he would seek out her company, she didn't mind, simply saying if he wasn't there when she set out, she wouldn't wait for him.

As the month slid by, the two of them could often be seen tramping over the moors surrounded by the four dogs, an easy camaraderie springing up between them. Jake realised how much fun Alex was to chat with, sending him off into gales of laughter over tales from her uni days, or anecdotes from her job in Chichester. In her turn, Alex had to acknowledge, Jake didn't have such a massive stick up his arse.

Jake did notice that Alex never mentioned her home, her family, or her life prior to uni.

He had tried to press her, but she clammed up, refusing to say another word. It took Jake the rest of the walk to get her to talk about *anything*, and, of her bright smile, there was no sign. That day, she remained markedly uncommunicative, turning on her headphones, and applying herself to her job with far more vigour than was necessary.

Jake mentioned her reaction to his father, and Reuben recalled what she had said about coming between people. He ruminated over whether Kassie St Germain might be able to shed some light on the matter, without giving away a confidence. For now, he left it, it hadn't affected her work and, to be honest her past had nothing to do with them.

By dinnertime Alex was her usual bubbly self, chattering enthusiastically about a breakthrough she'd made with some of their research. Being crabby and ignoring everyone, obviously paid off.

⁂

Jake stayed for two months. Alex never thought to ask why; she just assumed he was working from home. He had the opposite, much larger, wing of the house to her, vanishing after breakfast, reappearing for the evening meal. Totally engrossed in their research — the first draft of the book beginning to take shape — neither Reuben nor Alex questioned his continued presence.

As the days unfolded, Jake found himself wanting to spend more time with Alex. He walked with her every morning, and a casual friendship blossomed. He still went into Whitby to see Diana, a fellow engineer whom he met on a previous project, and had been dating for the past three years.

He never mentioned her to Alex, or Alex to Diana, and had anyone asked, he couldn't have said why. Neither did he talk about either woman with Reuben, who considered Diana far too sophisticated for her own good. She didn't like the countryside either, which in Reuben's eyes was an immediate black mark.

So, Alex remained ignorant of Jake's romantic entanglement and, given the last thing on her mind was falling in love, would have denied anything other than a passing interest, anyway.

· · ·

Until the day she got lost on the moor.

It was mid-July; the weather was blisteringly hot, and a storm had been predicated for days. Reuben grumbled it was about time. A good storm was needed. It would clear the air, which had become oppressive, and stop everyone being so short-tempered.

Alex, was less than enthusiastic at the prospect, being terrified of storms. She kept that little gem to herself not wanting to sound childish, hoping should one occur it wouldn't be too bad.

This particular morning, Alex got up with the dawn as usual. The air was muggy, and she speculated as to whether Reuben's longed-for storm was in the offing, crossing her fingers it would be later rather than sooner. The clouds seemed low, but they tended to burn off as the sun rose, so she wasn't unduly perturbed.

The dogs were skittish. It was only just after five, and Alex was worried they might disturb Reuben with their irritable whining. When Jake didn't show his face, she didn't hang around — thinking he'd probably stayed in Whitby overnight — and set out along one of the paths.

While she walked, Alex noticed the light was changing, becoming an odd hue, almost yellow, shedding an eerie glow over the moor as the sun rose behind the dense veil.

It was probably about an hour later when Alex turned for home and froze.

Her route home was obscured. It wasn't cloud. It was fog. Spinning back in the direction she had been walking she wondered whether there was a way she could either get above or below this level, but the heavy mist was thickening rapidly, and she didn't want to risk getting lost.

Crouching, she could see the track she had followed. As long as she stuck to it, it would bring her to the back of Moorview. The dogs tugged on their leashes. Presuming they had an innate sense of direction, Alex allowed them to pull her along. Turned out they had smelt a dead rabbit and by the time she realised this, she was no longer on the path. She hadn't brought her phone, she never imagined she would need it.

The yellowish sky was becoming grey, and she felt the first twinges of panic.

An hour or so earlier, at Moorview, Jake was puzzled. Granted, he'd been a little later than normal, but only by minutes. *Why hadn't Alex waited?* He recalled saying, at lunchtime the previous day, he was heading into Whitby and wouldn't be home for dinner. Maybe Alex assumed he had stayed over. He glanced at his watch, and considered following her, but there were two or three different paths and he had no idea which one she'd taken.

Deciding not to bother, he started to organise breakfast, then went into the lounge to watch the news. When Reuben stuck his head around the door to say good morning, Jake registered that he hadn't heard Alex come in, and as he got up from the chair, the lack of a view through the window could only mean one thing.

Fog!

"Dad, have you seen Alex this morning?"

Reuben shook his head. "No, she's probably out with the dogs or having a shower. Why?"

Jake pointed through the window.

"Bugger, I hope she's not out in that. I'll bang on her door see whether she's home, mind there's no sign of the dogs."

Within seconds it was clear Alex and the dogs were not in the house or the garden. Both men were concerned. It was bad enough getting caught in the fog when you were familiar with the moors, and even then, it could be hazardous. Alex was a recent arrival and although knew the lie of the land in daylight, if she became disoriented, the risk of falling increased ten-fold. Jake rang her mobile in the hopes she had taken it with her, only to hear it trilling merrily away in her bedroom.

"Dammit!" Jake's tones, frustrated. "Problem is, I have no idea which path she took but we can't leave her out there. I'll try to find her. Best if you stay here in case she comes home another way. I've got my phone."

While Jake got ready, Reuben brewed a strong coffee, pouring it into a small flask, tucking it and a couple of cereal bars into a backpack to which Jake added a waterproof. Shrugging into his coat, grabbing a torch and a whistle, Jake set out.

CHAPTER SEVEN

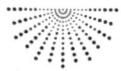

S omewhere on the moor, Alex was beginning to think she
would be stuck until the fog lifted, which, as the locals
had often warned her, could take hours. Deciding to find a safe
place to wait it out, she spotted a few thick bushes growing out
of a little rocky outcrop. They provided some shelter and there
was room for all five of them to huddle together.

The dogs continued to whimper softly, but did settle
against Alex, pressing against her side and sprawling across
her legs. Their coats were damp, but their bodies remained
warm, offering a modicum of comfort.

Checking her watch, Alex knew Reuben would now be
aware she wasn't home and cursed her stupidity, hating that
she might cause him to worry. Why hadn't she realised this
might happen? It wasn't as though she was ignorant of how
quickly the weather can change in such isolated countryside.
She grew up in Northumbria where, on occasion, you got all
four seasons in a single day. *Bloody hell.*

While she sat, willing the fog to dissipate, she felt the
temperature dropping, and an odd sound drifted on the air.

Thinking it was probably a bird, she didn't take much notice until a long low rumble reached her.

"Oh, that's just great, *now* we get the storm..." She groused to the dogs. Within minutes the breeze had picked up and, the impenetrable blanket of fog began to diminish, wraith-like tendrils swirling around her. The rumble came again, closer now, but still some distance away.

The odd sound became a high-pitched wail, almost a keen, heralding the storm, causing the dogs to growl and fidget, restlessly. Through the darkening sky, there came a flash of white, followed almost immediately by a roll of thunder.

Fear snaked through Alex. *This was bad, this was so very bad.* Out on the moor with four dogs, in a wild storm was worse than being stuck in a fog bank. Reuben would have something to say and rightly so. Thank God Jake was in Whitby. The two of them had just reached a kind of relaxed camaraderie — she didn't need him getting snippy and judgemental again.

Pushing herself as far back into the little hollow as she could, Alex held tight to the dogs and tried to stay calm.

⚬

Had Alex but known it, not far away, Jake was striding towards her, his long stride covering the distance quickly. The fog was thinning, but he could hear the fast approaching storm. He had chosen the track they walked most often, more on a hunch than any other reason, aware there was a chance Alex had taken a different route.

Every few minutes he blew the whistle, the shrill noise penetrating the dense air better than a shout, especially as the wind was beginning to howl. Good, in that it was blowing away the fog; bad, in that it would likely bring with it a torrential downpour.

The first drops of rain had begun to fall when Jake thought he heard a familiar yip. Standing still, he blew the whistle three times. Somewhere off to his left, a chorus of dogs barked. Relief coursed through him. It must be them; it being improbable more than one pack of dogs was lost on the moor. He was pretty sure they would have made their way home eventually, but he was thankful Alex hadn't let them go. It made her easier to track down.

When the dogs started barking, Alex lifted her head, gingerly, and tried to listen over the encroaching thunder. Lightning was flickering all around her, rain was lashing down, and panic had morphed into outright terror.

Wrapping her arms around her knees, trying to make herself as small as possible, Alex had clamped her jaw shut to keep from having the screaming habdabs. Not that it mattered if she did, it would be drowned out anyway, she just wanted to maintain some form of control. Ben licked her face, and whined. Alex ruffled his fur, hugging him against her, reaching out to pet the other three.

During a welcome gap between thunderclaps, Gus, who had been asleep on her feet, yipped, then all four started barking, frantically. Alex hung on as they strained at their leashes. Afraid either to trust their instincts and let them lead her or release them in the hope they found their way home. The storm was overhead. The fog had dissipated, but the day was so murky it was difficult to make out any landmarks and, for Alex, which direction would take her home to Moorview.

Hopeless, it was absolutely hopeless.

. . .

The dogs were still barking; desperate to get to something she couldn't see. Gus lurched forwards and Alex could hold him no longer, her hands were too cold and wet. He shot off into the gloom closely followed by Coco and Pip. Ben stayed with Alex, maybe sensing her distress, and offering a little doggy comfort. That's what she liked to imagine anyway.

Moments later they were back, bouncing happily around a shapeless bulk. Alex squinted, when the bulk crouched next to her, recognising Jake. He tried to prise her hands from around her knees, to get her to stand up, but she was gripping them too tightly.

"Alexandra, it's me, come on, we need to get home," he chivvied, relief making his voice sharp. Digging in the backpack, he pulled out the waterproof. He draped it around her, and encouraged her to sip some of the coffee, but her teeth were chattering too much, and it kept spilling.

She shook her head. "C-cant," she stuttered. "T-take the dogs. I-I'll be f-fine."

"You can't stay here. Trust me I'll keep you safe," he coaxed.

Alex stared at him, rain running down her face. *Was he mad? She wasn't going anywhere.* "N-no, p-please don't make me," she whispered, her voice catching as the remnants of her control seeped away.

"We can't stay here, Alexandra, you'll catch your death. You're an adult, only babies are scared of storms." Jake spoke roughly, forcing a reaction. It worked. He watched her face drain of all expression.

Unclasping her fingers, Alex straightened her shoulders and, ignoring his hand, used the rock behind her to push herself upright.

Looping Ben's leash around her wrist, she said in a cold

voice, which sliced through the cacophony. "My apologies, please…" She opened her hand, palm up, gesturing that she would follow.

Jake could see where her nails had bitten into the skin. For a split second, he was torn between yelling at her and kissing her, then common sense took over. Drawing a calming breath, he grabbed her hand, and set off. Alex tried to pull free, but he refused to let go.

"This way you can't get lost — *again*," he ground out.

By the time they reached Moorview, Jake was virtually carrying Alex. She was chilled to the bone and her legs refused to cooperate, which along with her fear, made every step feel as though she had lead weights around her ankles.

Had Alex registered this, she would have been mortified to be causing him so much difficulty, but the last few hours had taken their toll and she was beyond rational thought or action.

Windows glowing with warm light welcomed them as Jake dragged Alex the last few yards across the garden. She sagged against him while he unclipped the dogs, who shook themselves off and bounded into the house, seeking snug beds.

Warned of their impending arrival by a quick text from Jake, Reuben intercepted and gave each dog a quick rub with a towel when they tried to dodge past him, before letting them into the kitchen.

"Jake?" he called.

"Here, Dad," an exhausted voice replied. "Might need a little help." Jake got Alex to the back door, at which point even his strength gave out. He sank onto the wooden bench just outside, his chest heaving with exertion.

Alex swayed on legs, which no longer deigned to hold her upright and toppled forwards, Reuben caught her before she landed in a heap on the ground.

"S-sorry, s-so sorry," was all he heard as oblivion claimed her.

⌘

Reuben lifted Alex as though she weighed nothing, and carried her into the kitchen, laying her on the old leather couch in one corner, normally the dominion of the dogs. He didn't want to take her to her room while she was so wet, and for the first time in years, Reuben faltered. He, they, needed to get her out of her wet clothes but it wasn't his place.

"Jake, son, can you come here. I need… well we should… not sure…" he hesitated.

Jake appeared, rubbing his hair with a towel from the stack by the back door. "What is it Dad?" he asked wearily.

"We need to undress her and…"

"Oh, God." The two men stared at each other, then Reuben had a brainwave.

"Mrs Baxter."

"Mrs Baxter," Jake repeated. "Brilliant, Dad! You go ask her. I'll fetch a dry towel.

The two men disappeared in opposite directions, and at the same moment, Alex came round. Bewildered, she sat up, relieved to see she was home — hazy as to how she got there — and in the warmth of the kitchen. She was sodden, and dripping all over the floor.

Spying a scrunched-up towel, she began drying her hair,

every movement an effort. All she wanted to do was sleep, but her brain kept insisting she get out of her wet clothes.

Dragging herself off the couch, which she wiped down with the towel, Alex hobbled along the hallway to her rooms, the sight of her bed almost too much to resist. Skirting it, she tried to peel off her wet clothes. She was wearing three-quarter-length pants and a cotton T with elbow-length sleeves, but for all they were lightweight, they seemed glued on.

No matter how hard she tugged, they wouldn't budge. Cursing with frustration, she was about to give in to a bout of temper, when the door burst open, and Jake stormed in.

"What the *hell* do you think you're playing at? You've already caused enough trouble by being stupid enough to take a walk on a day anyone with an *ounce* of sense would have stayed home. I risk life and limb to find you, at which point you refuse to get up, behaving like a petulant brat. Then to top it off, when I finally get you home, I leave you for less than a minute, only to come back and discover you've disappeared *again*. You are a bloody idiot, and I wish to God, I'd left you out there!"

Jake bellowed this at Alex who, halfway into the bath-room, gawked at him, paralysed with shock.

Her mouth opened and closed, but no words came out. Trembling with cold and fatigue, she was sheet white, but in a fine temper, Jake didn't notice, and railed on.

"Jake…" finding her voice at last, Alex attempted to inter-ject,. He ignored her and, without warning, everything bubbled up. Extremes of emotion be damned. She was fed up of being walked all over, of being treated like an imbecile.

"Jake!" She shrieked his name, shrill tones cutting through his rant.

Her bedroom door was wide open, and two more figures appeared. Recognising Mrs Baxter from next door, standing alongside Reuben, Alex tried to rein in her outrage, but it was too late.

"Why didn't you? I daresay I would have made it back once the storm blew over. Or would you have preferred it had I injured myself, fallen down an old shaft, or died out there? Would *that* make you feel better? Then you could say it served me right, and because I didn't wait for you, it was my own fault? I had the dogs, Jake! They would have brought me home in one piece. You *honestly* believe I went out deliberately knowing both fog and storm were imminent? To spite *you*, to inconvenience *you*! You think I am *that* inept? You arrogant jerk! ***How dare you***?" She spat.

Spinning on her heel, she bolted into the bathroom, slamming the door behind her so hard it rattled the walls.

CHAPTER EIGHT

Jake, Mrs Baxter, and Reuben watched her go in stunned silence.

"For heaven's sake, son, what was that about?" Reuben demanded.

"I came back into the kitchen and she wasn't there." Jake realised how ridiculous his justification sounded. "Hell, I was worried. She'd fainted, then she'd gone, I…" He raised his hands. "I'm on it."

Mrs Baxter bustled over. "I think you've done quite enough for one morning, young man. Go on, I'll look after Alexandra, and then we'll see. Not sure as I'd want to talk to you again mind, after that little outburst. Of course, we could hear you," she said, when Jake spluttered. "I'm surprised the whole village didn't hear you. That poor girl, now off with you, make yourself useful and boil the kettle to make a cuppa."

She shooed out both men, then knocked quietly on the bathroom door. "Alexandra, honey, it's Mrs Baxter, may I come in?" Hearing a muffled response, which she took as an affirmative she pushed open the door. Alex was huddled on the floor, sobbing wretchedly, still wearing her saturated clothes.

"Come on, my lovely. Let's get you out of these wet things, you'll be ill if we don't." Mothering the girl, the kindly neighbour helped Alex get undressed and into a warm shower, after which she began to feel human again. "Now, hop into bed, I think a nap might help. Had a bit of a fright, haven't you?" She ran experienced eyes over Alex's face, which was too pale, her terror continuing to lurk.

Pulling on a baggy t-shirt and soft cotton shorts, Alex did as asked, and before Mrs Baxter had drawn the curtains and turned out the light, she was asleep.

In the kitchen, Reuben was sitting quietly, his hands wrapped around a mug of hot coffee, while Jake paced.

"Sit down, Jake, you'll wear a hole in the floor the way you're going."

Jake glared at his father, muttering about the ingratitude of certain people, their thoughtlessness and...

"Jake, get a grip and grow up." Reuben interrupted his grousing. "How was Alex supposed to know you'd gone for a towel? She comes to, on her own, in the kitchen, does the sensible thing, and heads to her room for a shower. She absolutely did not deserve to be told she was an idiot who should have been left out on the moor. Honestly, do you treat Diana this way? No, I don't suppose you do. I thought you two were getting along better. You've been quite amenable this past couple of months. A pleasant change from your usual grouchy self."

Jake raised a startled eyebrow at his father.

"Yes, you. You're always grumbling about your job or whinging about Diana. You've been so much nicer to have around lately, and now this. Are you annoyed because she left you behind this morning, or that she isn't falling into your arms like a damsel in distress?"

Jake gaped at his father. "I don't want her in my arms. Geez Dad," he refuted hotly, as unbidden, an image of exactly that filtered into his mind. Alex snuggled against him watching a movie, her expressive eyes sparkling with laughter, their bodies loosely tangled. *No, definitely not.* He shoved it aside and brought his attention back to his father.

"Well, this is not how I expected to start my day. Go and get yourself showered and changed, might help your mood." Reuben held Jake's gaze until his son inclined his head. Swearing under his breath, Jake stalked off to his bedroom.

Mrs Baxter bustled in, explaining she had left Alex to sleep. "Poor chicken, she was worn out. Long time since I've seen anyone that scared of a bit o' thunder. Makes you wonder why...?" She let that dangle; unable to answer her own question.

Her words gave Reuben pause, recalling those curious comments Alex made not so long ago. Maybe Jake was right. Maybe she was hiding something, only to realise how daft it sounded. He was coming up with wacky theories about someone who was simply afraid of storms. Offering Mrs Baxter a cuppa and a biscuit, they chatted until Jake came back, freshly showered and with dry clothes.

Before long the house was quiet again. Mrs Baxter returned home, Reuben and Jake were working together in the office — for a change. The storm, while continuing to reverberate around them, with an occasional loud clap, seemed to be abating, or at least moving away.

෧

It was late morning, when a scream rent the peace. It continued — scream after scream after scream. Jake and Reuben shot along to Alex's room, to see her tossing on the bed, grappling with the bedclothes.

"Now do you believe she's afraid of storms?" Reuben asked, pointedly.

"Leave her to me, Dad. Would you make another coffee?" Jake moved to the bed and sitting down, tried to get hold of Alex's flailing hands. He received a couple of good smacks to the chest, but he caught them, and drew her towards him. Shuffling until he was propped against the headboard, he tucked her snugly against his long frame.

Alex fought him off, but he didn't relax his hold. Her screams died away, to be replaced by shuddering sobs, which shook her body, words spilling unintelligibly from her lips. Unable to make neither head nor tail of what she was muttering, Jake didn't try, just stroked his hand up and down her back, trying to calm her.

Slowly, slowly, she quieted, her sobs becoming hiccups. She must have felt safe, because her hand crept over his waist, coming to rest on his stomach, and without thinking he entwined his fingers through hers, stroking her palm with his thumb. She settled against him, head now on his chest, falling back into a deeper sleep.

Reluctant to move, in case he woke her, Jake waited until Reuben came in with the drinks. His father said nothing. He placed the two coffees on the bedside table and left, closing the door behind him.

Jake studied the woman he was almost sharing a bed with, trying to work out why she evoked such powerful emotions in him. He had never reacted to a woman, to anyone, the way he reacted to Alex. Reuben was right, they *had* enjoyed being together. He loved her wit and humour; he loved her intelligence, and the way her face lit up when she talked about Ancient Rome, their lively banter, and her mischievous sense of fun.

He loved her... wait *loved her...?* Nope. Absolutely no way.

Love didn't come into this equation. If he loved anyone, it was Diana. As he thought this, Jake realised, with a sinking heart, he didn't. Diana was the perfect companion for any number of reasons but, although he enjoyed her company, there was no blaze, no desperation to see her again, no feeling of sadness when they parted.

Brooding over this, a series of pictures insinuated themselves into his mind. The day he came upon Alex curled up on the sofa, hugging a cushion while fighting back tears over a scene from one of her favourite movies. When she and Reuben fell about laughing at some badly researched historical documentary. Her wild gesticulations when she was excited about something — be it a new source she had teased out or simply because she had seen a fledgling finally take flight.

Her vivid face, her eloquent eyes, her soft lips... his thoughts spiralled out, and a line from one of those goddamn musicals she insisted on listening to, drifted through his mind. Alex had been singing it the other day, when she thought herself alone.

How did it go again? '...all at once it's you, it's you for evermore.'

Oh, bloody hell!

Alex slept on. Jake sipped his coffee, then drank the second cup before it went cold, and read a few articles on his tablet, thoughtfully brought along by Reuben. He was starting to feel drowsy, the morning's events catching up with him.

Promising himself it was just for a few minutes, he shut his eyes.

❧

Alex stirred. Coming awake, she noted several things. The most important being that, Jake was lying on her bed, one arm around her and she was using his chest as a pillow. *Really? How had that happened?*

Swallowing an exclamation, she raised her head cautiously, adjusting her weight until she rested on one elbow, spotting their clasped hands, and becoming aware his left arm lay along her back. *Oh bugger, this was a bit awkward,* recalling their most recent discussion, argument, fracas — whatever it was they had been doing before she stomped off.

Even with the curtains drawn, the room seemed lighter. Hopefully, the storm had passed. She listened, hearing nothing but Jake's breathing. Studying him in repose, Alex was visited by the most peculiar sensation. The urge to run her fingers along his jaw — currently covered with a smattering of dark stubble, giving him a slightly edgy appearance — up over his ear, the shape of which she wanted to trace, and into his unruly hair, was almost overwhelming.

Despite his job as an engineer for a prestigious firm, Jake seemed to cultivate a slightly crumpled appearance, as though about to go surfing, not deliver complex technical presentations.

She wondered whether he would be a good kisser as, dispassionately, she contemplated his lips. Not too full, not too thin. They looked to be the most kissable lips of any man she'd ever met — not that she'd met many and had kissed even fewer. Her gaze drifted lower, he was wearing a casual linen shirt in a dark sage green, the cuffs rolled up. She watched his chest rise and fall with each breath.

Her mind wandered and she recalled her panic on the moor, Jake's outburst and her response. She knew storms affected her badly, but that her reaction was acute after all these years, surprised her. She presumed she had outgrown it.

Carefully disengaging their hands, she fiddled, absently, with one of the buttons on Jake's shirt; unaware her movements had disturbed him.

Jake watched her through hooded eyes, trying to discern the emotions chasing across her freckled face. They didn't appear to be happy ones. She frowned and bit her lip, then shook her head as though to banish whatever was bothering her, at the same time as she lifted her head.

Their eyes locked.

Jake was convinced the world teetered. Alex's dark chocolate gaze bore into him, as colour bloomed up her cheeks. She snatched her hand from his shirt but could not stop staring at him.

"Alex," his voice sounded husky. He tried to concentrate, his head and heart behaving erratically. *This was madness.* "How are you feeling?"

"Better, my head aches a little, but I guess that's because… well probably owing… I didn't know…" she stopped and tried to make her mouth work. "I'm sorry, Jake. I never intended to cause such a flap. I assumed you'd stayed in Whitby, and it was okay until I turned back, but… well…" she spoke in a rush, her words tumbling over one another in her haste to apologise, to explain.

Jake raised his hand. "Alex, hush, it's me who should be apologising — again. I was annoyed because you hadn't waited for me, and worried sick when I thought you were lost, which translated into anger when you disappeared from the kitchen. "

"You were worried... about me?" Alex brought her legs up, shifting position until she was half-kneeling next to him, trying to ignore his hand which he hadn't removed from her back.

"Of course! You could have fallen down any number of steep banks, turned your ankle in a rabbit hole, suffered from exposure. The moors aren't safe in weather like that. Yes, I know..." when she started to interrupt, "...you didn't expect the fog or the storm, but you had no means of communication. Next time you go out on your own, please take your phone."

Even though his tones were gentle, Alex was aware of his censure. She knew he was right, but that didn't mean it was easy listening. Heat washed up her cheeks — *would she ever stop doing that?*

"Well, errm... anyway... thank you for rescuing me. Maybe you should go now. I didn't mean to keep you from your work." Gruffly spoken, her voice cracked a little. *Oh, for God's sake, Alex*, she chided, *stop being so pathetic...* her internal dialogue was interrupted, when Jake growled,

"Hell woman, you really know how to push my buttons." His hand against her back increased its pressure, pushing her closer to him, as he used his other hand to cup the back of her head bringing their faces together.

Without warning, he kissed her.

CHAPTER NINE

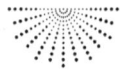

Alex would have gulped had she any air in her lungs, but astonishment left her breathless. Jake's mouth felt exactly how she anticipated, and he was *the* most amazing kisser, his lips moved lazily over hers, barely touching, but so inviting, a hint of more to come. She couldn't prevent a quiver rippling through her, nor the soft moan which escaped.

Jake slid down the pillows and drew her closer until their bodies were aligned, his arms around her. He could not believe the sensations this kiss was eliciting. Alex's response seemed part-hesitant, part-reckless — a potent blend.

Caressing her slender frame, his fingers learning her curves, teasing her hollows, searching until they found the hem of her absurdly large t-shirt. His touch was gentle, his hand skimming the skin above the waistband of her shorts.

Alex trembled, her breath catching, but she didn't pull away. In fact, she leant in, their kiss becoming more heated.

. . .

Alex's mind was whirling, this couldn't be happening. She thought she annoyed Jake. *Why was he kissing her? Oh, please never stop kissing her. What about Reuben? Reuben! No, they couldn't do this, it was a gross breach of trust.* Reality reared its head and she shot away from Jake, gasping her agitation.

"Jake, we can't… Reuben, you're his son… not after the others… he'll think… I don't know what he'll think, Oh God, what am I doing?" She covered her face with her hands, shaking her head. "I don't… my job… he trusts… no, no, no."

Jake pried her hands from her eyes, reading the panic in their velvety depths. "Alex, we're adults, it was just a kiss."

When he said this, two things happened. Firstly, Jake realised it wasn't *just* a kiss, he wanted much more than a kiss, he wanted Alex, and not just her sublime lips, he wanted all of her. Secondly, Alex registered that he said, 'just a kiss'. *Is that what this was to him? Just a kiss. Did he think she 'just kissed' men willy nilly or, allowed them to kiss her in so cavalier a fashion. Did he think her shallow?* Frowning, she got off the bed, going to the chest of drawers in the corner.

"I should get dressed. I've already wasted enough of everyone's day. Thank you again, Jake. You have been so kind." She rummaged around, pulling out a lightweight v-necked jumper, jeans, and her underwear.

Jake was flummoxed by the abrupt change in Alex's behaviour at the same time as he was entranced by the lacy garments she withdrew from the drawer. The desire to remove them sending heat coursing through him.

"Alex…"

"Please let me get dressed, Jake. You're right, it was just a kiss and quite pleasant. Now we need to get back to the real world."

Quite pleasant! Did she refer to that heady kiss as quite pleasant? What the hell? And did she just thank him for being kind? He wasn't being kind, that did not even come close to describing what he was being. Jake raked his eyes over her face, sensing undercurrents but couldn't think what prompted them.

Determined not to let her get away with it, but astute enough to accept he wasn't going to get any answers right then, Jake nodded and left the room saying he'd put the kettle on and organise a sandwich for them both.

Alex remained motionless for several minutes, waiting for her head to stop spinning and her heart to stop hammering. That was *the* best kiss *ever*, not to mention the raft of other delectable thrills, which had rampaged through her at his touch. Could she trust them? Anyway, hadn't Reuben mentioned Jake was dating some woman in Whitby?

Dropping back on the edge of the bed, and uncaring that her clothes were getting crumpled, Alex tried to get her thoughts in order. Nothing made sense anymore. He ignored her. He apologised. They became comfortable with each other, maybe even friendly, then today it fell apart. He reverted to his old grumpy self, only to mess with her head even more by kissing her. Should she confess to Reuben? Did he need to know? If it was a one-off anyway, shouldn't she put it out of her mind?

Aaaarrggghhhhhhhh!

Alex hadn't had many boyfriends, and at nearly twenty-eight had stopped worrying about it, but because of this she wasn't really sure how relationships were supposed to go. The longest one only lasted about six months, and that was more about having someone to go to the pub with than anything else. They had held hands, enjoyed each other's company, but rarely kissed, neither caring enough to take it to the next level.

Unable to answer any of her garbled questions, Alex pushed everything aside and got dressed, slinging a warm cardigan over her shoulders. The day felt chilly after the storm, *after both storms...* she grimaced inwardly.

Alex stuck her head around the door of the office to see Reuben busy on a phone call. He grinned, making the okay gesture while raising his brows, to which she nodded. Giving her a thumbs up, he waved her out mouthing 'lunch.' Alex continued to the kitchen, taking her time, unsure how Jake would be.

She needn't have worried. It was as though their kiss had never happened — in fact it was as though the whole day had never happened. He was relaxed and casually friendly, pointing to a plate full of sandwiches, coming over with two cups of hot coffee.

"Thank you," she said shyly. "I didn't realise how hungry I was."

"Must be all that tramping over the moors," Jake replied.

Alex shot him a suspicious glance, reading nothing except mild amusement in his expression. She smiled slightly, and sat at the table, tucking into the turkey salad sandwich which hit the spot. She had no idea the simple act of licking her fingers to remove the traces of salad cream as she swallowed the last mouthful, did weird things to Jake's heart rate, not to mention other parts of his body.

"That was delicious," she complimented him, sipping the rich coffee. "Now I really must go and do some work, the day is all but over." She hesitated then said, rather diffidently, "I won't be going for a walk this evening, just so you know." Hurrying from the room before Jake could comment.

He watched her go, pursing his lips in thought. She wasn't unmoved by him, but something had shifted. He ran his mind back over their conversation, what little there was of it, but nothing stood out as cause for her sudden coolness. He went back to his own office, immersing himself in his latest engineering project for the remainder of the afternoon, but their encounter lingered at the back of his mind.

※

Life returned to normal — almost, except Alex stopped taking the dogs for a walk. The morning after the storm, Jake was outside at five on the dot, but she didn't appear. In the end he took the dogs on his own, perplexed at her absence. Neither did she come the following day, or the one after that. She seemed to be distancing herself from him, but the reason wasn't clear.

Around Reuben she was her usual cheerful self, but with Jake she had lost her spontaneity. She remained smilingly polite but didn't engage him in conversation unless he asked her a direct question.

Jake was baffled. He thought all that stuff was behind them. He kept revisiting that afternoon, the one which refused to leave his mind, but couldn't put his finger on what he had done or said to make her retreat into her shell.

Frustratingly, before he figured it out, Jake had to go to London, then onto the States and would be away for several weeks. Reuben was sorry to see his son go. He had become used to his presence, enjoying the opportunity to spend time with him on a more relaxed basis instead of the quick 'hello' and 'goodbye' of his usual whirlwind visits. Alex wished him safe travels, but that was all. Reuben raised an eyebrow at Jake when she said this, but Jake just shrugged, he had no answers.

Once Jake left, the atmosphere lightened perceptibly. Alex resumed her walks with the dogs, twice a day. She couldn't explain why she stopped, except it felt awkward. She thought she would be able to go back to how they were before that earth-shattering kiss, but she couldn't. It was easier not to spend any longer than necessary with Jake, than risk the likelihood she would throw herself into his arms and beg him to repeat that kiss, again, and again, and again.

Yeah, probably not the best approach...!

The book was coming along, and a week or so after Jake's departure, Reuben broached the possibility of going to Rome. He wanted to meet with one or two of his colleagues currently working at the British School at Rome as well as organise access to their library and archives. While there, he hoped to arrange similar entry to the American Academy.

Well known in both institutions, Reuben wanted to ensure Alex would be granted admission as his assistant, which required the completion of several forms. Once assured her presence was necessary, Alex began to plan, thrilled at the prospect. She had never been to Rome, in fact, she had never been out of the UK, but had a passport — organised on a whim, for a holiday that never happened.

All that was left to do was book flights and accommodation — and with the latter, Reuben was lucky enough to secure two rooms in a hotel ten minutes' walk from the British School. Mrs Baxter, as she usually did when Reuben was away, generously offered to look after the menagerie. Now all they had to do was pack.

Three weeks later, shortly after dawn, Alex walked out of their hotel into the late August sunshine, the air already warm, but not unpleasantly so. It was almost midnight when they had arrived the previous evening.

Tired after a long day of travelling, Alex had fallen asleep the instant her head touched the pillow. Excitement, it seemed, wasn't prepared to allow her a lie in. She stood for a moment on the path, letting the serenity of the street envelop her.

Turning left onto the Via Ulisse Aldrovandi, Alex followed the path until she came to one of the entrances into the Borghese Gardens, through which she wandered for a good hour, returning to the hotel for a tasty breakfast.

The first few days were busy. Prior to their departure, Reuben had scheduled several meetings. In her capacity as his assistant, Alex accompanied him to some, but most he attended alone.

During these times, and once her pass was approved, Alex found a spot in the library to conduct her own research. Being able to read texts on Roman history actually in the city where it had been made was something Alex could not get her head around, hardly believing her good fortune.

On the fourth morning, Reuben suggested they treat themselves to a walking tour of the city. Rome is very easy to get around on foot, most ancient sites are within a few minutes of each other, if not there's always the metro.

"I thought we could start at the Piazza del Popolo then head down the Via del Corso to the Piazza Venezia.

Depending on time and our legs there's the Colosseum or the Forum. Of course, breaking for coffee and lunch."

"Is there any chance we could see the Pantheon?" Alex ventured. "Kassie always talks about it in her emails, she says it is incredible. I've seen photos, obviously, but I'd love to see it in the flesh so to speak."

"Are they in Rome at the moment?"

"No, I think they're running one of their intensive courses in Greece. Lucky things," she grinned. "I don't think they're back for another week. Maybe just before we leave, so I might get a chance to catch up. Typical hey, first time I get to Rome, and she's not here." She pulled a face.

Reuben laughed. "Well, if you miss her, it gives you a great excuse to come back."

"True enough. Now I'm here, I'm appalled it's taken me this long to visit. Rome is my…" she paused "…this probably sounds crackers, but it feels as though I've always known it. Perhaps because I've studied everything, I could get my hands on about it for so long. It's already part of me."

"I don't think that sounds crackers at all. Okay then, let's explore. Have you got your camera? You'll kick yourself if you forget that."

Alex made sure she had everything in her little backpack, along with a bottle of water, and they set out.

CHAPTER TEN

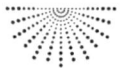

Discovering Rome with an expert was an eye opener. Alex was well versed in ancient history, but Reuben brought a whole new perspective to each site, as well as the modern city, which clearly, he knew well.

They meandered through the Piazza del Popolo, where Alex stopped to admire the obelisk and its lion guardians. Down the Via del Corso and its abundance of shops, glimpsing the Spanish Steps beyond the Via dei Condotti, marking both for another day.

After grabbing a coffee in one of the side streets, they continued on, coming out onto the Piazza Venezia. In front of Alex rose the magnificent *Altera della Patria* — Alter of the Fatherland. Also known as the *Monumento Nazionale a Vittorio Emanuele II*, or National Monument to Victor Emmanuel II, and to the locals, *la torta nuziale* — the wedding cake, because of its colour, shape, and prominence.

Whatever they called it, Alex was awestruck. The huge white edifice, glistened in the sunlight, watched over by twin statues of the winged goddess of Victory, each riding a horse drawn chariot or *quadriga*.

"It's spectacular," she breathed, clicking away with her camera. She turned to get a different angle of the piazza, and squealed, "Oh, is that Trajan's Column, no it can't be... it is?" When Reuben nodded. "No way ... truly?" Her astounded delight was infectious, making Reuben chuckle.

"Yes, it's Trajan's Column. Come on, time for lunch, more exploring later."

They enjoyed a plate of delicious pasta accompanied by a glass of cool beer — Reuben assuring her it was Rome, and therefore, the done thing. Energy restored, they strolled along the Via dei Fori Imperiali. Ahead, Alex could see the Colosseum, and to her right the Forum Romanum.

As they approached the Forum, she sucked in a breath. This was it. The chaotic, bustling, dynamic, throbbing heart of the Ancient Roman world. Where business deals, sacrifices, speeches, trials, triumphal processions, finance, the judiciary, and all manner of shenanigans, converged.

A place of riots and murders, of popular assemblies and games. Where senators brushed shoulders with plebs, where conspiracies, plots, and counterplots were formed and foiled. Where men of power held sway, where emperors were created, occasionally killed, and frequently deified.

A place of unprecedented significance, arguably, *the* most significant in history.

Alex was transfixed.

She stood unmoving, letting the ancient site speak to her. In her mind a magnificent vista superimposed itself over the bare stone and broken pillars. Everything became colour and light and sound and movement.

This was Rome.

. . .

"Reuben," eventually, she spoke, her voice lifting on an exhilarated sigh. 'I cannot believe... this is beyond... it's so..." Alex spread her arms in an all-encompassing gesture, her face glowed with rapture. "Thank you," was all she could manage.

Reuben grinned and patted her arm. "It's quite something isn't it?" He said, in one of his classic understatements. "Come on, we need more than a couple of hours for this. We'll come back at the weekend. How about we detour past the Pantheon, so you can see what Kassie was raving about, then we'll find somewhere for dinner?"

Alex glanced at her watch, surprised to note it was already well into the afternoon. Happy to fall in with Reuben's suggestion, she snapped several more photos of the Forum and the Colosseum, then they headed back. Through the Piazza Venezia, skirting the Torre de Argentina and its cat sanctuary, and coming upon the Pantheon from the rear.

Alex was unprepared for the majesty of the monument. Sure, Kassie went on and on about it, but Alex had always suspected her friend was exaggerating. As they rounded the front, she gasped at the soaring Corinthian columns, and the vast dome which seemed to float above the simple yet spellbinding interior.

It wasn't too busy at this hour, and they didn't feel obliged to rush through so as not to impede the next mob of tourists. The chatter of those within was absorbed by the lofty coffered ceiling, leaving only peace. Alex understood Kassie's love for this place — a temple created to honour all the gods, now honouring just one — it offered the illusion of serenity in the midst of this vibrant city.

Reuben pointed out one of the cafés in the rotunda opposite the Pantheon. Ordering another glass of chilled beer each, they chose a shady table and watched the world go by.

Alex settled into the chair, and as the pair relaxed, she wondered if it was worth talking with Reuben about his son.

She would like to clear up her confusion but didn't know whether it would be weird to talk about Jake to his father. *Duh*, yes it would be totally weird, but he might be able to help her understand Jake's attitude a little better.

She worried at her bottom lip while she tried to pluck up the courage. She didn't want Reuben to think she was being forward or trying to trick his son into something that wasn't there. She hoped he knew her better than that, but after what Jake had divulged about the previous two assistants, she couldn't be certain.

"What's up Alex? You look fierce enough to scare small children." Reuben's voice broke through her deliberations.

She glanced across the table. "Reuben would you mind if I asked you a question about Jake?"

Casually, Reuben sipped his beer. He had known this was coming since the day of the storm. He had no clue what upskittled their burgeoning friendship, attested by the sudden coolness between them, or rather from Alex to Jake, but knew his son well enough that there was more going on than reaction to their spat. Especially because Jake himself seemed utterly bemused by Alex's change in demeanour.

"What do you want to know?" His expression giving away nothing other than polite interest.

"After the storm, when he was… errrm…" unsure *how* to phrase what happened, Alex plumped for, "…making sure I was okay. He… that is… I didn't instigate it… more well… oh hell." She flushed bright red and ran her fingers through her hair. It was no use she couldn't say it. It sounded juvenile.

"Did he kiss you, Alex?"

She nodded. Her eyes wary now.

"Did he try something inappropriate?" Reuben's voice rose. *Dammit, Jake how could you be so stupid?*

"No, no, no, it wasn't that at all," she was quick to mollify. "It was quite the most wonderful kiss ever," the words flew out of her mouth before she could stop them. "It was only, I panicked. I mean you're his... he's your... you're my..." once again coherence abandoned her.

She inhaled a steadying breath. "You're my boss and he's your son, it's a breach of trust. Anyway," she rushed on before Reuben could comment, "when I tried to explain, he said, and I quote, 'Alex we're adults, it's just a kiss.' I don't just kiss people, Reuben. It was out of the blue, and while I can't deny I wanted it, I didn't give him any reason to think so, at least I didn't mean to. Then when he kissed me, I didn't want him to stop, but it's him, and it's you and..." she trailed off, looking down at her hands in which she was folding and refolding a napkin.

"So, what happened next?"

"I agreed. I agreed it was just a kiss and that it had been quite pleasant, then I asked him to leave so I could get dressed. I was in my pj's," she hastened to clarify, which really didn't help. *Bloody hell Alex, way to sound like some kind of trollop.*

Reuben shouted with laughter. "You told him his kiss was *pleasant*. Hahahaha! I wish I'd seen his face. It's about time someone cut him down to size. Don't worry about Jake, Alex. For long enough he's virtually had to fight women off, they seem to fall for him like ripe plums from trees. As far as I know, he's had few serious relationships and they seem more into him than the other way around. Maybe that's his attraction. Anyway, he's been seeing this Diana for a couple of years, but I don't think it's all that serious. If it was, they'd be married by now. I think it's more convenient than anything. Then you arrive and you won't let him get away with being rude, you don't fall for his charm, and when he yells, you yell back."

Alex flushed again, and fidgeted on her seat, needing to be honest. "Problem is, the reason I put a distance between us, was those words. That he could just kiss me, and it mean nothing. Oh God, I'm so sorry, you don't need to hear this. I knew it would be weird. I blame Kassie and her Pantheon. It makes you spill secrets."

She laughed a little tremulously, trying to lighten the mood, which was threatening to become serious. "Thank you for listening. I'm not who Jake would be attracted to anyway, storms are the least of it." She suggested another drink and maybe a pizza, going to order them at Reuben's nod.

Reuben mediated on her words. He knew it. He *had* recognised the a spark of something between them. Jake had never been so irrational about a woman, and Alex admitted she wanted him to keep kissing her. An idea began to nudge at his consciousness. Before the rational voice in his head quashed it, Reuben pulled out his phone and sent a quick text, hoping it wouldn't backfire.

The next three days were dedicated to research and libraries and meetings. Alex attended most of the meetings, taking notes, and jotting down references as they were flung out during conversations. They were so busy she all but forgot her conversation with Reuben outside the Pantheon.

Every afternoon, once they had finished, Alex went sightseeing. Reuben came with her once, but the other days she explored on her own. She didn't mind, happy with company as by herself — and anyway, was one ever truly alone in Rome?

Saturday was devoted to the Forum and the Colosseum, and that evening over a plate of pasta, Reuben asked whether Alex would like to visit Hadrian's Villa at Tivoli, the following day. Pointing out that since his book concentrated on an aspect of Hadrian's reign it seemed appropriate.

Did she ever!

⚜

Setting off early, the two made their way by public transport, arriving just as the site opened. Alex was eternally grateful to have Reuben with her because she would undoubtedly have boarded the wrong bus. Reaching their destination without incident, Reuben asked whether she wanted him to give her a guided tour or discover it on her own terms.

Grateful for his offer, Alex nevertheless, chose the latter. She frequently found herself getting caught up with minutiae on sites like this and it was easier when you didn't feel obliged to hurry along to suit another's time frame.

Reuben was more than happy, telling her to go for her life. He had been so many times he knew it as well as he knew his own home and was friends with most of the staff. He would get himself a coffee and enjoy a chat with them, agreeing to meet her at the entrance when she was ready.

Alex was like a kid in a Christmas store. She began at the poecile — the lake, which in antiquity was surrounded by a colonnaded arcade. From there, she strolled around to the Maritime Theatre, the island where Hadrian was said to isolate himself from everyone. On through the two bath areas. The grand thermae, a structure to behold in its current state, must have been breathtaking in antiquity, eventually coming out near the Canopus.

This pool, representing a branch of the Nile, is over 120 metres long and 18 metres wide. Embellished with graceful

Corinthian columns, and marble depictions of caryatids and satyrs, it leads the visitor to the remains of a domed temple.

Taking a seat on a convenient bench, Alex soaked up the serenity of this beautiful space, while reading in the guide-book, that in ancient times it was notorious for sumptuous banquets and noisy parties, in complete contrast with the tranquillity to be found in the modern era.

Closing her eyes for just a moment, she let her mind wander, a wicked grin forming when images of wild Roman orgies snuck into her head.

CHAPTER ELEVEN

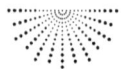

Tilting her head back and relaxing under the dappled sunlight filtering through the trees above her, Alex may or may not have drifted off. The warmth of the day, the unexpected peace of this incredible complex, the lazy buzz of insects, and the soft whoosh of the breeze through the umbrella pines, having a soporific effect.

She had no idea how long she had been sitting, when the quiet was broken by the crunch of footsteps on the gravel. Alex shot up, aware time was ticking away, and Reuben would likely be waiting for her.

A figure was walking along the Canopus, a tall man and, momentarily, Alex felt uneasy. Squinting in the sunlight, she observed his approach, trying to decide if he was any threat and whether it would be sensible to leg it around the opposite side of the pool, towards the less isolated areas of the site.

She was about as far from the entrance as she could be and, although there were a couple of groups wandering around, right now she couldn't see any of them. As the thought ran through her head, she realised how stupid it sounded. It was unlikely anyone with nefarious intent would pay the entry fee on the off chance they could steal a camera or someone's wallet.

She remained on the bench. Her face shadowed under the broad brimmed sun hat she was wearing.

The figure came closer. Alex found her eyes drawn to the man's long easy stride. It looked familiar somehow. Her jaw dropped in astonishment.

It was Jake.

No way? *What was he doing here? How did he even know where they would be?* The answer was obvious. *Dammit Reuben!* She wished she had kept her mouth shut. Now it would be awkward. Jake probably felt obliged to explain why the kiss meant nothing. Honestly, he could have waited until she was back in Moorview, sent an email or a text. To fly to Rome was excessive.

❧

Jake had reached Alex's bench. He stopped a few feet away and studied her. When he had received his father's text, Jake's initial reaction was outrage. First because his father had seen fit to interfere in his life, and secondly that Alex thought it appropriate to discuss their relationship, or lack thereof, with Reuben.

He had chewed on it for a day or so. His anger lessened to annoyance and the thought of spending time with Alex in Rome proved irresistible, overruling his irritation. Booking a week's leave, secured a seat on a flight, which had landed late the night before.

Letting Reuben know he had arrived and was staying in the same hotel, Jake hired a car for the week, confirming he would follow them out to Tivoli. He knew Hadrian's Villa as well as his father did, having spent hours wandering its majestic ruins when he was growing up. He had already seen Reuben, who was chatting with one of the curators. His father informed him Alex was somewhere in the grounds.

Now he was here, and Alex was sitting a hand's breadth from him and, bearing in mind her apparent indifference to him, Jake experienced an unaccustomed hesitancy. With Alex, he was treading on shifting sands.

One minute he thought he understood her, the next it was as though she was a complete stranger. He was used to calling the shots, to be the one in charge of the relationship, but Alex refused to follow his rules, and it was unsettling.

Even more unnerving, he longed to explore why. He wanted to see who was under that remote veneer, to draw out the bright young woman he had spied a glimpse of during those hours walking together across the moors.

⚜

"Hello Alexandra," the rich timbre of his voice sent shivers through her. Notwithstanding her reserve prior to Jake's departure for the States, it was all Alex could do not to fling herself into his arms.

"Jake," she acknowledged, relieved her voice sounded normal — aloof almost.

"I wonder whether I might join you?"

She held his gaze for a moment, before inclining her head slightly, sliding along the seat so there was room for two. She didn't want to ask him, but the words tripped over her lips before she could stop them.

"Why are you here? I thought you were in the States. Wait... sorry, none of my business." She turned away and stared out across the water, traitorous heat licking up her cheeks.

"What's wrong with wanting a holiday?" His mildly

spoken response prompted Alex to shoot him a sceptical glance. *Was he deliberately baiting her?* His face remained impassive. She went back to studying the mirror-like pool, with fierce concentration.

"Why here though? Why this place?" She flung her arm around.

"I love history, and Dad told m—"

"Yes, I might have guessed Reuben had a hand in this," she interrupted. "Okay, I should not... but I was confused... I didn't know... anyway it doesn't matter anymore." Not very coherently.

"Why doesn't it matter anymore?" His tone one of polite interest.

Alex shrugged carelessly. "Because if it had, you wouldn't have, but you did and so that's the way it is." Her answer was less intelligible than her previous statement.

"Alex, what are you talking about? You're making no sense." Jake was baffled. He thought he had a handle on this woman, then she went and threw him for a loop. He had no clue what she meant.

Alex got up and walked a few paces along the edge of the pool, admiring the reflections shimmering in the still water; deciding whether to 'fess up. Problem was, the minute she admitted anything to him, a possible friendship, which might be repairable, would be lost.

Did she want to be friends with him? *Hell no!* She wanted him to love and adore her, to want her and need her. If, to him it had been nothing more than 'just a kiss,' and he remained unmoved, no desire to explore it further, she have would no alternative but to leave her job — ruining the greatest opportunity ever — all because of a simple error in judgement. *No pressure, Alex, just your typical rock and hard place.*

Jake could almost hear her thoughts, see the way she kept flexing and bunching her hands as though arguing with herself. He watched her heave a huge sigh, and she turned around, retracing her steps to where he sat, legs outstretched, apparently unconcerned. The only outward sign of tension, a muscle pulsing along his jaw, but Alex was too agitated to notice.

"I suppose if I tell you, it might clear the air, but I need you to promise you won't tell Reuben. I don't want to lose this job, because of a petty upset between us. I have vested too much of myself in it, and I love it." She glared at him, daring him to do anything other than agree.

Jake nodded.

Alex continued to pace. She couldn't sit, he was too close.

"The day of the storm, when you... after you... well you know, was that all it was to you? Just a kiss?" She stopped, twisting her fingers together. "I don't... I haven't... it's not something... oh, bugger. I don't 'just kiss' men, and you initiated it and I really enjoyed it, but then..." Alex was mortified. This was not going well.

She always found it difficult to talk about feelings. Feelings were never to be discussed. In fact, it would be better if you didn't have them — at all. Growing up, Alex had it instilled into her that any display of emotion was considered feeble and somehow lacking. Her parents had perfected the British 'stiff upper lip,' their only child forced to adhere to their draconian values.

She had never been allowed, or even knew how, to vent the turmoil of being a teenager. All those raging hormones and emotions. How to figure out the best way to deal with the transition from youth to adulthood. How to cope when things overwhelmed her. Such things were frowned upon.

Kassie was the only person she ever talked to about her home life, and that was only because she had a nightmare while staying with her, interestingly, following a storm. Her best friend had been shocked, unaware of what was going on, but did help Alex deal with much of what she had buried under her seemingly unflappable façade.

Terrified, even a small crack in her composure might lead to a more violent reaction than any given situation warranted, Alex preferred to maintain a tight grip on her emotions. This probably explained her nightmares. They were rare now, but sleep was the only time her mind was free to express itself.

Covering her embarrassment in a burst of temper she bit it out, "How is it possible to kiss someone, the way you kissed me, and it leave no lasting impression? Why did you bother? Am I so unattractive, you would rather pretend it never happened, than... than...?" she dried up, unable to enunciate it.

Jake watched the confusion flit across her delicate features. He needed to discover whatever was bothering her, but right now he wanted to kiss her more. He wanted to see her smile, that infectious smile, and drown in the dark, brown depths of her beautiful eyes. That she could conceive of herself as being unattractive, floored him.

"Alex..."

She ignored him, continuing to stride up and down, muttering to herself about being an idiot, and what was she thinking, trying to talk about this, waving her hands around erratically.

"Alex!" He tried again, to no avail, so he stood, walked over to her and, grabbing her elbow, swung her to face him.

"J-Ja—" her squeak of surprise was cut off when, without another word, he pulled her to his long lean frame and bent his mouth to hers. Alex struggled a little, which only encouraged him to tighten his hold around her and let the kiss deepen. He was gratified by the breathy sigh that slipped out, when she stopped fighting and relaxed into his arms.

"Jake, oh Lordy, Jake..." she murmured against his mouth, as his lips began to trail a heated path down her throat and across the skin at the v of her t-shirt.

His hands roamed over her body, one coming to rest on her waist, the other sliding up to her nape, his fingers tangling through her curly hair. After several minutes, during which Alex was positive Hadrian's wild parties had started up again, Jake lifted his head, his eyes slightly glazed, and both were breathing heavily.

"Alexandra Mallory, never ever think you are unattractive. You are the most beautiful woman I have ever clapped eyes on, and the only reason I called it 'just a kiss' was because I didn't want to freak you out." He tucked a curl off her forehead and dropped a kiss on her nose.

"From the moment we met on the moor road, you have intrigued and fascinated me. I might have been worried about your motives in applying for the job, but I couldn't stop thinking about what it would be like to kiss you. The day of the storm, when you didn't come home, I was terrified. The thought you might come to harm almost brought me to my knees, and the reason for my regrettable behaviour when I found you huddled against those rocks."

Alex felt a quiver run through him when he spoke, her head whirling. *He cared about her? He thought she was the most beautiful woman he had ever met?* Involuntarily, she hugged him, relishing in this, *the* most magical moment of her life.

"Anyway, then you had the worst nightmare, something we need to revisit soon madam, and the only way I could think of to calm you was to hold you. You fitted against me as though you were born to do so. My head was screaming at me that we were all wrong for each other I was probably just an irritating blip on your radar, but all I could think of was kissing you senseless. Then, when you woke, and you looked up at me. Oh God, Alex, it was as though I was falling off the world. Which reminds me," he tilted her head back, just a little, "I need to kiss you again…" which he did with devastating efficiency, sending Alex's heart rate skyrocketing.

"What was I saying? Hell, I can't believe I've just told you all that. I sound like a schoolboy with his first crush."

"It doesn't matter what you were saying, just keep kissing me." Alex interrupted him, the taste of his lips on hers utterly divine.

So, he did.

The world around them faded, the peace of the Canopus enveloped them and for a little while, they lost themselves in each other.

CHAPTER TWELVE

I t seemed as though hours had passed, which of course they hadn't, when the sound of an approaching tour group disturbed them. Alex made to step away, but Jake caught her hand, entwining their fingers.

"No, you don't, come on, let's grab your backpack and find Dad. He probably thinks you've clocked me on the head, and dropped me in the Canopus, for my loutish behaviour," He winked, making Alex giggle at the image this evoked.

"Jake, before we go," she tugged on his hand, aware the group would be on them momentarily, and had no wish for their conversation to be overheard, strangers or not. "This is unexpected, and a bit mind-bending. What do we... errr...? I mean... do you...?" She hesitated, and rubbed her forehead distractedly, her brow creasing.

"Alexandra Mallory, I love you. I could tell you how many ways if you think we have the time, but I love you, simple as that."

Alex gawked. *He loved her ... whaaaaaaat? Ooof!* Her insides went gooey. She guessed she loved him too, but couldn't bring herself to say it, not so soon. To admit to that depth of emotion, opened you up to hurt, and she wasn't ready for the vulnerability it came with. She had to say something. Jake had risked everything to come here, to find her. To confess how much he cared, took some guts, especially when he couldn't be sure of her feelings.

"Jake, this isn't easy for me." She gulped, trying to regain her equilibrium and, still holding his hand, headed in the direction of the entrance. The group now gathering alongside them were too close for comfort. "Come on, let's get away from this mob."

They walked for a little while in silence then Alex continued, "Jake, if this... errr... if we... hmm... well anyway... there are things about me, about my life, which you need to know. It will take too long to explain now, but when I tell you, I hope you understand why I can't say those words back to you. Not yet, even though I believe I am, I do."

Alex was clutching his hand and, although her voice was steady, Jake discerned a mix of candour and anxiety in her tones. Both he, and his father, long suspected there was something she hadn't told them, but he didn't want to push, content to wait until she felt able.

He squeezed her fingers gently. "Whenever you're ready, love."

Alex relaxed her death grip, and they strolled back to where Reuben was waiting for them, enjoying the leafy shade of an ancient olive tree. He stood at their approach, a suspiciously smug expression on his face.

"Nice to see you two have settled your differences," was all he said, smiling at Alex. "Happy Birthday."

Alex grinned self-consciously while the two men high-fived each other. Pleased with the outcome of their texts and phone calls over the past couple of days.

"I didn't know you knew, but thank you, both of you. I can safely say this has been the best birthday ever!"

Jake pulled her to him, and kissed her soundly, making her blush. "Happy Birthday, sweetheart," he murmured into her ear, taking the opportunity to bite the soft lobe, causing goosebumps to trickle down her spine. Then, including Reuben in his comment, "I think this calls for dinner and champagne, not necessarily in that order."

"You don't need to. Turning twenty-eight is nothing to shout about," Alex muttered, "I do like champagne though," she added, ingenuously.

"Any birthday is worth celebrating, doesn't matter the age, eh, Dad?"

Reuben concurred, as they strolled through the gates and along to the carpark, where Jake led them to a very swanky looking hire car.

"Couldn't you have found anything more expensive?" Reuben asked wryly while they buckled themselves into the charcoal grey Alfa Romeo. Jake proved himself a competent driver and managed not to give Alex a heart attack by driving like a mad thing on the autostrada, pulling up in front of the hotel by mid-afternoon.

Jake handed the keys to the concierge and went to check for messages at reception. Alex and Reuben followed more slowly, Alex wanting to talk to her employer before this whole thing with Jake ran away with her.

"Thank you, Reuben. I know it was your doing, Jake being here 'n' all. I didn't mean you to tell him, but I'm glad you did. Only I don't want this to be a problem. If you feel I have overstepped my boundaries, please, please tell me and I'll—"

"Alex, stop panicking. Don't you think I guessed what was likely to happen if I told Jake? Just don't let him rule you — he will if you give him half a chance. It's your refusal to let him walk all over you that snagged his attention in the first place. Don't let him take you for granted." Reuben patted her on the arm and said he was going to shower and change. The three agreed to meet back in the lobby in an hour.

Alex was hungry and, if she didn't eat, she would get tipsy on the bubbles from the champagne, never mind actually drinking it. Jake said he'd like to join her, and the two enjoyed a crisp Caesar salad... an appropriate choice given their location. After they'd eaten, Jake walked Alex to her room. He didn't seem to want to leave her side, which was as confounding as it was gratifying.

"I'll knock on your door as we're going down," he said as he kissed her — again!

This was becoming a habit; one she was partial to. Alex slipped into her room, leaning on the closed door for a moment trying to get her head to come down from the clouds. Dropping her clothes in an unceremonious heap on the floor, she went into the bathroom and stood under the huge showerhead, letting the water drum over her skin and through her hair, as though somehow this would wash the confusion away.

Eventually, she shampooed her hair, and soaped herself down using her favourite shower gel, the heady fragrance of *d'Orange Vert* hanging in the steamy air. Standing a little longer while the jets rinsed off all the bubbles, she hopped out, towelling herself dry quickly. An absurd desire for Jake to see her as more than just an admin assistant, had her choose a neat summer dress, teamed with a pair of flat sandals.

She had thrown this outfit in at the last minute — just in case, and her birthday warranted a bit of effort. The sleeveless cotton dress, in daffodil yellow, was scattered with tiny embroidered white flowers, had a broad waistband, and a flared skirt, which fell in soft pleats to her knees. It recalled the 50s, and suited Alex's slight stature. Slipping her feet into flat, white sandals, she studied herself in the mirror.

Using a tiny amount of product, she ran her fingers through her hair, taming the curls a little, but letting them dry naturally. It took ages to straighten it, and the slightest hint of humidity curled her hair, regardless. It was easier just to let it do its own thing. A touch of eyeliner, followed by a dash of lip-gloss finished the look, and she nodded at her reflection. She was about to pick up her purse, when she heard Jake's promised knock.

Checking she had everything, Alex popped the room key into her bag and opened the door. Jake and Reuben were there, both wearing smart trousers and casually smart shirts. Reuben opting for short sleeves, Jake for long, but he'd rolled back the cuffs, the hint of tanned forearm, *the* most delicious sight. Alex swallowed as she stepped into the hallway and pulled her door closed.

"You look gorgeous," Jake breathed, almost reverently. She grinned and throwing caution to the winds, reached up on tiptoe to brush a kiss on his lips.

"You don't look so bad yourself," she complimented, and they walked along to the lift. "Thank you for this, you have no idea." She didn't elaborate, but Jake took note and added it to the list of questions he hoped he'd get the chance to ask.

The day was still warm, the sun on its slow descent, bathing the city in a golden haze. The air smelt balmy, hints of cooking and wine and coffee teased the nostrils, begging to be followed to some quaint trattoria. Reuben said he'd booked a table at Hostaria de' Pastini, a trattoria he frequented when in Rome. They meandered through the streets, passing the Pantheon, to be welcomed by the staff who recognised Reuben, even though it was almost a year since his last visit.

Seating them just inside the open doorway and leaving menus, their waiter brought over a bottle of Fantini Farnese, pouring the sparkling rosé into tall flutes, the soft blush of the effervescence reflecting like a miniature kaleidoscope on the pristine white tablecloth.

"Cheers and Happy Birthday, again," Reuben toasted. Alex, unused to being the centre of attention, thanked him with a shy smile, the colour blooming up her cheeks, matching their wine. For once, Alex had no problem with the men taking charge and choosing the food, something they clearly relished, while she sat back and let the ambience of the evening wash over her.

Every dish was sublime, pasta, salads, and fish, after which came the desserts. Alex could not believe the desserts, they were heavenly. Jake ordered a crisp white wine to accompany the main meal and then insisted a Muscat was absolutely the only drink to have with her tiramisu.

The evening lengthened, alcohol loosening their tongues a little more than normal and their chatter flowed around a diverse range of topics. The book, Rome, Pompeii, child-hood, university life, previous jobs and much more. It was late by the time they left the restaurant. Alex thanked Noli, their waiter and Claudio, the maître d'... who had persuaded them into a ubiquitous glass of limoncello with their coffee... for a wonderful evening.

"You helped make my birthday one of the most memorable, thank you so much." Alex shook his hand when they left. He bowed over her fingers and kissed her knuckles, as he accepted her praise.

"Non è niente, cara signorina," he assured her, his wrinkled face beaming with delight. Unthinking Alex brushed her lips to his cheek.

"Grazie, buona notte," she whispered, turning to find Jake waiting. He took her hand, his large one engulfing her slim one, and they moved away from the doorway while Reuben and Claudio said their goodnights.

Jake tucked Alex against him, her back to his chest, and his arms around her, chin resting on her head. Alex could have stood like that for the rest of the night; it felt both sensual and safe. She hoped, okay dreamed, this, whatever this was, might be the beginning of something tangible, but she wasn't naive enough to trust it yet.

There was also the matter of what she hadn't told either Jake or Reuben. She didn't think it should change anything, but one never knew, and what of Diana? Jake didn't talk about her, yet she had obviously been a major part of his life over the past few years. Was she still? Alex presumed Jake was not the kind of man to date two women at the same time, but what did she really know about him? Refusing to let her insecurities spoil what was left of her birthday, Alex shoved it all aside for now. That was for another day.

Reuben joined them, and they headed to the hotel. The night was mild, and there were plenty of people wandering the streets despite the late hour, muted sounds of laugher and chatter drifting on the air. Arriving back at the hotel, Jake asked Alex whether she wanted another drink.

She shook her head, "No, no more for me, that's more than I've drunk in years. I don't want a hangover. I think I'll just make a hot drink in my room."

"Would you mind if I walked you up?"

"I thought you'd never ask," she smiled, as the lift door opened.

Exiting the lift, Jake said they'd see Reuben at breakfast, Alex blushing with how that sounded. Unperturbed, Jake slung his arm around her shoulder, and they walked along the quiet hallway to Alex's room.

CHAPTER THIRTEEN

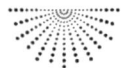

Alex slid the key card in the slot and stepped into the room. She'd left the balcony door open, and a gentle breeze wafted through, carrying with it the subtle scent of jasmine. Jake followed her. Inexplicably, the sound of the door clicking shut behind him, made Alex nervous. She dropped her bag on the little table and took off her sandals, curling her toes in the thick carpet.

"Would you like a tea? Coffee?" She asked, in a voice which was not quite steady.

"Sure, tea please." Jake smiled and walked over the balcony, to look out over the city, while she fiddled about boiling the kettle, dangling a tea bag in one of the cups. She didn't know what to do at this point. She *had* dated, but none of her previous and markedly few boyfriends had set the world alight.

To be with someone whose every move made your nerve ends tingle, whose body you wanted to spend hours discovering — and then rediscovering, and whose lips were capable of unleashing an almost primal need, was uncharted waters. The last thing she wanted was to appear clueless.

Jake's voice broke into her thoughts. "Alex, come here, come and look at the sky," holding out his hand as Alex walked over with the hot drinks. She put the cups on the table, and let him lead her onto the balcony, sucking in her breath when she looked up. Above her, millions of tiny pinpricks of light glistened in a sea of inky blue, and the moon — a mere sliver — seemed to be smiling.

"Oh..." she was mesmerised.

Jake squeezed her hand, then turned her to face him, stroking along her jaw with one hand, fingers coming to rest on the back of her neck, while the other drew her close.

"Quite a display isn't it," he murmured, his mouth grazing her cheek,

"Mmmm..."

He kissed the tip of her ear, then her forehead, then her nose.

"...it's beaut—" her words lost when he captured her lips. She stopped trying to overthink it and went with the moment. Not much she could do anyway, as heat simmered along her veins, every fibre of her being yearning for his touch, certain she was drowning in the mind-blowing sensations running riot around her body. Tentatively, her hands roamed over his back, tracing his muscles through the linen shirt, wondering whether she dared let her fingers glide under the material. Her desire to stroke his skin, almost uncontrollable.

Jake was experiencing similar emotions. He never wanted to stop kissing Alex. Her taste, her scent, her unrestrained response, and the way she fitted so perfectly in his arms was an intoxicating combination. Her soft curls tangled around his fingers like a caress, her hesitancy to touch him made him tremble. This woman, had she only known it, possessed the power to bring him to his knees. A small portion of his brain exhorted such power was dangerous, but the rest of him didn't give a toss.

Alex gave up caring whether it was okay to touch Jake and pushed her hands under his shirt, delighting at the quiver rippling through him when her cool fingers teased his warm flesh. She knew where this was likely to lead but, at the grand old age of twenty-eight, she had never done more than kiss a guy. Now she had to admit this to Jake. It wasn't that being a virgin bothered her particularly; she was just confused about the rules.

Reluctantly, she broke their kiss, and tried to step out of his embrace. Jake wasn't about to let her go, so she didn't get very far.

"Jake." She tried to get him to listen. He was otherwise occupied, trailing his lips over her throat, causing her to arch her neck allowing him better access. *Was it really that important? This was so much more... no, come on Alex get a grip, you have to tell him.* "Jake, please, I need to tell you something." Infinitesimal frissons shimmied through her slight frame. "Ohhhhh..." *Lordy he was good. She had to get this over with before it was too late.*

Alex pulled away.

Taken aback, Jake's raked his eyes over her, their stormy greyness hooded, his breathing a little fast.

"What's wrong Alex?"

Even his voice was dark — rich and sensuous — she had no chance.

"I have to tell you, before this..." she waved her hand about distractedly. "I don't want you to think I don't, because I do... it's only I haven't... and you might think... but it's not... oh sh—!" She bit off the expletive. Flopping onto the nearest chair, she dropped her head into her hands which, Jake was surprised to notice, were trembling.

He knelt next to her, tilting her chin with his middle finger, and tucking her hair out of the way with his other hand. "Tell me what?" he asked, gently.

Alex sat back, but grasped his hand, turning them through each other, rubbing her thumb up and down his. She couldn't seem to stop touching him. Unbidden, came the realisation, no matter how embarrassed she was about to make herself, she wanted to touch him for the rest of her life. *Did he want that too?* Gulping, as that thought registered in the turmoil, she once called her brain, Alex tried to make her voice heed instructions.

"I don't know what you want... err... how far you want to... hmm... go, but I don't... I mean, this is as far as I've been. That is to say, I've never slept with anyone before and I don't want you to think I'm a tease or leading you on because...well... but you might not... and then I just come off like a cheap wh—" Words tumbled over one another in her unintelligible rush to explain. When she got to what Jake quickly grasped, she was about to say, he placed a finger on her lips, stopping the flow.

"Please do not tell me you were about to associate yourself with ladies of dubious reputation?" he asked with the merest hint of amusement, before sobering again. "Alex, are you trying to say you're a virgin?" Her bright red cheeks gave him the answer. "Why do you think you might be leading me on?" He sounded genuinely curious.

"Well, because I'm kissing you and touching you, and you might expe... errr... like... to take it further, and even though I want to, I'm not sure I'm ready. I didn't want to go too far, only to pull away at the last minute, or make you think this is normal for me. That I kiss someone then hop into bed with them." She rubbed her forehead distractedly. *Was she making any sense at all?* She lowered her gaze, feeling like a complete idiot. This wasn't how she anticipated her birthday would end.

"Alex."

She stared fixedly at the carpet.

"Alex, please look at me." She raised her head, squirming uncomfortably in the seat. "I cannot tell you what this means to me, but how is it you have waited this long? Surely you have had other boyfriends?"

She narrowed her eyes at him. *Was he being facetious?* "What's that supposed to mean? Yes, I've had other boyfriends, doesn't mean I wanted to have sex with any of them."

"You didn't?" Jake was clearly incredulous she had made it to twenty-eight and was still a virgin. Alex was beginning to wish she'd never invited him into her room.

"What's it matter?" Tired and emotional, her voice took on a dangerous edge. "If it's such a big deal, forget I said anything." She growled. *How had she got sucked into this nonsense? What happened to 'I love you, Alex'?* "Would it have made a difference if I had slept around? Don't you want me? No longer lo…" the word lodged in her throat. She swallowed, "…now you know? Do you prefer your women experienced?" Her temper bubbled. "Look, maybe it would be easier to pretend today never happened and move on. Goodnight, Jake."

Alex knew she sounded petulant and churlish, but she couldn't help it. *How had they gone from first base to the third degree?* Yanking her hand out of his, she stood, and tried to push past him, not really sure where she was going, but away from his hypnotic charm.

Jake stood at the same moment and caught her by the waist. She hadn't taken a single step.

"Whoa, Alex, hang on. You misunderstood me. I am

simply astonished in this day and age anyone, male or female, makes it to their twenties without having sex. Old fashioned values are an unexpected bonus."

Refusing to speak, Alex folded her arms and kept her eyes straight ahead, which didn't really help because now, his chest confronted her. *Great, just great.* His muscles flexed as he talked, demanding to be touched. Resolutely she ignored the temptation. She was *not* capitulating without a fight.

Leaning away slightly, Jake studied her expression. Her face was pinched, and her mouth drooped. Her inflexible stance aside, she looked... he couldn't put his finger on it... wait... lonely. She looked lonely. *How could she be lonely?* Her words from earlier in the day filtered through his head, making him more determined than ever to uncover her secret.

He groaned soundlessly. *Boy, did he ever know how to kill a moment.*

"Alex, I didn't mean to upset you, or question your principles. I love you, and I *absolutely* want you. Can't you tell?" He pressed her against him, a roguish smile tugging at his lips. He heard her breathing stutter — his need for her was unmistakeable.

Before his body overruled his head, he continued, "To know I might be your first, better still, hopefully the only man you will ever know... intimately, takes some getting used to, which was what I was trying, apparently not very clearly, to say."

Alex's head shot up, her eyes widening during his little speech. *Really? So, this whole still being a virgin* wasn't *a bad thing? Who knew?* Her rigid posture relaxed a little. She wasn't ready to crumple back into his arms... *who was she kidding? Of course, she was, she just wasn't going to tell him that.*

"Fair enough. I'm sorry I flew off the handle, but you have

to know, that wasn't easy to admit. Makes me sound like a bloody teenager again and I hated it the first time around.

"I realise that, sweetheart and I'm sorry I hurt you." He kissed her forehead, and Alex surrendered, resting her cheek against his chest, listening to the steady beat of his heart. They stood in silence for several moments, neither speaking, simply enjoying being wrapped together.

"So, it's okay? It's okay if we don't... tonight?" she ventured. Unable to stop herself, she raised her free hand to cup his face, continually astonished by her strength of feelings for this tall, grave, yet incredibly sexy man, who evidently liked her too.

"Of course, it's okay, I have no intention of pushing you into anything. I'm not going anywhere, in fact, if I promise not to seduce you, might I sleep here tonight, with you?" He smiled his slow smile as he asked, but there was a wariness in his eyes suggesting, maybe he too was nervous.

"Can't think of anything I'd like more." Alex stretched up to kiss him. Their lips barely met, but it was enough for those delectable tingles to coil through her once more. "Well... maybe I can, but we'll save that for another night..." she left it dangling.

"No teasing," Jake warned, stealing one more leisurely kiss, before patting her butt. "Go on then, get changed. I'll be back in a jiffy." Jake hurried to his room, grabbing a pair of shorts and his toothbrush, returning to find Alex in a very cute pair of pyjamas. He imagined sliding her out of them, and vanished into the bathroom, so he didn't renege on his promise not to ravish her.

Alex was fast asleep, her back angled against his chest, their hands entwined. Jake was still awake, propped up on one elbow watching her. The pale glimmer of the moon, and mellow street lighting, cast a soft glow over her features, and he fought against the temptation to trace the outline of her body. Her confession, the expression on her face when she told him, made his heart both ache and swell.

He had guessed she wasn't particularly… worldly. Her response to him after the storm was testament to that, and to be the one lucky enough…! He grinned to himself. Honestly, he *really* did sound like a teenage boy on his first crush. Quite frankly, he was happy to relinquish his man-card for the bliss of having her right where he wanted, God willing, for the rest of their lives.

As someone who never seriously considered marriage, this was a revelation. Jake liked not being answerable to anyone. Even Diana knew better than to have any expectations from their relationship. He studied Alex, the gentle rise and fall of her chest, a secret smile on her lips, and recognised what a selfish git he'd been. No wonder Diana didn't seem unduly upset when he broke up with her.

When they first got together, he had been certain she was *the one*. Diana was clever, beautiful, cool, unflappable, and sophisticated. They dated, enjoyed each other's company, eventually slept together, but when he looked back on it now, it was almost as though they had just been going through the motions. Each step the next logical progression of their relationship, and they took it without either of them considering whether they actually wanted it. Well, perhaps Diana did, but Jake knew he hadn't. He, who was quick to judge others for thoughtless behaviour, was the worst offender.

Now there was Alex, with whom he seemed to share an unexpectedly passionate connection, one able to set him on fire just thinking about her. He wanted to do this right, he wanted her to know he was sincere, and he wanted to play her body until she was screaming his name.

Only to himself would he ever admit how terrifying was the depth of his love for this woman — and maybe one day, to Alex.

CHAPTER FOURTEEN

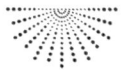

The sun was blazing through the gap between the curtains when Alex woke the next morning. She slept soundly, and for once without any of the troublesome dreams she was often afflicted with when her world was upskittled. Stretching, she became aware of something heavy on her waist. Delicious realisation swept over her and, turning slightly, she studied Jake while he slept.

He was lying on his side, his hair flopping over his forehead, his bare chest... *oh crumbs, best not look too hard*, a blaze beginning to smoulder... *that'll be it for the day*. His black lashes — *why is it that men are blessed with such long lashes?* she mused — a sooty curve on his tanned cheek. A shadow of stubble around his jawline, gave him a slightly swarthy look. She wanted to stroke his face, learn its shape, and then continue in the same vein over the whole of his body. He was utterly irresistible, and she was a lost cause.

In the quiet of the morning, in a luxurious hotel room, in *the* most incredible city she'd ever been to, Alexandra Mallory stopped ignoring her heart. She *did* love Jake. She rejected all the sensible arguments her head kept throwing out — that their coming together was implausible, improbable, and inconceivable — because, somehow, they had. For now, it was enough.

Glancing at the clock, Alex saw it was coming up to 8a.m. All thoughts vanished. Muffling a squawk, she dived out of bed. Without stopping to think — at all — she fled into the bathroom, shedding her pyjamas as she went. Her movements disturbed Jake, and he awoke to the vision of Alex disappearing into the bathroom without a stitch on, dragging a groan from his lips.

He had to get away from her or he wouldn't be responsible for the consequences. Shrugging into his pants and shirt, Jake collected the rest of his belongings, along with his key card, calling that he was going to his room. He heard an answering 'okay' and made haste while his legs obeyed him.

They walked into the breakfast room, where Reuben was already munching his way through a plate of poached eggs on toast.

"Sorry we… I'm late, Reuben," Alex apologised. "I can't think how I slept through my alarm."

He raised an amused eyebrow, flicking a glance at Jake, who grinned unrepentantly. "I could hazard a guess," he replied, blandly.

"No, oh God no, it wasn't anything like that," she assured him, her cheeks flushing bright red. "It's just…" she trailed off. *How to phrase this, hmmm… well, after a lot of kissing, your son slept in my bed, but it's okay, we didn't have sex. Probably not the thing to say to his father who also happened to be your boss.*

Taking pity on her, Jake interjected, "Not quite, Dad, and that's all I shall say. I'm starving." With that, he loped over to the buffet. Alex stood awkwardly, until the waiter who came over and asked whether she wanted tea or coffee had gone, and sat down. She stood up again, immediately, realising she too was hungry and followed Jake, missing Reuben's chuckle as he watched them attempt to behave in as nonchalant a manner as possible.

Any residual embarrassment faded quickly, when Reuben posed a seemingly innocuous question regarding his research. The three became embroiled in a debate about Antinous and Vibia Sabina, lover, and wife of Hadrian respectively.

The Emperor Trajan's niece, little is known of Sabina, who married Hadrian in AD100, at the tender age of twelve, and was honoured during her lifetime on coins and in statuary. Much more is known of her husband's lover.

Part of Reuben's book was devoted to the relationship, or lack thereof, between these two people and what impact it had, if any, on Hadrian's personal and political life. It was a subject previously documented, but to ignore their influence was unthinkable.

By the time they were draining the last drops of their tea or coffee, Reuben was satisfied he had diverted his son, and his assistant for the time being. He and Alex would be busy until after lunch. They had a meeting with one of the archivists. He had mentioned to Jake, while Alex was piling a plate with enough fruit to feed a small army, if he felt moved to call in at the School around 2:30, Alex would probably be done.

They all went off, as work or relaxation called. Alex and Reuben walked around to the International School, and Jake hopped on one of the free buses into the centre of Rome. Much as Alex wanted to spend the day with Jake, she was promptly immersed in all things Hadrian, and the hours flew by.

A knock on the wall of the cubicle she had been allocated for the duration of their stay dragged her mind, reluctantly, from the ancient world.

Twisting in her chair she saw who it was, a bright smile lighting her face.

Jake grinned back. "Your boss has given me permission to steal you away," he whispered, waggling his eyebrows and making Alex giggle. The room was supposed to be quiet at all times, and she clapped her hand over her mouth to stifle the sound, frowning at Jake. He didn't appear unduly contrite, and shouldering her backpack, took her hand.

"Thought we might take a walk through the Gardens," he suggested, on their way to the hotel, referring to the Borghese Gardens across the road from where they were staying.

"Perfect," she agreed. At the hotel, Alex freshened up and changed into something more comfortable. The pair was soon back in the sunshine and, as they walked into the Gardens, Jake drew her closer, slipping his arm around her shoulders, enjoying the contact of her arm when she slid it around his waist, hooking her fingers into his belt.

They meandered along the pathways, coming out at the Galleria Borghese. Checking his watch, Jake said they had time to go in if she wanted to, assuming there were tickets available for the next time slot.

"Well duh…" she said. "Who wouldn't?"

"More than you'd think."

Remarkably, given it was the height of the tourist season, they got tickets for the next slot and only had to wait ten minutes. Jake led Alex into the wonder that was once the villa of Cardinal Scipione Borghese, nephew of Pope Paul V. Even the building itself was a work of art.

They wandered through the numerous rooms admiring works by Canova, Raphael, Caravaggio, and Titian, to name but a few. Then there were the classical antiquities — including the mosaic of the gladiator, but it was the Bernini sculptures which entranced Alex.

She had taken a number of art history courses at university, and to see the work of one of her favourite artists in the flesh so to speak, was a privilege she never anticipated.

"I can't quite believe this," she murmured, her hand fluttering towards the first sculpture they came to, before dropping back to her side. The temptation to reach over the barrier and touch the work, almost irresistible. "Bernini." His name sighed across her lips with the same reverence she gave to ancient tomes.

"You like his work?" Jake glanced at Alex, catching her rapt expression.

"He is… well… look…" she spread her hands towards the sculpture in front of them. "Scipione was his patron, you know, and you can see why. This is flawless, especially bearing in mind how young Bernini was when he executed it." She flushed a little. She was probably telling Jake stuff he already knew. He surprised her.

"Go on then, impress me."

"Are you sure you want me to? I can go on and on and on. I love his work. It is exquisite."

Jake nodded. After holding his gaze for several seconds, to be sure he wasn't making fun of her, Alex started to speak. Jake listened and, knowing it must be at least four years since she left uni, was amazed by her recall of subject matter, he suspected she had little use for since graduating.

"This is the earliest major work in the collection. I think Bernini was about twenty when he completed it. It's Aeneas, founder of Rome, fleeing Troy, carrying his father, Anchises, on his shoulder, while his son, Ascanius, clings to his legs.

Aeneas' struggle to get his family to safety, is clear in the precarious, yet ingenious, vertical rendering of the figures."

She pointed out each part while she described it. "Aeneas' knees are bent under the weight, and his eyes are fixed on their path, but Anchises' body… look how Bernini has made him seem frail and withered…" Her tone one of awe. "… seems scarcely balanced, creating the notion that notwithstanding Aeneas' best efforts, the elderly man is slithering out of his grasp. Aeneas' fear his father will fall, gives the entire piece an urgency, that their bid for freedom is elusive and one misstep will bring them all tumbling to the ground."

She circled the sculpture. "Originally, this was believed to be the work of Pietro Bernini, Gianlorenzo's father, or maybe a joint work. Now, many consider it solely his son's. I think the experts are conflicted. Regardless who carved it, this is a masterpiece."

Jake was captivated by the animation in Alex's face. For all she loved Ancient Rome, this was undoubtedly another passion.

"Well, don't stop there, there are three more," he encouraged. Interlacing their fingers, he ushered her through to where Bernini's David waited.

Alex cocked her head and contemplated the slab of marble, carved into the boy who dared to face down Goliath. "This is the only sculpture in the collection with a Biblical theme," she began.

"Here, piled in a heap beside David's bare feet, is the armour offered by King Solomon. It acts as counterbalance to the rest of the sculpture, adding depth without seeming to. Look at his face. The intense concentration as he prepares to sling the fatal stone at Goliath. His body twists, his youthful form is unmarred, yet possesses a steely resolve."

Alex spoke with confidence and precision. Her words

were reminiscent of a seasoned tour guide or lecturer, but her voice was full of wonder. Jake surmised, to her, this was akin to a religious experience.

He was hard pushed to get her to continue through the gallery. It was only by dint of mentioning they'd likely be locked in overnight, that she was persuaded. If he thought getting her to leave David was difficult, Alex was so awed by the delicate beauty of the next sculpture, he realised it would be nigh on impossible to drag her away.

She sucked in a sharp breath, and stood motionless for long moments, her mouth open.

"Jake, look at this! Wow! I'm... no... I can't. There aren't enough adjectives to do this justice." She moved her hands as she spoke, fingers making graceful arcs to emphasise her words.

Jake couldn't decide which fascinated him more, Alex or the sculpture. Definitely Alex. He forced his attention back to what she was saying, but his eyes kept straying to her hands.

"So dynamic yet oddly restful, see how the fluidity of the figures encourages the viewer to follow the scene around as it unfolds," she said. "Apollo, struck by Cupid's golden arrow, pursues. Daphne, pierced by one of lead, triggering revulsion, flees. Her riotous hair and the drapery almost whipping around them, illustrates the chase.

"Bernini captures the moment when, recognising her predicament, Daphne begs her father for help, and he transforms her into a laurel tree. Does her heart still beat under Apollo's hand at the same time as her flesh turns to bark? The shock and heartache on Apollo's face impels us to believe so.

"See here, Bernini's skill when he fashioned branches from hands, roots from feet, and hair into leaves. They are so delicate, light filters through them."

Alex stopped speaking, and Jake was astonished to see a tear run down her cheek.

"Hey love, it's just a carving." He gathered her against him.

Alex scrubbed at her face, "Sorry, but this is as sad as it is beautiful. The desperation she must have felt that to become a tree seemed the only escape."

CHAPTER FIFTEEN

"Come on, there's one more and then we should go, or Dad will think I've kidnapped you." He chivvied her, with a grin trying to lighten the mood. Pleased when Alex's lips twitched a little as she squeezed his hand.

The last sculpture was The Rape of Proserpine. Alex walked around it three times before she spoke, entranced by how lifelike it appeared. She almost expected to hear Pluto roaring his frustration, as Proserpine tries to escape his clutches.

"This is based on Ovid's description of the moment a young girl, Proserpine is seized by Pluto, who wants to keep her in his Underworld realm," Alex clarified. "Ceres, her mother, hears Proserpine's pleas for help, and grants a reprieve. She permits Pluto to take his prize, on the proviso her daughter spends six months of every year on earth. This ancient myth is associated with the changing seasons."

"See how the heel of Proserpine's left hand crumples the skin on the side of Pluto's face, when she tries to flee. Everything about her is erratic. Her back is arched. Her hair is billowing around her, and, look at those tears spilling down her cheeks. Blind panic is etched in every facet of her body."

She huffed a breath. "In contrast, Pluto appears in control. Yes, it is clearly an effort to hold her. The bulging muscles in his powerful physique flex and clench with the effort, but you know there is no way he will let her go. See how his right hand grips her leg, his uncompromising fingers dig into her soft flesh."

Her voice softened, and she was virtually cooing when she came to Cerberus. The gaping jowls of the three headed dog seemed to drip, and his fur to ripple in response to the agitation in the air. "I love this. I want to stroke my fingers through his thick fur, talk to him, pet his head, calm his stress. Poor poppet is caught up in the tension."

Hearing Alex describe a hellhound as a 'poor poppet,' struck Jake as hilarious, but he swallowed his mirth, unwilling to break her concentration.

Alex ground to a halt, her chest heaving a little, her emotions catching up with her. Never had she expected to see these sculptures. Such things always seemed beyond her reach. She freely admitted she didn't have an artistic bone in her body, but found music, and art in all its forms, a balm to her soul.

One thing, probably the only thing, she could thank her parents for, was instilling in their daughter a love of art. Their home overflowed with an eclectic collection and Alex had been encouraged to study and, afterwards, discuss them.

When she was young, she had hated it. To her, the majority of the paintings were dark and dingy, but when she was at university, those boring evenings provided her with the basics to understand art history. Familiar with different styles, theories, principles, and some of the complex terminology lecturers like to bandy about, Alex realised she had a flair for the subject, which blossomed into a genuine interest.

She had enjoyed it so much, she ended up taking enough units to give her a double major, alongside her first choice — ancient history.

Disentangling her hand from Jake's she moved away from him, needing space to regain her composure. She felt idiotic, becoming sentimental over a few carvings, but they had the same effect as when she saw the Forum, or if she had found the Holy Grail.

Jake felt oddly bereft without her hand nestling in his. Her expression became wistful, prompting a responding ache in his chest, and all he wanted was to bring back her smile. After several minutes when she seemed lost in another world, he walked over to where she stood.

"Alex?" He spoke quietly.

She turned to him, her eyes refocusing, the room taking the place of wherever she had vanished to. "Thank you, Jake. I don't think I will ever be able to tell you how much this afternoon means to me. This place, these pieces..." she stopped, nope she couldn't find the words. Instead, she stepped close, stood on tiptoe and kissed him.

Jake's arms went around her, and his lips moved over hers; teasing, tantalising. She sighed against his mouth.

In the peace of the room, as the afternoon waned, under the tormented gaze of Proserpine, and no longer able to hold back the words, Alex whispered, "I think I love you."

Jake stilled, and lifting his head, cupped cheeks, searching her face. "Did I hear that correctly?" A smile beginning to form.

Alex nodded, shyly, blushing bright red. "Alex…" he reclaimed her lips, their kiss becoming heated.

Alex struggled a little, muttering about being locked in. Jake ignored her until they heard a not so subtle cough right behind them. A guard, his eyes twinkling, even as his mouth tried to remain stern, tapped his watch.

"S… sorry," Alex spluttered, mortified, trying to drag Jake back through the gallery. Jake wasn't in the slightest perturbed and said something to the guard in Italian. The guard beamed and shook Jake's hand, a stream of excited words spilling from his lips, his hands gesticulating wildly.

Alex gaped, but Jake didn't elaborate, just thanked him. Taking Alex's hand, he led her through the multitude of rooms, down to the main entrance. As they walked out into the late afternoon sunshine, Alex glanced at her watch startled to see it was coming up to six o'clock.

"Goodness, I had no idea we were in there so long, I thought there was a time limit for visitors?"

"We've only just exceeded it, anyway it's not busy today. They only hurry you out on the time limit if it's heaving."

"I still can't quite believe it," Alex said, pausing on the steps. Plenty of people milled about, enjoying the quiet of the park, their chatter and laughter drifting on the breeze. The air was balmy, and the sky clear, heralding a cooler night.

Hazy light cloaked the umbrella pines in a kind of aura, dust motes and flies catching the last rays of the sun, which was beginning its downwards journey to the horizon. The scene had an otherworldly quality.

"I've wanted to visit Rome for ages. Kassie's always badgering me to come, but I couldn't seem to get my timing right, and it never got further than a distant dream. Now here I am in front of the Galleria Borghese. I keep thinking I'm going to wake up. So much has happened in the last few days, especially yesterday…" she stopped, uncertain. She had just opened her heart, and Jake *had* said he loved her, but Alex remained wary of how exposed such declarations left a person.

It wasn't that she doubted his feelings. Well, okay yes, maybe a tiny part of her did. *What on earth did someone so worldly-wise, so charismatic, so intriguingly handsome, see in her?* She couldn't figure that out, yet she didn't think Jake was someone who said anything he didn't mean. Giving herself a mental shake, she shoved it aside and accepted that, for now, it was so.

Jake slid his arm around her shoulder in much the same way as he had earlier.

"Dad's right, I can read you like a book. I don't fly halfway across Europe to tell a woman I love her, and not mean it. Neither do I share a bed with someone I don't care about; and before you ask, because I expect it's nagging at you, Diana and I are no longer together. Haven't been for months. Alex, you're not the only one who finds this a little overwhelming. I was so afraid you would tell me to bugger off, I nearly chickened out."

Alex spun around to look at him. "You did?"

He nodded, encircling her in his arms.

"Wow, I'd never have guessed." Letting that revelation sit for a minute. "Jake, I've never been in love. I said I *think* I love you because, to be honest I'm not sure I even know what love is. Such things were not..." she cut herself off, leaving Jake once again curious about her past, "...but when you're near me, my pulse quickens, and all I want to do is touch you, and kiss you. I worry you think I'm someone I'm not. I'm very boring, you know. Not at all sophisticated, or beautiful, or gregarious, or any of those things, men find attractive. I am happiest in quiet spaces with few people — like the moors. I prefer books and music to endless rounds of parties and socialising."

She took a breath and moved out of his embrace. "Jake, I don't want to take this any further unless you're sure. Whatever this is I'm feeling, I'm falling deeper into it every day, and the thought of losing you…"

Jake reached out to gather her back against his tall frame. He held her close, his face buried in her hair. "Alexandra Mallory, I've learnt a fair bit about you over the past four months. I know I didn't trust you to begin with, but I'm glad you didn't put up with my crap. I love that you love history, and music, and books. I love that to you, a picnic on the moors, or by a quiet lake, is the perfect day out — not shopping in a crowded city. This is not to say I don't want to wine and dine you. I absolutely do. Even given your *terrible* taste in movies, you are all I will ever want from now until the day I die."

He held her gaze.

It wasn't so much his words — *although they were pretty freaking awesome* — it was the sincerity in his voice, the slight tremor of his hands, and the tenderness in his eyes, which convinced Alex as nothing else would. Her doubts fell away, and she stopped questioning.

Jake knew the second it happened, her whole demeanour relaxed, and a radiant smile lit her face. Their eyes met, and he felt the world pitch, as it had done the afternoon of the storm.

"I love you, Alex."

"I love you too."

Hand in hand they walked back to the hotel.

The rest of the week seemed to pass in the blink of an eye. Jake arrived every afternoon to take Alex somewhere she hadn't already seen. Sometimes Reuben went along, but mostly it was just the two of them. As had Reuben, Jake proved to be a knowledgeable tour guide, and Alex already knew much of the history of Rome, even if this was her first time seeing any of it.

While they explored ancient sites, or wandered through museums, or simply enjoyed a gelato in one of the piazzas, they talked about everything, slowly coming to know each other. Jake was interested in Alex's experiences at Fishbourne and her time at uni, while Alex was fascinated, if occasionally baffled, to hear about the engineering projects Jake was involved in.

It was during these conversations, Jake elaborated a little about his mother, whom he and Reuben didn't mention. Erin Faulkner had left her husband before Jake was three years old. Originally from San Francisco, she hated the cold, and the isolation of Moorview. Unable settle into rural life, Erin decided being married to an academic was not glamorous enough for her.

One day, she simply up and left, without a backwards glance, and had not contacted either Reuben or Jake since. Neither knew whether she was still alive. Reuben's mother had stepped into the breach, helping out until Jake finished high school, but from then it was just the two of them.

"Thank you for telling me, Jake." They were sitting under the shade of a brightly striped umbrella outside a café in the Piazza Navona, a glass of wine each, watching the world go by. Alex was holding Jake's hand, absently circling his palm with her fingers as she listened. "That's a tough break. I understand why you were leery of me when I first arrived."

"I have no memory of her, Alex. The photos we have could be of any woman, but Dad struggled for a long time.

He loved her, I think he probably still does, or at least the ideal of what they shared. I can't risk him being hurt again."

"I appreciate how much you care and worry about him, but he's a grown man and not stupid. Have a bit of faith in his judgement. We're not all bitches, out to bag a husband." Alex chided gently. "You never know, he might enjoy a fling." She fell about with laughter at Jake's horrified expression. "I was joking. Be there for him, but don't coddle him."

They chatted about it some more, but talking wouldn't change what happened, so after a while, they moved onto other topics. While Alex expressed her sorrow that Erin had abandoned her husband and child, without thought or consideration, she didn't seem unduly shocked.

Some of her questions suggested she recognised a pattern of behaviour. This, along with the fact his disclosure didn't prompt Alex to reveal any further details of her life prior to starting at university, perplexed Jake enough that he mentioned it to Reuben, leaving both men somewhat perturbed.

It was as though she had blinked into existence at the age of twenty. Her C.V. stated she had achieved the qualifications required to enter uni. Even the name of the high school she attended wasn't listed.

It was a mystery, one Alex seemed determined not to disclose, although Jake hoped she would eventually trust them enough to share her secrets. He did speculate, briefly, whether Alex was her real name, but that led down a dark path — one he wasn't prepared to take.

Between work and sightseeing, they indulged in *a lot* of kissing and, by tacit consent, shared a bed every night. Respecting Alex's wishes, Jake managed not to surrender to his baser instincts, although one evening, as her fingers tormented him, he confessed — in a very hoarse voice — it was touch and go.

Too soon their time in Italy came to an end. They returned to Moorview on a mild September evening, as the sun was setting, to a riotous welcome from the dogs, who had been spoiled rotten by Mrs Baxter during their absence. Alex relished the peace.

She loved Rome, but the North Yorkshire moors had become home to her and as she unpacked her bags and threw open the French doors to let the evening air freshen up her room, she realised she never wanted to leave. Yes, going away on holiday, or in this case for work, was great fun — but this; this stark, wild land, was now a part of her.

She prayed it always would be.

CHAPTER SIXTEEN

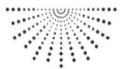

They settled back into their normal routine, as though they had never been away. Jake had to leave almost immediately, heading back to the States. One of his company's projects was ending. He needed to conduct on-site inspections and would be away nearly a month.

Alex was concerned, after spending so much time together, it would seem like a lifetime. As it happened, Reuben and she were so busy collating all the papers, research material, documentation, and innumerable photographs, gathered during their two weeks in Rome, she didn't have time to miss him.

She found being alone in bed the hardest; amazed she had grown used to sleeping next to him in so short a space of time. Thankfully, during the day, she was able to disappear into the world of Ancient Rome. Buried in work, winnowing out trustworthy evidence from that which was hearsay. Or had been written down so many years after the fact, she would need to establish whether it could be traced back to an earlier source. Or invented to suit an emperor's whim, to connect him to an earlier rule as a way of legitimising his imperial claim.

Some of the material they found, although after the period Reuben was concentrating on, was worth deciphering, because there was often a ripple effect from emperor to emperor. Small snippets of information occasionally led to something wholly unexpected, sending the researcher on a different tangent.

Engrossed, the pair easily lost track of time, and more often than not Reuben and she worked late into the night, tracking down a squirrelly piece of information, or elusive inscription.

❦

It was mid-October before Alex next saw Jake. They spoke on the phone nearly every day, sent texts and emails, but when he called to say he was on his way home, Alex became unusually flustered.

The day he was due to arrive, she spilt the tea when brewing it up, dropped a mug on the floor, tripped over a non-existent piece of something, and was so distracted she kept calling Hadrian, Augustus, during a discussion with Reuben over some notes she had been making.

"Alex, go take the dogs for a walk," her boss insisted, grinning at her expression.

"They've already been today," she grumbled, truculently, blithely ignoring the fact she would be taking them later anyway.

"Well, take them again. It's cool enough and they'll not complain. You need to get out of this house, or you'll be a wreck by the time Jake gets in. Honestly, I hope he's in a better state, or he'll have missed his flight. Go on." Reuben shooed her out of the office, breathing a sigh of relief when he heard her call the dogs. The five heading through the back gate, Alex surrounded by a flurry of wagging tails.

Alex had been gone about an hour when Jake's car drew up. He was out and into the house almost before he'd switched off the engine. Barging into the study, his stupefied expression when the only person there was his father — comical.

"Where's Alex?"

"Nice to see you too. Have a good trip? Yeah thanks, Dad, it was great," Reuben replied taking both parts, grinning at his son. Jake dragged his fingers through his hair and grinned back, sheepishly.

"Sorry, Dad. Hi, yes, it's great to see you too, and the trip was worthwhile. All done and signed off. Now where's my girl?"

"Out with the dogs. She has been useless to me today, all fingers and thumbs and could not keep her head in the game so I dispatched her onto the moor. I daresay you…" whatever he had been going to say died on his lips. Jake had dropped his suitcase and disappeared along the hall.

Seconds later, Reuben caught sight of him striding purposefully out through the wicket gate and chuckled, devoting his attention once more to his work. Finally, someone had tamed Jake. He'd given up believing it was possible. That it was Alex, the icing on the cake. Buried in his latest chapter, Reuben forgot about the couple, presuming they'd turn up when their stomachs told them it was dinnertime.

⁂

Up on the moor, Alex in an attempt to walk off her agitation had covered a good distance, the dogs gambolling along beside her. It was chilly; they were well into autumn now. In a couple of weeks, the clocks would change, and the days would seem much shorter. A pale blue sky, dotted with a few wispy clouds, was framed by the odd contrail, high above, as a plane passed over.

In spite of the lack of warmth in the sun, it was a pleasant afternoon; the light was soft, almost pearlescent, and the air — crisp. Most of the heather had long since flowered, but here and there tenacious smudges of purple could be seen in sheltered nooks, adding a splash of colour to the changing landscape.

Standing for a moment to catch her breath, Alex gazed out over the endless vista, occasional coils of smoke from distant bonfires, reminding her of childhood. Turning for home, her heart lifted when she spied the little village, the sight of which never failed to make her smile.

She had an urge to sing, and without thinking, burst into an enthusiastic rendition of 'The Hills are Alive' from one of her all-time favourite movies. Arms out, she spun in a slow circle, to the joy of the dogs who thought it a great game and barked along — not quite in tune.

This was the vision which met Jake when he reached the top of the rise. Alex singing at the top of her voice, surrounded by several leaping balls of fur, yapping their heads off.

He halted in his tracks, laughter bubbling up at the sheer abandonment of the woman and her canine companions. Alex was waving her scarf like a flag, and he vaguely recognised the song, but the dogs were making so much noise, he couldn't be certain.

He strode into the midst of the melee and, grabbing her by the arm, hauled her against him, cutting off her startled squeak with a searing kiss.

. . .

Alex found herself enveloped in a strong embrace, being kissed as though he would never let her go. Pretty darn glad to see him, she returned his kiss with passionate interest. Only because the dogs were jumping up desperate to be petted, did Jake eventually lift his head. Alex's eyes were glassy, and she was unsteady on her feet.

"Welcome home," she murmured huskily. "I think the dogs missed you."

"Did you miss me?" he growled in her ear, duly patting each of the dogs.

"Nah, too busy," she replied pertly.

"Oh, is that right?"

She nodded, a saucy grin beginning to curve her lips. Her joy at seeing him, shining in her sparkling eyes. "What, you think I have time—"

Jake stole her words, his mouth on hers. Encouraging her to open to him, tongues tangling, sending her into a dizzy spiral.

"Oh…" she husked when he finally relinquished her lips. "…well, maybe I missed you, a tad." Giving up the pretence, she flung her arms around him for yet another kiss.

Jake smiled against her mouth, gratified by her uninhibited response. "I missed you too, sweetheart."

"Good. I'm glad," she said artlessly, twiddling with the buttons on his jacket, needing to feel his skin, to re-learn his body. Her hands crept under his shirt, and she heard his breath catch when her chilly fingers sought warm flesh. "It's a shame we're in the middle of the moors," she murmured, "I really, really want to tear off all your clothes and ravish you."

Jake stopped her hands before her touch sent him over the edge. "Precisely *what* do you mean by that, madam?" he enquired, his tones curiously bland.

"Exactly what you think I mean."

Their eyes locked.

Jake felt his heart rate triple, as blood rushed to his head, not to mention other parts of his body. She nodded slowly, a wicked smile playing around her mouth, and for a split-second Jake lost the ability to function.

"Can you wait 'til this evening?" he croaked. "I would like to take my time, and not worry about giving some poor unsuspecting hiker the shock of their lives."

Alex started to laugh at the image his comment evoked, the merry sound echoing around them. "Come on then, you'll probably require some sustenance, you know after your long journey..." she left that dangling, and corralled the dogs who, bored, were sprawled across their path. "Let's go, gang," she chivvied them, and as ever with dogs, they bounded up, tails wagging, ready for their next adventure, which turned out, to their great disappointment, to be going home.

They arrived back at Moorview, chattering and laughing, flanked by a cluster of legs and tails, threatening to become hopelessly tangled up. The dogs desperately trying to get to full bowls before Jake unclipped their leashes.

While he was occupied with the dogs and their food, Alex slipped along to her room for a shower, taking the time to pamper herself, in anticipation of the night ahead.

The three gossiped over dinner, peppering Jake with questions about his trip, which he answered, patiently. Alex struggled to eat, and the meal one of her favourites — Thai green chicken curry, owing to the thousands of butterflies partying in her stomach. She drank three glasses of wine more quickly than usual, which didn't stop the butterflies, but meant she didn't notice them as much.

The evening slid away, over more conversation and some mindless television. When the late news came on, Jake noticed Alex was no longer joining in the discussion. The wine had taken its toll and she was dozing off.

"Come on sleepy head." He pulled her to her feet.

Alex murmured something unintelligible. Jake bade his father a goodnight, and virtually carried her along to her bedroom. Despite her best intentions, Alex had barely finished using the bathroom, before she fell asleep fully clothed, spreadeagled on the bed.

His hopes dashed, Jake chuckled ruefully, and carefully removed her jeans, socks and long-sleeved t-shirt. Getting undressed, he eased them both under the covers, without waking her.

Alex snuggled against him, her back to his chest, unconsciously hooking her leg over his and pulling his arm around her. Jake inhaled several deep breaths in a bid to get his desire under control and closed his eyes.

The house fell quiet.

❧

In the early hours of the morning, Alex awoke. She had no recollection of coming to bed; amazed she didn't have a hangover and was momentarily confused by the weight wrapped around her. A hint of aftershave hung in the air and she smiled in the darkness.

He was home and now she was awake.

Vaguely registering she was almost naked, Alex wriggled until she faced Jake, the light from the moon just enough to make out his craggy features. Angles and planes softened by the stubble dusking over his jawline. As ever, his body called out to her, demanding her attention. Lightly, she stroked his chest, catching the smattering of dark hair, resisting the urge to wind it through her fingertips.

Shoving back the covers, she raised herself onto one elbow, and trailed one finger up his arm, across his shoulder and down his side, tracing his muscles, then his ribs — one by one until she came to the dip of his waist. Following the outline of his hip, a little frustrated he was wearing shorts, she stretched until she could no longer reach, her hand curling around his thigh.

She was about to venture further when a hand ghosted up her leg. Swallowing a shocked yelp, she tore her gaze from the delights of Jake's lower torso, lifting her eyes to his face. He was staring at her, features shadowed, but she discerned the pulse leaping in his throat.

"Hi," she said, with a hint of a smile, running her tongue over suddenly dry lips.

"Hi," His large hand gliding higher, teasing at the lacy edge of her underwear, before splaying around her back, the tips of his fingers resting on the catch of her bra.

The whole of her body thrummed.

CHAPTER SEVENTEEN

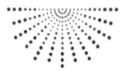

Deliberately, leisurely, Jake played Alex as though she was a delicate musical instrument, creating his own harmony with his hands and his lips. Bewitched by his seductive symphony, she never recalled him removing the last silky barriers, her body resonating under his expert touch, as he drew her inexorably to the crescendo.

Almost delirious with the sensations Jake was creating, Alex writhed underneath him, her hands searching, teasing, and tormenting. Her tentative movements threatening to tip him over the edge faster than he anticipated.

He wanted this to be one of the most memorable nights of her life. It was her first time, and to rush wasn't in his plan. "Alex," he groaned. She had removed his shorts. Her lips were kissing him anywhere they could reach, her fingers swarming all over him.

Slowing her journey, she raised her eyes. Silhouetted under the pale moonlight, Jake couldn't read her expression.

"Oh, God… am I doing this wrong… did I hurt you…?" The anxiety in her voice caused his chest to tighten.

"Hell no, you are doing this so right, I'm losing my mind,"

he hastened to assure her, sliding his hand over her butt and bringing her up his body until she was flush on top him, her face inches from his. "I don't want to cause you any more discomfort than necessary, so please, let me make love to you, there'll be plenty of time for you to return the favour."

He kissed her nose and her eyelids, recapturing her mouth. His hands seeking her most sensitive parts, as he brought her back to the peak.

His name a ragged moan, Alex was spinning in a vortex, and at the same instant she became convinced her body was quietly detaching itself piece by piece, Jake claimed the last part of her, making her forever his.

Shattering around him, Alex was sure time lurched forward, it seemed hours passed before she floated from high in the stratosphere, heart pounding, and breathing erratic. Jake moulded her against him, and she was oddly pleased to feel the chaotic drum of his heart and the heaving of his chest — knowing she wasn't the only one. They lay together, limbs entwined while everything gradually came back into focus.

"J-Jake..." Alex stuttered, sucking in air. "I c-can't..." she lay a bit longer, until she felt able to speak without gibbering like an idiot. "Jake, I, never in my... when did you learn... is that how...?" she stopped speaking, her words were garbled — *so much for not gibbering.*

Unexpectedly, a tear trickled over her lashes, and she didn't know whether it was because this whole making love thing exceeded her wildest imagination, or simply because her emotions had been bundled up, hurled around, then splattered from a great height.

"Hey, love... what's wrong?" Jake, cradling her in his arms, ran his thumb along her cheek catching the solitary drop.

"I'm sorry, I don't know why I'm crying. That was... oh god, that was mind-blowing. I didn't want it to end and now

I'm blubbering wreck." She dipped her head so he couldn't see her face. "I… hope it wasn't… because I'm not… because I've never…" Hectic colour blazing across her cheeks. *It's sex. You've just had sex. Jake knows what it is, sheesh, Alex, spit it out.*

Lifting her arms around his neck, he brushed his lips to hers. "Sweetheart, you have no idea. This," grazing light fingertips along either side of her body, feeling her shiver, "what we've just shared, is the most terrifying, and at the same time, most incredible sensation." Jake kissed her nose and tucked a wayward curl off her forehead.

"What? You've lost me. This is nothing new to you, how can it be terrifying?" Unwinding her hands from around his neck, she trailed one finger along the curve of his ear, her other hand sneaking down over his hip.

"I can't think, never mind speak when you do that, so if you want an explanation, stop torturing me, woman." His breathing stuttered when her hand reached his thigh.

Alex bit down on a giggle. "Sorry, have to touch you." Gasping, when Jake caught her wandering hands and anchored her legs between his, effectively trapping her. "Hey, not fair."

"Totally fair, madam. Stop wriggling, honestly you're like an eel."

By now Alex was shaking with laughter, her convulsive movements almost his undoing.

"Do you want me to tell you or not?" His voice hoarse.

"Tell me," deliberately stretching along his body, Alex kissed the hollow of his neck, wrenching a growl from the back of his throat. Her eyes were dancing with mischief, her mouth formed a cheeky grin, the tip of her tongue darting out to wet her top lip.

He might be the one holding her captive, but Jake acknowledged was he who could not escape. *Man down! Man down!*

"Right, while you're in my power..." grinning at her disgruntled huff, "...hush and listen. You know those dreams you have when you fall and think you'll never stop? It was like that, but just when I thought I was going to slam into the ground, I landed on a cushion of ecstasy. I adore that you are innocent, that you have never been with another man, and I want to be the only man you ever make love with." This last almost a growl.

"You're like a drug I can't get enough of. When I was away, all I could think of was you; of your smile, your laugh, your eyes, your lips. Of kissing you, holding you, touching you, craving that moment we'd be together again."

He stopped. He sounded poetic, okay — really, *really* soppy, but knew Alex needed convincing, wishing she would open up to him. Whatever she was hiding would not, could not, change how he felt. Releasing her hands, he cupped her face, staring into her dark eyes. Moonlight glimmered on her hair, highlighting the sheen on her skin. This moment would remain with him for a lifetime.

"Alex, I remember what you said in Rome, and I realise you may be unsure about what is happening between us, or at least your feelings. I also know there is something you are holding back from me, but it makes no difference. It's too late. I love you. I will love you until the stars fall from the sky, or the universe explodes, or the world stops spinning." He kissed her then, letting his mouth, his touch, and his body articulate what he feared words could not — not yet.

Stunned, Alex nevertheless responded, and by the end of the night any lingering qualms, apprehension, and uncertainty had been well and truly quashed — for the moment at least.

The weeks vanished in a blur. Alex and Reuben were consumed by their work. On top of everything else, a pile of facsimiles arrived and required translating. Some of the inscriptions were less than decipherable, prompting Alex to spend hours poring over ancient sources, texts, and other inscriptions to ascertain whether the fragments they had, fell into recognisable patterns so they could make a best guess. It was painstaking work, but riveting, and late evenings became the norm rather than the exception.

Jake was working on a new project, which entailed his being away much of the week. He contrived to come home most weekends and did his best to drag Alex away from all things Hadrian related as often possible. Days out exploring Whitby or York — visiting museums or art galleries, or simply wandering the old streets, and pottering around craft shops. Closer to home, Alex fell in love with the local villages, such as Helmsley and Hutton le Hole, Goathland and Grosmont. Hunting out books on the best walks from these centres, she aimed to do as many as possible before the approaching winter made it too difficult.

Used to wide open spaces, with little habitation, to Alex, this moorland landscape was different — no less wild, but somehow more welcoming. She couldn't explain it and occasionally wondered whether it was to do with how she felt here compared with the environment in which she grew up.

A little further afield, she discovered the Yorkshire Dales, and the first time Jake took her for an afternoon's drive through them, Alex had to stop from behaving like an excited child. The scenery changed again, and while not completely tamed, it was softer somehow, more mellow. The profusion of autumn colours, yellow, orange, red, and purple made it seem as though the countryside had been draped in a jewelled blanket. It was breathtaking.

During these jaunts, Jake introduced Alex to the Cistercian ruins littered throughout the countryside. Three abbeys — Jervaulx, Rievaulx, and Fountains, were within striking distance, and it wasn't long before they became her 'go to' destinations.

Jervaulx is England's largest privately-owned Cistercian Abbey. Not as extensive as the other two, it has its own charm and is relatively unknown, making it a peaceful place to while away an afternoon.

Rievaulx, nestled in a dip just outside Helmsley, was the closest to home, and the easiest to get to. Already a member of English Heritage, Alex found it relaxing to drive over for an hour at the end of a hectic day, if only to enjoy a quick potter around the grounds.

Fountains Abbey quickly became her favourite. The first time they visited, she was blown away by its magnificence. Jake drove, choosing the Studley Royal entrance, pointing out the herds of deer as they entered the grounds; parking above Studley Lake.

Strolling hand in hand along the water gardens, Jake gave Alex a potted history, noting that in the fifteenth century, the Mallory family inherited the property, until it was passed to John Aislabe two hundred and fifty years later.

"You never know, you might have some claim to this," he joked, spreading out his arm to encompass the whole of the estate. Alex went bright red. She shoved him in the shoulder, told him not to be daft, and laughed along with him, but Jake gained the oddest impression his quip had hit a raw nerve.

The moment passed, but he didn't forget, consigning it to all the other curiosities surrounding this woman who had stolen his heart.

Distracting her, he urged, "Close your eyes and hold my hand."

Alex narrowed her gaze in suspicion.

"Trust me, it's worth it."

Dubious, nevertheless, she did as he asked, allowing him to lead her along the path beside Half-Moon Lake. They walked steadily until Jake stopped, and turned her to the right.

"Open your eyes."

Alex did so, and gasped. The abbey rose up in front of her, and although still some distance away, its impact was astonishing.

"These are the largest monastic ruins in the country, the best-preserved ruins in Europe and a World Heritage site to boot." Jake assumed the slightly superior tones of a seasoned tour guide, to Alex's amusement.

"It was founded in the twelfth century, by Benedictine monks from York, who not long after, joined the Cistercian order. The lay brothers created a prosperous settlement through farming, mining, and quarrying. Surmounting numerous challenges down the centuries, Fountains remained important, until good old Henry VIII ordered the Dissolution in 1539. The abbey was closed, the monks retired, and the estate sold." He paused for breath.

"Wow, colour me impressed. You should apply for a job as a guide." Alex beamed at him. "Hurry up, I need to be inside, it's calling to me." She blushed when she heard the words trip off her tongue, but it was true. There was something about the setting. It's history, its grandeur, and today, at the end of October with so few visitors, it's surrounds, tranquil.

Once in the midst of the abbey, Alex was determined to see everything. She lost herself in the sheer scale of the stunning architecture. Taking her time, she started at the infirmary, meandered along to the church, where she admired the Chapel of the Nine Altars. She had visited Durham Cathedral many times and knew this to be the inspiration for its chapel of the same name. Through the choir and into the nave,

Abbott Huby's Tower soaring overhead, the whole of the church surviving nearly to its original height.

She was unable to stop herself skimming her fingers over the locally hewn sandstone, marvelling at the changing hues and textures within the stone. Tilting her head back, she soaked up the elegant simplicity of the multitude of Romanesque arches. The sturdy yet perfectly rounded pillars, and the minimal decorative features.

In those areas no longer protected from the elements, grass had taken the place of flag stones, but to Alex this enhanced rather than detracted from the grace of the ruin. Not expecting to be any more awestruck, Alex almost forgot to breathe when Jake showed her the vaulted cellarium.

Three hundred feet long, the undercroft would have been used as a storage area, as well as a support for the lay brothers' dormitory directly above. So well preserved, the cellarium appears as though it is only days, rather than the almost five hundred years it has actually been, since the monks were forced to abandon their home.

In his turn, Jake enjoyed viewing the abbey from a new perspective. It was one of his preferred spots, if he fancied a day out, but he had a tendency to overlooked certain areas because of how frequently he visited. Alex wanted to investigate every nook and cranny and it was refreshing seeing the abbey through her eyes.

CHAPTER EIGHTEEN

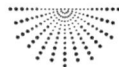

They spent the whole day exploring, inhaling a hasty snack at the visitors' centre, before rushing back down the hill to the watermill. On their way back to the carpark, along the alternative path towards the water gardens, Alex kept glancing over her shoulder, unwilling to say goodbye to this place, which had enthralled her from first sight.

Reaching the corner, beyond which the ruins would disappear from view, Alex turned for one last glimpse, to be halted in her tracks.

The sun almost at the horizon, had thrown the abbey into silhouette, its last rays like ghostly fingers filtering through the lofty arches. The sky was morphing from bright blue to soft pink, edges already darkening to purple. Alex was transfixed. Something about the light had transformed what was already a remarkable view into something utterly magical.

"Jake, look," she exhorted, in undertones, for to speak any louder seemed irreverent. "I wish I could capture this moment. It is one of the most wonderful of my life."

Jake smiled and came to stand behind her. Looping his arms around her, he rested his chin on her head.

"It's certainly something," he murmured, spinning her to face him. Threading his fingers through her curls, he tilted her head and kissed her.

Alex felt the inevitable blaze spiral through her as she moved into him. She didn't care that they were right in the middle of the path — it was quiet, any visitors likely long gone — revelling in the seductive combination of his lips, his embrace, and the extraordinary setting.

When Jake relinquished her mouth, the light had changed again. Aware the afternoon was waning fast, the pair hurried to the entrance, neither particularly wanting to be locked in overnight. The drive home was mostly silent, they didn't need to chat. At some point, Alex dozed off, confident Jake knew these roads like the back of his hand.

That day was the first of many trips to the abbey. As was becoming a habit, Alex was comfortable going by herself should Jake be away. Occasionally, Reuben accompanied her, but mostly she went on her own. More often than not, she found somewhere to sit and watch the world go by, enchanted by the ever-changing scenery.

Autumn became winter, and Christmas loomed. Unsure what Alex had planned, Reuben didn't want her to think she was expected to work, during what would be a proper break. One evening, while the three of them were enjoying a large glass of red wine, while watching a sit-com on the television, he broached the subject.

"I meant to say, Alex. We'll have a two week break over Christmas. We, Jake and I, would love you to stay here, but understand you'll probably prefer to go home to your family."

Alex, who had been convulsed with laughter at a scene on the show, stilled. Her mirth evaporated and expression went from animated to unreadable in an instant. Surreptitiously, Reuben glanced at Jake, saw he too had noticed, the atmosphere becoming strained.

"I have no plans, but neither do I wish to intrude on your festivities. I don't celebrate Christmas. I'll probably book into a hotel or something." Her painfully precise phrasing was in stark contrast with her nonchalant tones.

Jake gaped. "Don't celebrate Christmas? Good grief, woman, why on earth not?" He didn't wait for an answer. "You most certainly will not book into a hotel, and how could you possibly think you would be intruding? We'd far rather you were here with us anyway. You're quite useful to have around, plus, Dad doesn't invite just anyone you know." He grinned and patted her knee, trying to lighten the mood.

Alex smiled and shrugged, maybe a bit too casually, taking a large gulp of her wine. "Thank you, that's very generous, and if you're sure, I would be glad to." Still polite, she at least seemed less tense.

"That's settled then, three for Christmas. I need to start planning." Reuben picked up a notepad to jot down what they would require by way of food, and drink, and tasty treats. Before long he was asking for their opinion, the discussion, aided by another glass of wine, quickly descending into the nonsensical.

"Jake and I were planning to go to York on Saturday. If there's anything you'd like me to pick up while we're there, I'd be happy to. Just need a list," Alex remarked, as they were getting ready to call it a night.

"I'll have a think," replied Reuben. "I'm pretty sure I can get everything in Whitby, but I'll let you know."

"Okay," she hesitated. "Thank you, Reuben, I didn't mean to sound ungrateful for your kind invitation, it's just Christmas usually slides by without much bother. The last few years I've been working and before that..." she didn't finish her sentence. Reuben, tactful enough not to pry, reiterated their pleasure she would be sharing the holidays with them.

As they were getting ready for bed, Jake contemplated her words. *What could possibly be too awful to tell him?* His train of through was interrupted when Alex shot in from the bathroom and jumped into bed.

"Brrrrr, it's cold tonight. Glad I have you to keep me warm." She beamed at him, stretching out like a cat, her outline under the bedclothes, taunting him. Jake hurried through his night-time routine and was soon beside her. All thoughts of who she was and what she might be hiding, pushed to the back of his mind while he proceeded to make sure Alex didn't get chilled — at all.

The days rushed inexorably towards Christmas, most of them dominated by work. The weather grew colder and, to Alex's joy, the day after Jake and she went to York, it snowed. It was a long time since she'd seen real fluffy deep snow.

Reuben and Jake did not share her excitement. Here on the moors, you could become cut off very quickly. Snowploughs tried to keep the main roads cleared and gritted, leaving individual householders to ensure their properties remained accessible.

Alex offered to help clear the driveway but was smart enough to recognise when three was a crowd. She had no mind to interfere in what was obviously a time-honoured father-son ritual and, instead, took the dogs for an afternoon's romp on the moor.

During the evening it started snowing again and didn't stop for most of the week. Jake made it into Whitby on the Monday, but the weather was so bad, he decided to stay in his flat, not prepared to risk travelling home until it let up.

He had only been gone two nights when Alex's cocoon of happiness started to disintegrate.

When he was away, Jake was the one who called Alex, rather than the other way around, saying it was because he knew she got distracted when she was working and often forgot the time. Also, during the day, he was in and out of meetings. It was easier for him to get hold of her than spend the day playing telephone tag.

This particular evening, Alex had finished early. The notes she was transcribing had not taken as long as anticipated. She had fitted in a walk with the dogs before it got dark, and there was probably at least half an hour before dinner. Looking forward to a chat, she dialled his mobile number, surprised when a woman answered.

"Hello, Jake Faulkner's phone." It was a woman's voice, low-pitched, sultry. Alex pulled her mobile away from her ear and stared at the screen as though an image of the speaker would miraculously appear.

"Hello," the woman repeated.

"May I speak with Mr Faulkner please?" Alex asked, politely.

"I'm sorry, he's not available at the moment, may I take a message?"

Alex dithered. Who was this person? She glanced at her watch. It was after half past five. Was Jake in a meeting, leaving his mobile with his secretary? She didn't want to ask, stating it wasn't important and she would try again another time. The woman commented he would likely be tied up for a while and cut the connection.

Nonplussed, Alex sat for a moment. She imagined Jake had her name programmed into his phone. When she called it would flash up on the screen in the same way his did when he rang her.

Presuming it to be an innocent mistake, she didn't say anything when Jake called her a couple of hours later. After they had said goodnight, she realised he didn't mention her earlier call.

The next afternoon, a nagging doubt which refused to be quieted, prompted her to call at the same time as the previous day. The same woman answered, but her response was entirely unexpected.

"I'm sorry, he's in the shower. Shall I ask him to call you back?"

Alex nearly dropped the phone. Who *was* this woman and how did she know Jake was in the shower? A strange feeling washed over her, somewhere between devastated and furious. Was that why he wanted to be the one calling her?

"Hello... are you still there? Would you like to leave him a message?" The woman's voice came over the air, tinnily. Alex put the phone back to her ear.

"No, no, don't worry. I'll try in an hour or so."

"Tomorrow will be better. He has plans for this evening, which I expect will run late. Are you sure you wouldn't like to leave a message? I'll make sure he gets it."

"I'll bear that in mind, and th-thank you no." Alex managed to stammer out.

"Coming, Jake," The voice sounded slightly muted as though whoever this woman was had moved her mouth from the phone, to answer, presumably, a question from Jake, but there was no disguising her seductive purr. "Sorry, must go, and you are most welcome," she trilled, and hung up.

In shock, Alex sank onto the bed. *Did that really just happen?* Was there a woman in Jake's flat while he was in the shower? Had to be — where else would he shower? *We...ll, think about it, Alex, who might he spend time with, in Whitby?* The voice of doubt tortured her. An unpleasant image swam over her vision.

She felt sick.

Leaving her phone on the bedside table, she went along to the kitchen where Reuben was ladling out spicy chicken curry on a bed of fluffy white rice. It smelt heavenly, but Alex's stomach roiled at the thought of food.

"You feeling okay?" Reuben asked, after watching her push food around her plate for about five minutes.

"A woman answered Jake's phone, one with a really sexy voice." The words blurted out before she could curb her tongue. "She did the same yesterday. Today, she said he was in the shower, and he has plans for this evening 'til late. She sounded very pleased about it. How could she know that unless...?"

She raised her head and Reuben saw the despair in her eyes. "Why? Why did he tell me he loved me? Why did he bother...?" she stopped. "I'm sorry, Reuben, I can't eat this. I'm sure it's very tasty, but I've lost my appetite. Please excuse me." She pushed back the chair and returned to her room, not re-appearing until the next morning.

Reuben tried to ring Jake, but the call went to voice mail, and his son had never bothered connecting a landline in the flat, because he didn't need it. He left several snippy messages and at least three texts but didn't hear back. This in itself was unusual, but until they reconnected there was nothing Reuben could do.

☙

Alex didn't refer to the call again, and turned off her mobile, unwilling to listen to what she assumed would be excuses and platitudes, if he bothered contacting her. She didn't know whether Jake had tried the landline, because she refused to answer it and Reuben didn't enlighten her.

The weather deteriorated. Severe conditions were forecast for the next several days. There was no chance of crossing the moor, and Alex welcomed the isolation. No one could get in, no one could get out. It gave her space, and time to adjust. To accept and move on.

If that's what he wanted, she wouldn't stand in his way. She had no intention of questioning him on it, she would not give him the satisfaction, it was his life. She had enjoyed their time together and yes, she had hoped, even believed, it would lead to something more... enduring. He told her he loved her, many, *many* times.

Maybe people did that, so they could have sex. She couldn't equate that notion with the Jake she thought she knew. He came across as an honourable man. Alex recalled how worried he was about Reuben when she first started, all those months ago. Someone, concerned his father's assistant was using him as a meal ticket, didn't seem the type to have more than one girlfriend.

Well he has never actually referred to you as his girlfriend, her logical side countered. *Yes, but he spent every minute he possibly could with you*, her idealistic side shot back.

The arguments went back and forth but she couldn't reach a satisfactory answer and stopped trying. She closed her heart and reverted to the Alex she had been before she met Jake. The one who had never trusted love.

CHAPTER NINETEEN

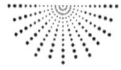

R egrettably, fate hadn't finished battering her heart.

Two days after the fateful phone call, Reuben and Alex were hard at work, and the office was quiet except for the clicking of keyboards. Alex was listening to a peculiar mix of classical arias and musicals, her head full of the theme from Gladiator, when her email pinged. It didn't look important, and she ignored it. By early afternoon, she noticed there were three, all from the same sender. Intrigued, she opened the first one and her breath caught. She blinked, rubbed her eyes, and read it again.

Dear Ms Mallory,

It is my sad duty to inform you, your parents were killed in a skiing accident. We have been trying to contact you by telephone, preferring not to deliver this news in so impersonal a manner but have been unable to get through.

We extend our deepest condolences for your loss and ask that you call the number at the bottom of this email at your earliest convenience...

etc. etc. ...

The email went on to provide detailed information as to who was handling the case and the relevant numbers, concluding with a very impressive logo.

Alex checked the other two, they were along the same lines, each one asking her to contact them immediately. She couldn't recall hearing anything on the news about a skiing accident, but they had rarely bothered with the television during the last few days — too busy doing other things. Plus, her head was so full of Jake, even if there *had* been a report, it was doubtful she would have registered the significance.

Going to her bedroom, Alex retrieved her mobile from the bottom of one of her drawers. Turning it on, she listened to what sounded like hundreds of beeps, while voice and text messages came in.

Most were from Jake, which, had she been in a better frame of mind, might have found interesting, but as it was, she disregarded them, concentrating on the five messages from the legal firm.

Returning to the office, she slumped into her chair, wondering whether anything else could go wrong, at the same time as Reuben glanced across.

"Alex? Alex what's happened?" He noticed her white face and trembling hands. "Alex?" Walking around to where she was sitting, he knelt next to her chair. "Alex, love, please tell me what's wrong."

She raised bewildered eyes to his. "My parents have

been killed. Skiing accident. I have to call these people…" she stared at him helplessly. "What do I do?" Her voice cracked.

Swallowing his consternation, Reuben took control. "Just sit tight, I'll handle it," his tones brisk. "What are their contact details?" She pointed to the email.

Reuben dialled the number and waited. A lady with a cultured accent answered, and he asked to speak with Mr Tomlinson, explaining he was calling on behalf of Alexandra Mallory. He was put on hold for what seemed like an age but was actually less than a minute.

"This is Mr Tomlinson. To whom am I speaking?" The man's voice exuded power.

"This is Dr Reuben Faulkner, Alexandra Mallory's employer. Your email has given her a tremendous shock and she is struggling to process the news. Is there anything I can do, any information you require, or that you can provide to help me walk her through the formalities."

"It is rather irregular. We prefer to speak to the next of kin.

"Just a moment." He turned to Alex. "Alex, can you tell them it's okay to give me the pertinent information?"

She looked at him, trying to make sense of his words. He repeated them, and she nodded slowly. He handed her the phone.

"Mr Tomlinson. Thank you for the messages and emails. Please might you speak with Dr Faulkner? I don't think I can retain anything at the moment." Mr Tomlinson asked a couple of questions to establish she was, in fact, the correct Alexandra Mallory, before agreeing to discuss the matter with Reuben.

Alex passed the handset back to Reuben and tried to listen to the one-sided conversation but was too dazed to concentrate. Her parents were dead? That didn't seem possible. They were always so… vital. Forbidding, terrifying, stern, and unyielding, but still vital.

&

Her father, Terence was a strapping man. Her mother, Imogen, taller than average and handsome rather than beautiful. Amongst her peers and in front of Alex, Imogen affected a veneer of permanent boredom. As soon as Terence appeared, she became the embodiment of sweetness and light.

The two were well matched, but they only ever had eyes for each other. Alex wasn't the son they hoped for and worse, she was needy — *how irritating*. She wanted to be played with, talked to, cosseted. If she was unwell, she wanted her mother to sit with her or read to her… *too, too tedious*. Neither Terence nor Imogen were remotely interested in this small, skinny child, and Alex was palmed off on a series of nannies and governesses.

As soon as she was old enough, they dispatched her to boarding school. Her parents, hoping she would stay there until her education was complete, were appalled when informed the exclusive establishment could *not* keep their daughter for the duration of the long summer holidays. *Why were they paying those exorbitant fees if this was the case? Gracious me. Still, that's what their staff was for, thank goodness they had sufficient.*

From the age of eight until she finished university, Alex could count on the fingers of one hand how often she encountered her parents. The staff spoilt her rotten, but that never made up for the knowledge she was unwanted. Then there was the time… with the pony… *no*, she forced that one right out of her mind. It was pointless dwelling on it anyway.

After university, she went home for about six months,

where her mother made it clear she didn't want a twenty-three-year-old daughter outshining her. Her attitude prompted Alex to apply for, and be offered, a job almost as far away as she could get without actually leaving England.

She hadn't seen them since.

Now they were dead.

♊

After a long discussion, Reuben concluded the call, thanking the solicitor, confirming he would ensure Ms Mallory completed and returned all the forms she was about to receive.

"Come on, I think you need a break. Let's go and make a coffee and talk this through, shall we?"

Not altogether with it, Alex followed him through to the kitchen, and watched while he brewed a strong coffee on the stove. The rich aroma permeated the room and starting to clear her head, which was rapidly becoming fuzzy.

Adding milk, sugar, and a healthy dash of brandy, Reuben set down the coffee in front of her. Alex wrapped her fingers around the mug and inhaled deeply, her nose wrinkling when she smelt the alcohol.

"For shock" Reuben was pleased to see a slight smile tug at her pinched lips, while she sipped the brew. They sat for a while in silence, then Reuben continued.

"I realise this might be difficult for you, but some of what Mr Tomlinson told me, needs urgent attention. He is going to send you, probably already has, a series of emails regarding the return of your parents' bodies. Their travel insurance covered all possibilities, and Mr Tomlinson has initiated the process of repatriation. They will be transported to your family home where, as next of kin, you are required to receive, and formally identify, their bodies.

Anything subsequent to that, such as the funeral arrangements and so on, appears to have been set down in their joint will."

"Do you have any idea when their bodies will arrive?" she asked quietly.

Reuben shook his head. "I imagine Mr Tomlinson will apprise you of each detail as they come to hand. You can't travel today anyway. For one thing, your head is not in the right place to be behind the wheel of a car, and for another the roads are impassable."

Overnight, the snow stopped, and the traffic report on the radio said snowploughs were out in force, but their priority was the major routes, outlying villages would be a long way down the list.

"I wish Ja..." Alex clamped her mouth shut. She wanted Jake, desperately, to feel his arms around her, to draw strength from him. It was futile desire, especially since she had ignored every one of his calls. She wished she could cry. If she did, it might offer some release. She couldn't, emotional outbursts, once suppressed are not easy to revive.

Neither was it as though she had lost a loving, caring family. Her parents had been cold, hard, and indifferent, yet she was aware of a curious sense of regret. Whether that was because they were essentially estranged, or because their death absolved them from explaining their neglect, she couldn't tell.

The peace of the kitchen settled her turbulent thoughts. The hiss of the fire and the gentle snoring of the dogs, familiar and restful. A second cup of coffee appeared at her elbow, Alex did not realise she had drunk the first, almost in one gulp.

"I don't want to go home. I don't want to accept their bodies. I don't want to do anything expect be here, in the quiet, with my work." Her voice was devoid of inflection, but her body was quivering.

Reuben, sensing a meltdown knew the best place for her, right at this moment, was bed. Removing the mug from her hands, he pulled her up from the chair, walked her along to her room and told her to have a snooze. His practical tones pierced the fog in her head. She lay down and within minutes was fast asleep.

Checking her computer, Reuben saw a stream of emails from the lawyers and printed them off, setting them aside for later. He mused over the Jake and Alex debacle, wondering whether he should interfere again. He had the feeling there was more to what Alex assumed was going on.

His son might be an idiot on occasion, but Reuben had never known him to be two-faced or thoughtlessly cruel. He needed to get to the bottom of it before the pair ruined what was obviously more than a brief affair.

Unable to do anything until either his son called him, or the roads became navigable, Reuben returned to his desk and spent the remainder of the afternoon immersed in the ancient world.

Three days after receiving the email from the lawyers, Alex, a small suitcase tucked in the boot of her car, was ready to set off. She had no intention of being away any longer than was absolutely necessary, not even sure she would go to the funeral — should it be permitted. She wouldn't put it past her parents to include a stipulation in their will, barring her attendance.

The previous forty-eight hours had been spent filling out innumerable forms; signing, scanning, and emailing them back to the lawyers; an exhausting process, but it was done. The one remaining thing was to settle the estate, the procedure for which she hoped to set in motion the following morning. A meeting at her childhood home with a representative from the legal firm, already scheduled.

The road out of the village, down to the A170 was clear, and from there she could get onto the A19 north, at Thirsk. All she had left to do was say goodbye to Reuben. They were standing in the office; Alex indicating she didn't want him to wave her off.

"It's easier this way," she explained quietly. "I think if I was to see you at the door, I might lose it." She smiled a little wryly. "Thank you for everything, Reuben. I wouldn't have coped without you. I'll keep you updated, and hopefully be home by next Wednesday."

Reuben grinned, gathering her into a warm hug. "Take care on those roads Alex, and don't feel you have to come back until you're good and ready. These next few days will be hard, but never forget, you'll always have a home here."

While trying to make sense of all the forms, Alex had shared some of her life. After all his help, Reuben deserved to know, and now he understood why she was so reluctant to reveal anything of her past.

When she had admitted who her parents were, Reuben was astounded. More so because as far as the rest of the world was concerned, they were childless. Even the numerous news reports about their deaths had failed to mention Alex. Renowned for their philanthropy, it seemed Terence and Imogen Mallory were generous to all, except their own daughter.

CHAPTER TWENTY

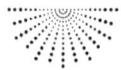

Neither heard the sound of a car pulling up or footsteps along the hall. Reuben was pressing a kiss to Alex's forehead, when the door flew open.

Jake halted on the threshold. His hair was wild, and his clothes rumpled, as though he'd slept in them. Taking in the scene, his girlfriend in the arms of his father, Reuben kissing her, his face darkened. *This was why Alex hadn't bothered returning any of his calls or texts the last few days.* Conveniently forgetting, in his fury, everything they had shared, prior to this moment.

Cursing the weather that had caused this delay, and without giving either in the room the chance to speak, he launched into a tirade about women pulling the wool over his eyes. Tricking him into thinking they cared, when in reality they were after his father, and how sick that made him feel. That he'd always known she wasn't to be trusted. He barely paused for breath, ignoring Reuben's repeated pleas to shut up.

Eventually he did, glowering across the room.

Alex had turned at his entrance, butterflies erupting in

her stomach at the sight of him. Tall, handsome, and oozing charisma, even when angry. She bit the inside of her cheek, willing herself not to jump into his arms, floored by his invective.

Inhaling a deep breath and forcing all expression from both her voice and her face, she said, "Are you quite finished?"

Jake snarled something unintelligible.

"Before you dare to start casting aspersions, you might want to take a long, hard look at yourself. I believed you to be an honourable man. I assumed, after all this time, considering how often you swore you loved me, you also trusted me. Clearly, I was mistaken on both counts." She looked at Reuben. "Thank you again, I'll text you when I get there."

Without so much as a glance at Jake, shoved past him and was gone.

❧

Seconds later, the two men heard the spin of car tyres on the gravel as Alex floored the accelerator. Reuben flinched, hoping she calmed down before she reached the end of the driveway.

"Well, I hope you're satisfied," was all he said to Jake, who was lurking in the doorway.

Jake dragged his hand through his hair. "What the hell, Dad? How could you do this to me?"

"Seriously?" Reuben perched on the desk and folded his arms. "Do enlighten me." His tone, deceptively neutral.

"Alex. Dad, you know I love her, how could you..." his voice trailed off, and Reuben took a moment to study his son. Jake looked terrible, his face was grey and gaunt, and he hadn't shaved in days.

"What gives you the right to question what we may or

may not have been up to, when it seems you weren't missing Alex at all?" Reuben countered; his eyebrow arched.

Jake looked perplexed. "What are you on about? I've been desperate to get hold of her for days. I tried the landline, too but no one answered it."

"I think there were problems because of the weather. Every time it rang, all I got when I picked up was static." Reuben went to sit in his chair. He made himself comfortable and stretched out his legs.

"Alex rang you twice at the end of last week, both times a woman answered and the second time, said you couldn't come to the phone because you were in the shower, and that you had plans for the evening. Whoever answered must have known who was calling because I presume you have Alex's name and number programmed into your mobile."

Jake's jaw dropped. "What… wait, hang on a minute… say that again."

Reuben repeated himself. "I don't quite know what you expected Alex to do, son. Then if that wasn't bad enough, three days ago she received an email from some random legal firm in London informing her that her parents have been killed. Now this today. Honestly Jake sometimes I wonder what goes on in your head."

Exasperated, Reuben sat upright, rolling his chair closer to the desk, and shuffling the mouse to bring his computer back to life. "I have work to do. Go, have a shower, and make yourself look half decent, for goodness sake."

Feeling like a recalcitrant child being dismissed from the headmaster's office, Jake slunk out, heading to his room, where he unpacked, and did as his father suggested. Freshly showered, shaved, and looking much less crumpled, he was sitting in the lounge watching television, when his father popped his head around the door asking whether he wanted a cup of tea.

Accepting this for the peace offering it was, Jake followed Reuben into the kitchen, and sat at the table, patting the four dogs who pushed themselves against his knees.

"Tell me, Dad, all of it."

Reuben did, leaving Jake in no doubt how low his current opinion was of his son,

"I'm sorry I flew off the handle, but after Mum and then Tricia, and I'd been so worried when I couldn't get hold of Alex. All sorts of horror stories were running through my head. Then I get home and I see you two..." Once again, he couldn't finish his sentence.

"Why on earth you would *ever* think there might be the remotest possibility of a romantic entanglement between Alex and I is beyond me, you numbskull. Even if I did harbour feelings for her — which I don't, before you ask — I wouldn't dream of tearing the two of you apart. What kind of man, father, do you think I am?" Reuben tsked in exasperation. "Anyway, now Alex has gone home to sort everything out. Why don't you follow, she might appreciate some support?"

"Do you think she'll give me the time of day?"

"If she has any sense, no—"

"Dad..."

Reuben chuckled. "Unfortunately for the poor girl, she's hopelessly in love with you. You just need to persuade her you haven't been screwing around, which might involve *a lot* of grovelling What did happen by the way? Was it Diana?"

"I guess it must have been. Can't think it would be anyone else. I've been in and out of the office a lot and had so many meetings, I didn't know whether I was coming or going. I left my phone with Janice, in case anyone needed to get hold of me urgently. Diana certainly hasn't been in my flat, and I never noticed any missed calls from Alex."

"That's because they weren't missed, were they? Unless you

scrolled through your recent callers you wouldn't see them. It couldn't have been Janice, because Alex said she sounded provocative. That leaves Diana. Unless you have a bevy of women intent on seduction, working with or for you?"

"Damn the woman, I need to ask her." He plucked his mobile off the table next to him. Alex's face smiled back at him from his lock screen. Jake closed his eyes and took a breath. *Hell's teeth.* He found Diana's number in his address book and pressed call. Both men heard her answer and, making sure he was recording their conversation, Jake put the phone on speaker. He needed his father to hear this.

"Hello, darling, miss me already?"

"Hi, Diana, quick question. Did you answer my mobile a few days ago, actually two days in a row, maybe late afternoon?"

"Yes, it was that funny little thing Alex. The one you think you're in love with. I think I persuaded her you are no longer interested. You're welcome, by the way."

Jake ground his teeth but held onto his temper. "Why would you do that?" His tone, one of mild interest, reflected none of the fury Reuben could see in his eyes.

"Well, it was obvious you just needed to get her out of your system. I knew you'd tire of her sooner or later. I was surprised it took this long, but there you go. You can't possibly prefer her to me Jake, she's a nobody. You have nothing in common, whereas we have three years of shared experiences, not to mention our love of engineering. We are well suited, you and I. You *must* see that, darling?"

Jake was astonished. He gaped at Reuben who shrugged. Jake felt hot colour wash up his cheeks. His dad had always claimed Diana was superficial, and only with him because he fit her criteria of what a husband should be, but he hadn't believed him.

"Diana, we broke up months ago. I told you it was over. You didn't seem particularly bothered."

Her voice dropped to what was probably supposed to be an alluring pitch but had completely the opposite effect on Jake.

"Hon, it was easier to go with the flow. I knew you'd come back to me. Why settle for beer when you can have champagne." She flung the last sentence out with a hint of hauteur, to be met with silence.

Jake was speechless.

"Jake, honey..." Diana sounded less assured.

"Diana, for the last time, we are through. We were through six months ago. We were probably through for longer than that, only neither of us was ready to admit it. It was lovely, I enjoyed our time together, and until this afternoon, I never regretted any of it. To mislead someone, deliberately, two people in fact, is something I cannot condone. I am appalled you thought it acceptable to behave in such a manner."

There was the sound of stammering, but Jake cut her off. "Goodbye Diana." He severed the connection and threw his phone carelessly back onto the little side table. His leant forward, resting his elbows on his knees, his forearms hanging loosely.

"Dad...?"

"Go get your girl, Jake. Just don't drive like a maniac to get to her. I'm worried enough she's driving all the way up to Northumberland in this weather." The day was gloomy, more snow in the offing. Hoping it was localised, Reuben added. "If you set off now, you'll probably avoid getting snowed in again."

"Do you have her address?"

Reuben jotted something down. It seemed very short to

Jake, and when he read the scrap of paper his father handed him, his eyes widened.

"You have *got* to be kidding me?" he breathed, in disbelief.

"Nope. All true."

"Wow, well that explains why she was so embarrassed when I said she might lay claim to Studley Royal. It's entirely possible she *is* a descendent of the Mallory family who lived there in the fifteenth century. Lordy." Letting that one roll around his head for a minute, Jake tucked the note in his back pocket and, saying he was going to throw some clothes in a bag, left the room.

While he was gone, Reuben heard from Alex. She had arrived safely. No other information, but he didn't expect anything more. Texting a quick reply, he sipped his tea and waited for Jake.

Jake motored across the moors, following the same general direction Alex had taken hours earlier. It was mid-afternoon, and the light was already fading, the winter days short. He hoped the snow would hold off until he got to the hotel near the airport, where he had secured a room.

He didn't want to turn up on Alex's doorstep this evening, it wouldn't be fair. Reuben told him she had a meeting with one of the lawyers the next morning regarding the estate. He was going to take a chance on her agreeing to see him afterwards.

It was late when he pulled into the hotel carpark. The traffic was heavy as he approached Newcastle, and the weather had closed in. Parking the car, he scuffed through the thickening snow to the hotel, checked in, and found his way to the room.

Ordering room service, he rang Reuben to let him know he'd arrived in one piece, enjoyed his meal with a large glass of red wine, and went to bed.

CHAPTER TWENTY-ONE

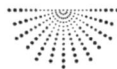

Alex turned her car up a long, winding driveway, crunching to a halt on the gravelled frontage of Lanchester Hall. An imposing mansion, and her family's home for generations. Stepping out of the car, she sucked in a gulp of the sharp air, feeling the odd twinge in her back and shoulders after the wearisome drive.

A voice hailed her, and she turned to see Dominic Winters — Kassie's oldest brother and estate steward to the Mallory family — who greeted her with a warm hug. Friends a long time, Alex had spent every possible moment with the Winters family when she was at the Hall, and it was lovely to see his familiar face.

"Long time, no see, Alex. I'm sorry it had to be in these circumstances," Dominic consoled.

Alex shrugged. "Thanks Dom. I suppose I ought to feel sad. I wish I could feel sad, but to be honest, I don't feel anything."

He nodded in quick understanding; wholly aware of the fragile relationship she shared with her parents. She moved towards the boot, intent on collecting her meagre luggage.

Dominic shook his head. Signalling to Mr Nelson, the butler, he ushered Alex out of the frigid air into the slightly less cold, cavernous entrance hall.

"I expect you're hungry and tired," he said as they walked into the library. A fire crackled merrily in the huge hearth — the smell of pine logs, polished leather and old books pervading the space.

Alex heaved a sigh... this was the only room she was ever comfortable in. Being able to lose herself in one of the hundreds of tomes lining the shelves was almost the only solace she got. That and escaping into the wilds on her pony.

"How is everyone?" she asked, aware they must be worried.

"You know, stoic as always." Dominic grinned. "I'll be back in a moment. I think Mattie has concocted something tasty for dinner." Inclining his head politely, he left the room, formalities, it seemed were ingrained — even with her friends.

In the blink of an eye, Alex had gone from research assistant to countess, probably with a seat in the House of Lords. It was farcical, even though she knew this day would come. She was the only child of the Count and Countess of Lanchester.

This was her birthright, yet as the peace of the room enveloped her, she could feel the weight of the title beginning to bear down. This house, okay stately home, was too much for her. *What did she want or need with a vast estate?* There was nothing of her in this building. Not so much as a photograph. She had never existed in the minds of those who came before her and, while recognising sorrow should be her overriding emotion, she was conscious of only a gaping emptiness.

Mindful of this, during the drive up from Yorkshire, an idea had begun to percolate. She believed it was feasible, but would have to make sure, if she carried it out, there were no loopholes. No way for some distant relative or interfering busybody to contest it.

She let the idea blossom in the quiet, watching the fire devour the logs, sparks billowing up the chimney as the wood popped and settled. The dancing flames reminded her of evenings at Moorview and unbidden, images of Jake filtered into her mind.

"No," she growled to herself. "He's not worth it. Let him go," but she couldn't. However angry she was with him, she hadn't stopped loving him, probably never would. "Grrrr... no more... enough," she muttered, furious he thought it acceptable to skulk around with some skanky female, then jump to preposterous conclusions without taking a moment to use his stupid brain. *Talk about double standards.*

Refusing to let him waste another moment of her time, Alex consigned Jake Faulkner to the fringes of her consciousness. Hopefully he would do the decent thing and stay there.

The evening passed pleasantly enough. After a hearty meal, eaten in the dining room in isolated splendour, Alex sauntered along to the kitchens where she knew the rest of the household would be gathered. She had virtually lived in the domestic quarters as a child. It was a hub of warmth and activity.

Irresistible to a youngster, and she had loved helping Mattie prepare the food. Looking back, Alex acknowledged with wry humour, she must have been a royal pain in the butt — definitely more hindrance than help. Her parents were harsh taskmasters and her interference in the smooth running of the kitchens must have been a nightmare for

Mattie and those under her wing, but they never shooed her out or complained.

Smiling, she recalled Mr Nelson remonstrating with her when she was about ten years old saying, 'it weren't right her bein' in yon kitchen, not the place for young ladies.' Her response had been along the lines of, 'she'd never be a lady, she was too unruly and headstrong; doubtless the title would pass her by' — waving her hand like a miniature princess, making the butler chuckle.

Happy days she mused, with a trace of melancholy. Not really, she corrected herself, she was never truly happy within these walls. There were too many strictures, but the time she had spent with Kassie, and the stolen hours behind the baize door, had been as close as she ever came to it.

Knocking, Alex pushed open the door, separating master from servant. Heading along the brightly lit corridor, she called a 'hello' to whoever was within the archaically named Servants' Hall. A designation which amused the current staff, and one they took great delight in deliberately overemphasising.

In the cosy lounge, to one side of the kitchens, she found Mattie, all alone, sitting on the sofa, engrossed in a television programme, mug of tea in her hands. The cook turned when the door creaked open, a huge beam warming her face when she saw Alex, who hesitated on the threshold, suddenly unsure.

"Alex, well now, bonny lass, you're a sight for sore eyes and no mistake. Come in come in," Mattie put her mug on the low coffee table and enfolded the young woman in a bear hug. The buxom cook, dragged Alex over to the sofa, sat her down and searched her face, simultaneously patting her hand. "How are you holding up, my sweet? It's a sorry mess so it is." Her familiar Northumberland burr, somehow soothing.

"I'm fine thank you, Mattie. It's a bit surreal, but…" She opened her palms in a philosophical gesture. She had no need to expound on her words. The household knew where Alex stood in the hierarchy of Lanchester Hall — somewhere below the pigs in the orchards. "It's you I worry about. This place is too big for me, and in all honesty, I don't want to live here. I think I might have a plan. Do you think the others might join us, and we can have a chat?"

"'Course hinny, you stay here. I'll round 'em up. Most are just finishing off. I'll make us another cuppa while we're waiting."

Alex smiled gratefully, sinking into the sofa, the noise from the television distracting her. By the time the kettle had boiled, everyone who lived in had gathered, and sipped their hot drinks while Alex outlined her plan.

"If I can come to an agreement with the lawyers, you should be able to keep your jobs. They will need people of your calibre to ensure the estate remains profitable."

Heads nodded all around

"What will you do, Lady Lanchester?" queried Connie, who had been her mother's personal maid.

Alex grinned. "Don't you dare 'Lady Lanchester' me, Connie, my name is Alex."

Connie blushed.

"I mean it, that goes for everyone…" grinning at their faces, which ranged from amused to astonished — one or two of the staff, new to her.

"I have a wonderful job in Rosedale Abbey." She expounded, telling them about her work for Reuben. For the first time since Alex had set foot in her old home, her eyes glowed.

Well-versed in interpreting even the most subtle facial expression, the staff knew something — or more likely someone — was the cause, and it wasn't her current boss.

Despite their relaxed camaraderie, they didn't pry, she'd tell them in due course.

Chatting over hot chocolate laden with marshmallows, and listening to the local gossip, Alex took comfort in the informal atmosphere, until deciding it was time she left them to their evening.

"Am I in my old room?" She turned when she reached the door.

"That you are, my lovely. I hope you sleep well. We'll hold breakfast until you're ready. Don't feel you have to get up with the birds." Mrs Nelson, the housekeeper, affirmed, not forgetting Alex's penchant for dawn walks.

"I have a lot to do tomorrow, Mrs Nelson. If I might have breakfast at seven, that would be perfect, and please, if you don't mind, I'd rather eat it here than in that soulless dining room." She winked, and the housekeeper smiled back.

"As you wish, my dear. Now go on with you, doubtless Bruno will be in his favourite spot." Referring to her father's aged wolfhound.

"Bruno? No way!" she exclaimed, and Mrs Nelson nodded. "I can't believe he's still alive! He must be ten if he's a day." The dog had been her faithful follower, since a puppy, more because he knew she was a pushover for letting him sleep on her bed, than any other reason. It had amused her no end when Bruno had shown his preference, during the break between school and university.

Their affinity didn't please Terence Mallory, and it remained a constant surprise to Alex that he hadn't got rid of Bruno, whom she begged to be allowed to take with her when she moved to Boxgrove. Her father refused point blank, and she hadn't seen the dog for five years, amazed he was allowed in her room.

"He howled if the door was closed. His lordship stopped caring," Mrs Nelson explained.

Her heart contracting for the lonely dog, Alex mentally kicked herself for abandoning him. *Would Reuben agree to Bruno living at Moorview?* She didn't think he was likely to object, and she was certain the other dogs would be accommodating.

Thanking the housekeeper once again, Alex trudged up to her bedroom. The door was ajar, a lamp lit by the bed, and Bruno was sprawled across the luxurious comforter, snoring.

"Bruno, you bad dog," Alex murmured when she entered the room. Glancing around, she noticed nothing had changed since she last set foot in there. It was both heartening and weird. She half-expected her parents to have removed all evidence of her from here too.

Bruno snuffled in his sleep, shifting his body on the bedcover. She spoke again. The dog blinked drowsily, then blinked again, as though in disbelief of what he was seeing. With a kind of choked howl, he uncoiled his great length and hurled himself at her, whimpering in ecstasy when she tickled him behind the ears and stroked his shaggy fur.

"Hello boy," she crooned, dropping to the floor, in front of the fire, letting the dog re-establish his bond. Much later, snuggled under warm covers, Bruno lying next to her, Alex contemplated the coming days.

The arrival of her parents' bodies, the funeral, and the settlement of the estate — hoping the latter would be organised without too much fuss. The funeral was in three days' time. After that she could leave. There was nothing to keep her here.

❧

The next morning, not far from Lanchester Hall, Jake Faulkner sat at the desk in his hotel room, deliberating over how he could possibly explain his behaviour to Alex.

He didn't think marching up to her and requesting a hearing would go down too well, but he wasn't very good at approaching a situation obliquely. In his line of work, there was no point beating about the bush. You had to come straight the point and be very clear, otherwise lives could be at stake.

The irony that this time his heart was at stake, not lost on him.

He realised he was afraid. Afraid she would look at him with that empty stare. Her dark eyes no longer smiling up him when she teased. Or twinkling with mischief while they debated a topic — her playing devil's advocate, just to rile him up. Or gazing at him as they made love, her passion for him brimming over.

He smacked his hand against his forehead. Stupid! How could he have been so stupid?

Reuben long-believed Jake had a self-destructive streak where relationships were concerned. Until Alex, Diana had been the longest liaison Jake indulged in, and at thirty-five, it was not the best track record.

Whenever things became serious, he backed off, and Reuben had a hunch Jake stayed with Diana for so long because she never pressured him into a long-term commitment. Now Alex had blown into his life like a miniature gale, turning all his arguments inside out.

Without trying, she had undermined Jake's resolve. He was teetering on the brink of an abyss, yet he wanted nothing more than to open his heart, and let himself fall into Alex, and keep falling for the rest of his life. Was he too late? Did he still have a chance?

There was only one way to find out.

. . .

He glanced out of the window. The heavy sky indicated more snow was in the offing. The grim greyness suited both his mood and the situation.

Slipping his wallet into his back pocket, he picked up his phone, and unhooked his thick winter coat from its hanger. Checking to make sure he had the room key card, he left. The sound of the door slamming shut behind him had an ominous ring, and he hoped it wasn't an omen.

CHAPTER TWENTY-TWO

I n the library of the great house, Alex was preparing for
the solicitor. The hardest part, she believed, of her visit
to Lanchester Hall was over.

Two sombre black hearses arrived on the dot of 8:30, and
a smartly dressed gentleman from the local funeral home had
handed her a sheaf of papers to read and sign. She was
expected to confirm the bodies were indeed those of Terence
and Imogen Mallory, but that was all.

As previously arranged, the caskets would be returned to
the funeral home, where any who chose to do so could view
the earl and his countess. Alex thought this macabre in the
extreme, but seemingly there were always those with a
ghoulish desire to see the dead.

Relieved, once that was completed, she spent the next
hour or so researching on the Internet, finding, and printing
out, any relevant information. She had accumulated a neat
pile of documents on the desk, in anticipation that the representative from the legal firm would attempt to dissuade her.
Her mind was made up. This was the only way she could

trust the staff would reap the benefit of their many years serving her family.

Alex had forgotten the almost feudal constraints her parents had insisted were observed. While she understood the need for respect between staff and employer, some of her parents' expectations were positively medieval. Had she walked into the Hall, unaware it sported all the modern conveniences, she would be forgiven for thinking she had blundered onto the set of a BBC historical drama.

Cup of strong coffee in hand, she sauntered over to the French doors, propping herself against the frame to stare out over the winter wonderland. The majority of her memories of this place might be cheerless, but she had to concede the view was breathtakingly beautiful.

Under a layer of snow, neatly manicured gardens, carefully tended by Mr Potts and his team, rolled out towards, what in years gone by, would have been the Great Park. Now it was the domain of the horses when not confined to the stables, as they were currently.

Opening the door a crack, Alex breathed in the frosty air, enjoying its bite for several minutes until she heard the roar of an engine coming up the drive. Shutting out the chill, she checked her watch. He was right on time. Mr Tomlinson was attending this meeting; apparently, her parents' will warranted a senior partner, not some underling.

Alex had asked Dominic to join them, more so all the legalese, and technical jargon lawyers loved bandying about, wouldn't confuse her. Dominic was a clever man, with a double degree in business and commerce, as well as a master's in management. Head steward of Lanchester Hall for the last ten years — not much skipped Dominic's notice.

There was a knock, and Dominic entered at Alex's invitation. On his heels, a burly, florid-faced man, who in spite of his impeccable suit, looked more like a rugby player than a solicitor. He carried a legal archive box, on top of which balanced several more files, and as he approached the table, Alex realised her hands were trembling.

A glut of mixed emotions threatened to swamp her, and she instructed herself to get a grip. Her parents' lives — a combined total of over one hundred years — had been reduced to this box and a few papers. Much as any love had been extinguished long ago, they were still her parents, and Alex had believed them invincible. She never expected, at twenty-eight years old, to be dealing with their deaths.

To Alex's relief, Mr Tomlinson proved an affable man, and sensitive to the situation. He explained the will. It was very simple. To her everlasting astonishment, everything came to Alex, and there was a lot. Some of which she had an inkling, most she didn't.

The Mallorys owned an estate in Switzerland, and a villa in the South of France, she knew that. Two houses in London, two in Paris, one in New York, and one in San Francisco. She knew about one of the properties in London and the house in New York, of the rest she had no clue

Then there was this estate and all its holdings, the tenant farmers, and the accompanying stock, both animals and crops. The Lanchester estate was vast. It stretched for miles and kept umpteen people in employment.

Finally, he came to the financial endowment, and when Alex heard the sum, she had to concentrate on not bursting into hysterical laughter. It was more than she ever imagined, an astronomical amount, her stupefaction apparent to the solicitor.

"Your parents were shrewd with their investments, Lady Lanchester. Your father had the knack of knowing just when to buy and sell, and they chose their portfolio wisely." He smiled, genially.

"Thank you, Mr Tomlinson. I see that, but this…" Alex spread her hands over the desk, "…this is ludicrous. I could buy a small island with all this."

"And the rest." The solicitor winked.

Alex shook her head and took a breath. "Sir, might there be a way we, I, can channel these funds elsewhere? Charities and so on, you know several anonymous donations. To have such an enormous sum of money at my disposal, not to mention all those properties, without considering others, smacks of self-indulgence. I shall bank only a small percentage and hope you might arrange for the remainder to be distributed among several charities of my choice. In addition, I should like to sell this house and its estate to an organisation like the National Trust or English Heritage, along with enough money to maintain it in perpetuity." She concluded, diffidently. "Supposing that to be possible."

Aware her words sounded formal, stilted almost, Alex wanted to be sure this man understood she was serious.

"Mr Tomlinson, all I need is enough to keep me comfortable, with a little extra for a holiday. The rest can go."

At this, Dominic intervened. He suggested, in his calm, unflappable way, that perhaps they needed a few minutes to discuss this, and would Mr Tomlinson appreciate a quick tour of the Hall.

The solicitor readily agreed. Dominic rang for Mr Nelson, who led Mr Tomlinson off towards the remainder of the house.

The room fell silent.

"Alex, please think long and hard about this. I don't want you to rush into something, only to regret it later," Dominic ventured after several minutes of quiet. "What about any children you might have? You should at least keep enough for possible school or uni fees. Also, you need to remember, this would become their heritage too. Do you want to eliminate any chance they have to be part of this?"

He opened his palm in an all-encompassing gesture. "Perhaps you ought to consider retaining this estate. Let the others go by all means, but this has been in your family for centuries."

Alex stared at Dominic. His words struck a chord. He was right, but the thought of being responsible for Lanchester Hall made her feel physically unwell. Most of her memories ranged from unpleasant to downright horrible. There was too much negativity for her ever to feel comfortable here.

Even if she had children, her lip curling at the distinct lack of probability, did she really want to saddle them with the same obligations? The estate cost a significant amount to maintain, was it fair? A point she voiced now.

"I can't answer that, Alex. All I can say is, if you sell you are denying them the option. Are you prepared to do that? Plus, there is the, not inconsequential, matter of inheritance taxes and how they would affect any sale. I believe, regardless of what you decided to sell at, the tax relates to the market value, not the sale price. Your liability could be exorbitant."

Alex stood from the table and paced the floor. Her grand plan had sounded so easy in her head; maybe it wasn't possible at all. Going over to the French doors, she gazed out at a landscape which ought to evoke pleasant nostalgia, but its magnificence didn't touch her heart.

Shutting her eyes, she let all the noise fade away,

emptying her mind of the rational arguments, and the sensible, appropriate alternatives. An image of the Yorkshire moors at sunset swam over her vision, making her smile — and she knew.

Coming back to the desk, she resumed her seat and looked at her friend.

"Dom, I can't be responsible for this place, never mind the other houses, it's absurd. What use have I for eight houses? What am I supposed to do with all their thousands?"

Dominic creased a brow.

"Millions?" she queried, faintly. He nodded. "Okay, millions. Millions… oh Lordy…" she trailed off as that finally sank in. "I have a job I love, a car, and a little flat in Boxgrove. What more could I possibly need? Yes, this place may have been in my family for centuries, but that doesn't mean it should remain so.

"Think of how many people could benefit from it being in the public domain. I'd far rather that was my legacy. My parents didn't love me, they never wanted me. I was the spare part, the part that didn't fit into their perfectly ordered world. I don't want what they coveted, what they craved. If I'd been a boy, things might have been different, but there you go."

Dominic heard the edge in her voice, keenly aware of how little Alex's parents had cared for her. Members of his family had worked at the Hall, in one capacity or another, for generations. His own father had little time for Terence and Imogen Mallory, in part, owing to their treatment of Alex.

Alex had spent more time at the Winters' home than she did her own. Kassie, his soft-hearted sister, had acted as a stabilising influence on the child who had a tendency to run wild, to flout the strictures she was forced to endure when at home.

They had believed her tales of discipline and punishment

to be the result of her vivid imagination, until the day the storm hit, the storm that changed everything. After that, without making it obvious, Dominic's family shielded Alex from her parents as much as they were able, but the damage had been done.

Alex was never quite the same happy-go-lucky, spontaneous kid. She remained friendly but became reserved, retreating behind a protective shell. Her uninhibited laughter, exuberant chatter and joyous spirit, subdued. Since that day, Dominic had never seen her cry. It continued to bother him twenty years after the fact.

He watched Alex stand again to stride around the room, thumping her fist into her palm, rattling off all the reasons why handing over the majority of the endowment was the most logical and practical choice.

Letting her vent, he turned his attention to the documents on the table, scanning them, mentally adjusting them to fit Alex's suggestion.

"Alex, come sit here a minute."

She continued to pace.

"*Alex*!"

She swivelled around to stare at him, her mind elsewhere.

"Come and look at this with me. I've had a thought."

She walked over and, resuming her seat, listened while Dominic explained.

It was unorthodox, but as Alex mulled it over, she acknowledged it had definite potential. Although it would undoubtedly involve a lot of discussion with the tax people, it could be the answer.

Asking a few pertinent questions, she grudgingly — seeing the sense in Dominic's argument — acquiesced on the financial aspect. There were one or two things she refused to budge on, but by the time Mr Tomlinson reappeared, Alex was satisfied.

. . .

"This is a wonderful house, Lady Lanchester," the solicitor gushed. "Mr Nelson informs me, some parts date back four hundred years."

"Thank you and yes, it does. Most of the Hall was refurbished early last century, when the wings were added to the original building. It was rewired about fifteen years ago I think, so that's one less expense any new owner would need to consider. Father hated open fires, and had central heating installed, at around the same time. I think it has been as modernised as is appropriate in a house such as this, we even have access to the Internet." Alex elaborated, while the solicitor organised himself.

Once he was settled, she made her pitch. "Mr Tomlinson, I am aware there are all sorts of arcane rules and regulations involved in the sale and purchase of properties like Lanchester Hall, not to mention inheritance tax. What I propose, should it be approved by the relevant government department or departments, is to donate the property to either National Trust or English Heritage."

Mr Tomlinson blinked.

Then he blinked again.

His eyes swung between Alex and Dominic, he started to say something, faltered, and clamped his mouth closed.

The silence lengthened, no one broke it.

After several minutes, when Alex speculated whether the distinguished gentleman was about to have a heart attack, Mr Tomlinson finally spoke with a modicum of coherence.

"Miss Mall… Lady Lanchester, this is a most unusual request. Its market value is in the millions."

"Yes, I realise that, which is precisely why I want to donate it." Alex leant forward. "Don't you see? There is no way any one organisation could justify buying at the current value. As a gift, with a trust set up to cover everyday expenses for staff, maintenance, wages and so on, it is a far more attractive prospect. It could be administered on the same lines as places like Chatsworth or Castle Howard. Open to the public, to school groups, whatever.

"The new owners would reap the rewards of having people working the land, as they have for centuries. We have cattle, sheep and deer. The orchards are plentiful, as are the crops. I imagine the stables are still full of horses?" She looked to Dominic for confirmation, seeing the slight incline of his head.

"They could run a riding school. There are so many options available, they would be fools to ignore the opportunity. It would also save the property from being divided up for development."

Alex was in full flood, her enthusiasm contagious and the three began to debate the merits of her plan, including what she wanted to do with the remaining properties, and the monetary balance.

It took some time, but slowly her idea coalesced into a viable scheme.

CHAPTER TWENTY-THREE

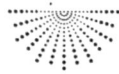

I t wasn't long before they had an outline. Mr Tomlinson agreed to act on her behalf. He would arrange to meet with someone from HM Revenue and Customs to discuss the proposal and all it entailed. With regard to the remainder of the estate, he confirmed he would have the papers drawn up for her perusal as soon as possible.

Another tray of coffee was brought in, and while the three sipped the heady brew, Alex signed the numerous legal documents the solicitor assured her were necessary. It was a lengthy process but eventually, with an aching hand, she was done. Resting against the back of the chair, she rolled her shoulders and flexed her fingers, watching Mr Tomlinson gather the last few sheets together.

"Thank you, Lady Lanchester. I shall be in touch regarding these," he waved the papers enthusiastically. "I admit to being shocked that you have no desire to keep anything other than the amount you have stipulated but respect your wishes."

"If you knew anything of my life, Mr Tomlinson, it wouldn't seem so outlandish," she demurred. "As long as those people maintaining any and all of my parent's properties are not left destitute, the rest can be distributed amongst that list of charities."

A new thought teased her. "Might we also consider a couple of bursaries for students from low income families wanting to study the Classics? I'm sure the local universities — Durham, Newcastle and Northumbria — would know how that works." The idea solidified. "Yes, definitely, I would like each of the three to have an annual grant available to those studying ancient history."

The solicitor made another note on his legal pad. "I'll email you when I have everything organised. The sale of the overseas properties might take some time, international law being what it is, but we'll get there. Now, I have taken up enough of your day. I know you have other things to organise. Thank you very much, Lady Lanchester, it has been my great pleasure to meet you."

He shook her hand and Alex, uncaring it might not be entirely appropriate, drew him close for a quick hug. "No, thank you, Mr Tomlinson, and please call me Alex. We are doubtless going to be working together for many months until this is concluded, and I cannot countenance being 'Lady Lanchester'd' all the time."

She grinned, for once a wholly unrestrained gesture eliciting responding smiles from the two men standing there.

"Fine, Lady... Alex, and my name is Richard. No, please you don't need to bother," when Dominic moved to show him out. "I can find my own way." He nodded a goodbye. "I'll be in touch."

"Drive safely, Richard," Alex called, as the solicitor strode from the library, his footsteps fading as he reached the front door. Alex dropped back into the chair. It was exhausting all this talk of money and left her feeling oddly grubby. "I need another shower," she chuckled as Dominic shut the door. "I hate talking about money."

"Maybe so, but it has to be done, this isn't some pitiful bequest, it's unheard of sums, and demands careful thought."

"I know," she sighed, "and I'm stunned they left it all to me. I was certain mother would have named every single one of her friends, their families and any enemies before allowing me a single penny of her fortune."

"Maybe she did care for you in her own way."

Alex was about to make a derisive comment when there was a knock, and Mr Nelson's head appeared around the door.

"You have a visitor, Lady Lanchester"

"Show them in, Mr Nelson, and what did I say about using that title?" She reproofed with a mischievous smile. "I used to slide down bannisters and pinch biscuits from the kitchens. There's nothing 'Lady' like about me."

He bowed, and with a hint of a grin left the room, returning seconds later with a tall gentleman.

❧

Dominic was about to welcome the stranger and ask his business when a strangled sound from Alex stopped him. He glanced across, noticing she had gone pale.

"Alex?"

Alex didn't hear Dominic's soft voiced question, staring in shock at the visitor.

"J… Jake. What… when… because… did you…?" She bit her lip and tried again. "Why are you here?"

"I came to talk to you, to explain… if you'll listen." His voice was uncharacteristically hesitant, and Alex felt her chest pinch. She wasn't about to fall back into his arms —

however muscular and inviting they might be. *No, she absolutely would not.*

"I'm not sure we have anything to talk about," she replied, with arctic hauteur.

Dominic sensing undercurrents, and astute enough to realise this man was far more than a passing acquaintance. Excusing himself, he said he would come back later to finalise the funeral arrangements.

Alex nodded absently, her gaze never leaving Jake's face. He looked exhausted, and she had to stop herself from rushing over and stroking his weary features or kissing the tired lines at the edge of his eyes, or better still his pinched mouth. *No*, she admonished herself, *no, no, no!*

Forcing all expression from her face, Alex waited.

Jake came a step closer, then stopped, seemingly irresolute.

He opened his palms. "Please hear me out, Alex. There was, *is*, nothing going on between Diana and me. Nothing! I swear on all your ancient books." Haunted eyes held hers, willing her to trust.

Alex studied him, letting the silence drag out. She was unwilling to give him a minute, never mind long enough to hear him out. It dawned on her, *he looked afraid.*

Half of her, the angry, upset and hurt part of her, wanted him to suffer the same gut-wrenching pain she had experienced at the thought he was playing around. The other half, the half that loved him beyond measure, wanted him to wrap her in his arms and kiss away the ache.

Crap!

Jake watched anger, sadness and hurt play across her face, then a mask fell. He guessed he had blown it, she wasn't interested in what he had to say. Fair enough, he couldn't blame her, but he couldn't stay to hear her reject him.

His shoulders slumped, and he turned to leave.

"Where are you going?" Her voice warming from frigid to chilled.

He spun on his heel. "I supposed you weren't in a forgiving mood. I can understand that." His voice was quiet, resigned.

"I'm not sure what to think, Jake, but you came after me, that's something." She didn't elaborate further. Reaching out, she tugged on a long wide ribbon of material with a tassel on the end. Almost immediately, a young woman appeared.

"Connie, please could you arrange for some more coffee, actually make mine tea, or I'll be bouncing off the walls, and some sandwiches for lunch?"

The maid nodded.

"Thank you very much. Now," she said, when Connie vanished into the depths of the house, "come and take a load off, you look knackered." Her use of slang in these refined surroundings surprised Jake into a tentative smile.

He walked over to where she stood by the hearth, a roaring fire crackling in the grate, and took the seat she indicated. He would have preferred to whisk her into his arms and kiss her senseless but was too wary of her reaction.

"Okay, tell me," she urged, remaining by the fireplace. She didn't trust herself to be too close.

_&_

He did. He told Alex everything. At this point he had nothing to lose.

"First off, I had no clue Diana had answered my phone. I leave it with Janet when I'm in meetings, always have. How Diana found it is anybody's guess. Maybe Janet stepped away from her desk or had gone home. I'd been in and out of meetings all week, some of which had dragged on until well into the evening.

"The best part of my day was chatting with you, and then out of the blue, you stopped replying. I called, texted, emailed — nothing. You have *no* idea how terrifying that is when I had no way to reach you physically either.

"Alex, I didn't know why I couldn't get hold of you. All sorts of scenarios kept running through my head. I had no clue whether you were alive or dead. In the middle of winter, when you live out on the moors, it's not inconceivable. It was the worst week of my life."

Jake averted his gaze, staring at the flames, abject panic simmering close to the surface.

Alex flushed. She hadn't given any thought to Jake's feelings. She believed him to be in the wrong. Hadn't, for one second, considered giving him the benefit of the doubt, and never questioned him about the woman she had spoken to. Yes, she was afraid of his answer, but surely, even hearing him admit he was back with Diana would have been better than that awful week.

She had consigned every email he sent to the trash — unopened and switched off her mobile. It was only the email from the solicitors that prompted her to check her phone and, she had continued to ignore everything Jake sent.

Then he had turned up, in a flaming temper, accusing *her* of sleeping around. Wait... that was *exactly* what she had accused him of.

Double crap!

She forced her attention back to Jake.

"Finally, the road was passable, and I drive home like a mad thing, only to see you in Dad's arms. My head about exploded, and my heart shattered. Logic went through the window, and I lashed out. I had no right to accuse you of having an affair with my father. I knew you weren't capable of doing something so cruel, but everything else, Mum, Tricia, Jill..."

Alex furrowed her brow, quizzically.

"... she was the one before Tricia..." he clarified, seeing her nod in quick understanding, "...reared up and the words were out before I could stop them. Yeah, I was angry, but I was more gutted. I thought I'd lost you..." He raked his fingers through his hair in agitation.

Alex fought the urge to fling her arms around him and kiss him until neither of them cared about those bloody stupid misunderstandings, but they had to fix this first.

"I thought you'd gone back to her, she told me you were in the shower, that you had plans which would take up the whole of the evening. She said 'Coming Jake', as though you were calling to her. How could she know that, say that, unless...? Why did she...?" She couldn't finish either question.

"It never happened, Alex, and this is why..." Jake withdrew his mobile and replayed the conversation with Diana from the previous day.

Alex was flabbergasted. "She thought I was just a bit of something on the side? Not important enough to hold your attention for more than a couple of months?" Her face reflecting how much that stung.

"Alex, you know how wrong her assumption was, is. I love you. I have loved you, probably from the day you looked at me through those ridiculous magnifying glasses. Certainly, since the day of the storm." Unable to wait any longer, Jake got up from the chair.

Closing the gap between them, he caught her hand,

pulling her into his arms. "And I will love you until I draw my last breath."

He kissed her.

＊

While Jake talked, Alex studied him, his torment clear in his expression. The ache in her heart eased, her body yearned for his touch. *Why did he have to be so bloody handsome, and sexy? Even with all the misery she, they'd both, suffered this last week or so, she was a lost cause. Totally, utterly, and hopelessly in love with him.*

Remaining by the hearth, several paces from him was taking all her willpower, but when he gathered her against his irresistibly taut frame, the last of her outrage melted away — and then he went and kissed her. *Well that just isn't fair*, she thought, grumpily. *How am I supposed to...?*

The rest of her eminently sensible argument vanished as delicious heat flared. She stopped thinking, stopped rationalising, and stopped caring.

Jake was here. He'd come for her... for *her*... and now he was kissing her. It didn't get much better than that.

He kissed her until the sound of knocking registered in the mashed potato, which had replaced her brain. She broke away, calling a husky, "Come in."

Connie entered, carrying a tray piled with sandwiches and two steaming mugs — one of tea, one of coffee. She dipped a curtsy when Alex thanked her, and fled back to whatever duties she had yet to complete.

Jake raised an amused eyebrow.

Alex blushed. "I know, it's crackers. A week ago, I was Alex Mallory, your ordinary, average, common or garden research assistant. Now, I'm the Countess of Lanchester and people defer to me. To me!" A giggle escaped her lips and she sucked in a steadying breath. Hysteria, borne of trying to bank down way too many emotions, lurked.

"You have never been ordinary or average to me, love," Jake interposed. He spoke quietly, but she heard the sincerity in his voice as though rung from the village church bells.

Alex also had some explaining to do. She would have told him who she was eventually, but people always treated her differently when they found out about her family. They either ignored her altogether, because… obviously… the moment they learnt her status, she immediately considered them beneath her. A sentiment which made her roll her eyes, in frustration but still stung. Or, worse — became obsequious, like Uriah Heep in Dickens' David Copperfield.

It was easier not to tell anyone.

School was marginally tolerable because she had mixed with others from similar backgrounds. By the time she started at uni, she no longer divulged anything about herself, a practice she continued. Only a select few people were privy to who she was, and that was only because she had no alternative.

Handing Jake a plate, she passed the platter of sandwiches, placing the mugs on the occasional table between their chairs. Once they were sorted, Alex sat in the chair next to Jake's, curling her legs under her, and balancing the plate on her knees. She fiddled with the bread, pulling out a slice of tomato and nibbling on it, then doing the same with the wafer-thin slice of beef.

"What's going on in that muddled head of yours, my lady?" Jake quizzed, grinning when she narrowed her eyes at him.

"Don't you start," she groused. "It's bad enough the staff doing it. I usually eat at the table in the kitchen, for goodness sake. Anyway, it doesn't matter, because even though I can't divest myself of the title, most of the rest will go."

"What do you mean?" Jake asked, confused. Alex outlined her plans for the Hall as well as all other the properties and monies. Stunned at the sheer numbers she was talking about, Jake managed to stop his jaw from hitting the floor, and instead listened carefully, asking the odd question here and there.

"And you came up with this in… what… less than forty-eight hours? I am impressed."

Alex shrugged. "What do I want with all this?" She waved her hand around the room. "This is nothing compared with some of the other rooms. This place is only a building to me, it was never a home." She cut herself off, not yet ready to share that part of her life.

Jake reached across to interlace their fingers. "I'm here when you want to tell me. It's okay, I imagine anyone who covers their tracks as well as you, is either wanted by the police or has personal reasons for keeping her past hidden. I'm pretty sure it's not the former." He wiggled an eyebrow, prompting Alex to laugh, the tension in the room dissolving by the minute.

"I will tell you, Jake, but I've buried it for so long, I don't know whether I want to dredge it up. It's easier pretending it never happened." She turned their hands and traced his palm with her index finger. Unable to stop herself, she continued to stroke over his wrist, and under the cuff of his shirt, which peeked out under his jumper.

No, not yet. She let go as though his skin had scalded her and jumped up from her chair.

"Right, would you like the grand tour or the halfpenny tour?" she asked over-brightly.

Jake frowned at her sudden change, but determined not to read too much into it, unfolded himself from the chair.

"I would love one, and it absolutely must be the *grand tour* if it pleases, my lady." He winked, holding out his hand, glad she took it as she led him into the rest of the house.

CHAPTER TWENTY-FOUR

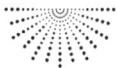

Following a comprehensive tour of the Hall, Alex and Jake were strolling through the formal gardens, the paths cleared of snow that morning. It was bitterly cold, but neither noticed, engrossed in their discussion regarding Alex's change of circumstances.

Rounding the building into the rear courtyard, off which were the outhouses, a few of the estate workshops and the stables, Alex came to a sudden halt. Rubbing her forehead, she stared at a row of dilapidated buildings at the opposite side.

It never ceased to amaze her, memories from that day still had the power to turn her into a quivering wreck. She took a step, and then stopped again, uncertain whether she should try to lay the ghost to rest or turn her back on it.

"What's up?" Jake queried, puzzled.

"It's just… there was… a long time ago… but…"

Jake spun her to face him, registering the slightly grey cast to her cheeks and the shadows lurking in her eyes. Bending, he kissed her nose. "Spill, Lady Lanchester."

Alex shuddered. "Please, please don't ever call me that."

She let go of his hand and went over to the line of buildings. It was strange to her, they looked so innocuous today, in the weak sunlight of a winter's afternoon.

On that scorching July day, they seemed like portals to hell. Of course, they weren't in such a sorry state back then. Alex frowned, as she got closer, wondering why no one had repaired them.

She walked slowly along the row until she reached the one farthest from the main house. Smoothing her hand over the wooden door, she traced the knotty grain of the panels. It was as solid as it had been back then, but the edges bore evidence of the flames.

Pictures reared up in her mind. She ignored them, forcing them aside as she tugged on the wrought iron handle. No padlock today, just a rusting loop of metal.

The door screeched when she opened it wide enough to slip inside, long unused hinges torn from their creaking brackets, warped wood dragging over uneven cobbles. She peered at the stone steps leading down to the lowered floor, covered in dirt and leaves. Tufts of grass struggled to stay alive through fissures in the flagstones, the tiled roof looked as though someone had taken pot shots at it, and pools of ice formed wherever water seeped in.

Nevertheless, it had a benign aura, serene even — the slightly damp odour, reminiscent of spring rains. Fingers brushing over the cool stone, Alex stepped through the gap, vaguely aware Jake was asking her something. She couldn't hear him properly, her head full of a long-ago afternoon. The sounds, the smells, that earth shattering crash, and the overwhelming fear she was about to die.

Image after image slammed into her consciousness, flickering like a strobe light. Her heart thudded, her breathing became erratic, and her legs turned to jelly. Alex thought by now she would be able to handle it; she was an adult, and so many years after the fact, there should be nothing here but an old shed.

Her hands went up as though to push away the memories, but they kept coming and it was all she could do to remain standing.

She had to get out.

Past and present collided. Alex couldn't distinguish what was real and what was imaginary, and for some reason she couldn't move. Then she smelt it... what was it? It tickled her nostrils and she inhaled, trying to pinpoint it. Wait... was that smoke? No, it couldn't be, but yes, delicate tendrils were making their sinuous way through the cracks in the walls. *How was it on fire?* The sheds were brick and tile.

She rattled the door, shouting for help, please someone let her out — then realised it would be okay, her father knew she was here. He would come and save her.

Confident her father wouldn't leave her locked in, Alex sank onto a pile of threadbare hessian sacks dumped carelessly in a broken wheelbarrow, and waited. It was so hot. The smoke got thicker, and she began to cough, her eight-year-old brain screaming at her to find clean air.

She banged and yelled and kicked and battered, until her throat was raw, her fingers bruised and bleeding, but no one came. She remembered it was important to stay low. The local fire brigade had visited her school, to demonstrate what to do if caught in a fire. Recalling the drill, she fell into a crouch, the dusty floor cool and the air less acrid.

. . .

She was going to die, all because she had ridden Clover against her father's express instructions. It seemed an extreme sort of punishment. *Maybe it would be easier if she was dead*, her inner voice mused. Her parents didn't want her under their feet.

They complained constantly about her singing, or her piano playing or her childish games or that she always ran instead of walking, or she spoke too loudly. This would deteriorate into bitter discussions about her lack of grace, lack of intelligence, lack of looks, and lack of all the genteel traits they had tried to instil in their only child. Each blaming the other for her shortcomings.

She was the reason for their arguments.

The one who caused dissent.

Alex could hear the crackle of the flames as they consumed the buildings in the row. There was so much noise; the storm, the fire, and her screams. Terror took over, and she hurled herself bodily at the door, at the same instant that it was yanked open from the outside. Alex fell into the courtyard, like a shrieking banshee — a black, bloodied and sooty mess.

She had no memory of what happened next. She woke hours later in the safety of her room, her hands bandaged, and Mrs Nelson sitting by her bed, reading a book. Her parents, it seemed, didn't care enough to make sure she wasn't injured or traumatised by her ordeal.

A month later they sent her away to school.

After exhausting every conceivable emotion in the space of a few hours, Alex had resolved it would never happen again and became almost an automaton. The only time she showed any feelings at all, was when she was with Kassie.

· · ·

Until she met Jake.

Jake waited in the courtyard, unsure why Alex wanted to investigate a rickety-looking shed, mildly concerned she didn't appear to have heard his questions. For no reason he could think of, he recalled the morning of the storm, her reaction and resulting nightmare.

He was about to go after her when footsteps crunching across the courtyard had him turning. It was the man, Dominic, who had been with Alex when he arrived. Jake inclined his head, and the other man grinned a greeting. The two began an amicable discussion about the estate. It was several minutes before Dominic asked where Alex was.

"She's exploring that old shed." Jake pointed to where Alex had gone.

Dominic shook his head. "No way! Shit, I don't think she should be..." he started to say, but was cut off by an unearthly wail, then came a faint cry for help, followed by a series of shrieks.

It took Jake precious seconds to register it was Alex. It didn't sound like her, the voice muffled by the walls of the shed. Presuming the roof had fallen in, he sped after Dominic who was already wrenching the door wide open, expecting to find a scene of utter devastation.

Instead all seemed undamaged. Alex was huddled on the floor, rocking back and forth, as unintelligible babble interspersed with agonised screams for help, spewed from her lips.

"Alex, Alex it's okay, you're safe. It's me, Dom." Both men bolted down the steps, Jake reaching Alex first. Scooping her off the dirt, he hurried out into the chilly afternoon, Dominic on his heels. In the throes of a waking nightmare, Alex wrestled against the arms constraining her, but Jake was stronger.

Dominic led the way into the Hall through the domestic entrance, sticking his head into the kitchen to ask Mattie to organise some sweet tea and perhaps a plate of ginger snaps. Mattie was another, present twenty years ago, the day's events clear as though they'd occurred only yesterday. Overhearing Alex's gibberish, she nodded in immediate understanding.

At Dominic's direction, Jake carried Alex to the library. He chose the same chair by the roaring fire, where he was sitting less than two hours earlier, and settled her on his lap. Holding her close, he talked, trying to bring her out of the horror gripping her mind.

It took a long time. Minutes ticked by with ever-increasing slowness but at last Alex began to calm down. Dominic came in with the tea and biscuits, then went over to a beautifully carved wooden cabinet in the corner to pour a generous splash of whisky into three tumblers.

Placing them, and the decanter, on the table, he lifted his own glass, swallowing the measure in one go; indicating Jake should do the same. Jake needed no second invitation and gulped a mouthful, the aged single malt clearing his head.

Dominic refilled both glasses, while Jake picked up the third, and wafted it under Alex's nose. She pulled away, unconsciously batting at the hand holding the tumbler, but he persisted and was rewarded by a moue of distaste as the distinctive aroma tickled her nostrils.

He repeated his actions one more time.

Alex opened her eyes.

Jake held his breath

Alex blinked, her focus coming back to the elegant, yet

comfortable room, with its blazing fire and shelves of books. The smell of aged leather, dusty tomes and the hint of cigar, although faint was familiar, and a sense of peace descended over her. Twisting in the arms still holding her, Alex smiled, tentatively, at Jake whose troubled expression was curiously warming.

"What happened?" she asked in a hoarse voice.

"I think you might have to tell us, sweetheart. You went into the shed, then you were shrieking for help and muttering about ponies and wickedness and fire." He dropped a light kiss on her forehead and offered her the whisky. "I think you need this."

She clutched the glass in trembling hands and sipped, spluttering when the fiery spirit caught her sore throat. "I thought if I went in, if I faced it, it would vanquish the ghosts, but it was awful. It was as though it was happening all over again," she explained, quietly.

"Faced what, love?" Jake asked, bewildered.

"The reason she's so afraid of storms," Dominic clarified, leaning against the mantel, swirling the amber liquid in his glass. Jake sent him a searching glance, but his gaze slid back to Alex. Her pallor hadn't lessened but the tremors had subsided.

"Is this why you were so terrified up on the moor that day?"

Alex nodded, her body language indicating she expected her fear to be mocked. "I know it seems infantile to you, but severe storms always trigger bad memories. I can't help it, I don't know how to deal with it, them, so I find somewhere to hide, usually under my bed." She offered another, self-deprecating, smile.

"Do you feel able to talk about it now?"

"I think it's time you told him."

Jake and Dominic spoke in unison, making all three chuckle, and the atmosphere improved.

"I didn't realise how much you knew, Dom," Alex remarked, while the two men raised their glasses to each other.

"Kassie told us, after one of your nightmares," Dominic confessed. "Don't worry, she made us promise to keep it to ourselves. She was worried in case something similar happened when she wasn't around, and we didn't know what was going on."

"She's such a good friend," Alex murmured, tracing the pattern on the glass in her hand. "I'm sorry, Jake, I should have told you after it happened at Moorview, but I didn't know you well enough. It had been drilled in me never to show any kind of weakness. My parents preferred an emotionless façade, regardless of the circumstance. To admit the reason behind my fear didn't enter my thinking, then time passed, and I hoped I'd never have to. Seems now I have no choice."

CHAPTER TWENTY-FIVE

"Regardless of anything else, Alex, you need to talk about it. Have you ever spoken with a counsellor about this?" Dominic asked.

Alex looked at him, her sardonic expression needing no interpretation. "You are kidding right?" she snorted. "The daughter of Terence Mallory does not need a shrink. Can you imagine the scandal if that ever got out? Deal with it, girl." She mimicked her mother's voice to perfection — had Jake but known it — causing Dominic to bite down on a laugh.

Alex sighed. "No, I have never seen anyone, and the only person I ever talked with about it was Kassie. I don't even know whether I *can* talk about it. It was so long ago."

"Yet today it was as though it was still happening. Sweetheart, Dominic's right. You need to talk about it. Definitely to us, here and now, but you might want to think about seeing someone, to get some perspective from a professional. Your reaction was violent." Jake's voice was threaded with concern, and Alex conceded he had a point.

"I give in. Now if Dom would be so kind as to top this up," she gulped down the last mouthful of whisky and waved her glass around, "I'll give it a shot. I apologise in advance if it makes no sense or sounds disjointed. I shall blame the whisky."

"Just tell us. We're quite clever you know. I'm sure we'll be able to work it out," Jake encouraged, winking.

"Okay." Alex stood and, trying to get her thoughts in order, walked around the room, stopping occasionally to stare through the windows still awed by the stunning wintry scene outside.

*

"I was eight, it was the middle of summer, end of July, I think. It was definitely the long school holidays. It's important for you to know that in this house, spontaneity was frowned upon. Tantrums were ignored. To cry or laugh or dance or sing was quashed immediately. One was expected to be undemonstrative at all times."

Parroting her mother again, Alex grimaced, recalling how many times she had been upbraided for sliding down the banister, or singing while she walked along the corridors.

"Anyway, this particular day I was supposed to be doing something for my father."

Jake noticed she never called either of her parents Dad or Mum, it was always Father and Mother. This, in itself, made him grieve for a child unloved.

"I can't recall what it was now, but I do remember fuming because I had to stay indoors when I could be outside in the sunshine. I wasn't allowed to have my friends around to play, so I used to go for rides over the Park or better still, sneak into the village where I nearly always saw someone I knew."

Alex spoke in a matter of fact tone. This had been her normal. It wasn't until she was at boarding school, that she came to comprehend how lonely and restricted her life was at Lanchester Hall. She had made a handful of friends during her time there, but remained reserved, and always acquitted herself in the manner expected by her parents.

This behaviour continued throughout uni, and into adulthood, even when she moved to Boxgrove. It was only the wilds of Yorkshire, which had stirred something in her. That and the attentions of certain gentleman who — recent upset aside — with a simple touch, could unleash emotions long suppressed, and spark a blaze she had come to desire more than anything in this world.

"It was lovely outside. I could see the Great Park from where I was sitting. It might have even been this room." She glanced out of the window, her voice becoming wistful. "Whatever Father had me doing, was boring and I was fed up. I asked whether I could finish it later, but he refused permission. Then he left, with strict instructions to stay put until I was done. I wish I could remember what it was he wanted me to do? He seemed to think it vitally important." She returned to her pacing.

"After a bit, I decided I didn't give a stuff about finishing whatever it was. I tidied the desk and snuck out. Checking no one was around, I marched my eight-year-old self, through the kitchens and out to the stables. Saddling Clover, my pony, I didn't even tell Tom, the stable boy — oh that's so weird, he's now head groom, then he was just a lad — I was off.

"There I was, a slip of a kid, riding out into the wilds of Northumbria and no one knew I'd even left the house. It was reckless, and wonderful, and I was free. I remember the wind was blowing my hair, messing it up, which made me laugh.

No, I didn't bother with my riding hat. Fiddlesticks to that, it was a rule and I hated all the rules. I rode for hours. At least it felt that way, only coming back when I spotted storm clouds building.

"The minute I arrived home, all hell broke loose. Father was waiting for me by the stables, his face blacker than the thunderclouds behind me. He ranted and raved about disobedient children, and pushing boundaries, and who knows what else. I was hot and tired by this time. I took no notice and flounced off."

Alex bit her lip. This was the hard part.

"He grabbed my arm and dragged me to the outhouses. I recall struggling and tussling with him, and I daresay I bawled at him, but his temper had reached glacial levels and he ignored me. He threw me into the shed, locked the door, and informed me I would be staying there until I regained my senses. I stomped around for a bit, assuming he meant minutes not hours. It wasn't the first time he'd locked me in, although never on such a hot day, and he rarely left me for long."

She didn't notice the look Jake and Dominic shared.

"He didn't come back. I was annoyed, I had things I wanted to do, and there was Clover to brush down. Plus, it was like an oven. The shed doesn't have any windows, and because the day was so hot, the air was stifling. I began to shout for him to let me out, saying I was sorry and wouldn't disobey him ever again. Looking back, I doubt he was within hearing distance, certainly no one came. Then the storm hit."

Alex stopped pacing and chewed on her thumbnail.

"You don't have to tell us, Alex, I think we can guess the rest," Dominic interposed, soothingly.

She shook her head. "No, I've gone this far I need to get it off my chest, it's just…" her voice wavered, and she looked through the window she had come to a halt beside.

Snow was falling again, light flakes of delicate beauty drifting from a laden sky. Alex didn't notice, she was seeing a whole other picture.

Her voice was calm and steady, at odds with the drama of her words.

"It was a terrible storm. The weather had been blisteringly hot for days, and it was predicted, but none expected it to be so bad. There I was, in the shed and feeling a bit frightened. I've never been very good with storms. It was so loud, I don't suppose anyone would have head me yelling anyway, but I kept trying.

"Without warning, there was *the* most horrendous noise. I thought the world had exploded. Everything was muffled, like I was going deaf, and I couldn't see. Later they told me a thunderbolt had hit the shed at the far end. At the time, I had no clue.

"I banged on the door as hard as I could. Still no one let me out. I gave up, and was sitting on the wheelbarrow, when I smelt smoke. That was impossible, because it was pouring with rain. How could anything be burning? Before long, smoke was filling the shed, and I realised the whole line of buildings must be on fire. Surely now my father would release me?"

A solitary tear ran down her cheek, and Jake had to suppress the impulse to wipe it away. He knew she hadn't finished.

"Over the cacophony, I heard the fire. It hissed and popped when heat met water, and through the cracks in the walls I saw the flames. I couldn't get out, and now I was going to die in this awful shed, simply because I'd dared to ride Clover without permission. Worst thing was, although I was terrified of being burned, I wasn't afraid of dying. What does that say about my life?"

Alex shrugged, in helpless resignation.

"For a few minutes I sat there in a kind of numb haze, but something inside me refused to give up and fought back. I started to scream for help, throwing myself at the door, hoping it might splinter. I was eight… it was never going to give. At what felt to me like the last minute before fire engulfed the shed, I tried again, and hurled myself at the door. It flew open.

"At the other side stood Mr Nelson. He had been looking for me, because Tom mentioned Clover was still saddled, but I was nowhere to be found. I never left a horse without cleaning the tack and brushing down the animal. Anyway, I guess I fainted or collapsed or something, maybe I'd inhaled too much smoke, whatever, I don't remember anything else until much later."

She walked over to the chair and sank into it, taking another gulp of whisky.

"Apparently, Mr Nelson carried me to my room. Mrs Nelson washed off all the soot, cleaned and bandaged my hands, and sat with me until I woke. The doctor wasn't called. I suppose that might have generated uncomfortable questions. Thankfully, I didn't get an infection, although it hurt to breathe for a while."

Jake checked a reflexive movement, incensed at such heinous treatment of a child. He met Dominic's gaze, both men equally dumfounded.

"My parents didn't even bother to check on me. The next day Father summoned me to his study and said it served me right for being a disobedient brat. That was it. A month later I was sent away to school. The next time I went home, which was the following year, Clover had gone. I hope she was given away, the idea he would stoop to having her destroyed because of my behaviour makes me want to throw up, even now.

"I rarely saw my parents again. They made sure to be on the continent or in the States during the few holidays I couldn't stay at school. I left home for good about six months after I finished uni, when I got the job in Boxgrove actually, and haven't seen them since."

Alex wound up. The telling had been difficult, and a headache threatened, but she felt as though a weight had been lifted. Perhaps Jake's suggestion of seeing a counsellor was worthwhile. She hadn't realised just how much she'd been bottling up.

The two men sat in appalled silence. Even Dominic had no idea how bad it had been. Jake was outraged, and wished Terence Mallory was still alive. He wanted nothing more than to beat the man to a pulp. *Hell's teeth, no wonder Alex was frightened of storms.*

"Didn't your mother care either?" he pried, gently.

Alex raised tired eyes to his and shook her head. "No. I was the daughter they never wanted, the child who craved attention, who was clingy and needy. I was a disappointment to them because I wasn't a boy, the son who would carry on his father's name. I was the reason they argued, well maybe not the reason, but any disagreement seemed to centre around my shortcomings."

She gave a parody of a smile. "It became easier for me not to care either. Which is probably why I had no idea what it meant to be in love... until I met you." This last spoken so quietly, neither man was sure they had heard her correctly.

Dominic, sensing the two might need time alone together, thanked Alex for sharing what happened. "I'll pop back in the morning. I think we'll delay finalising the funeral arrangements until then, Alex. I do believe you have endured enough stress for one day."

He grinned and excused himself, heading off to the estate office to finish what he had been intending to do before Alex, so effectively, diverted his attention.

CHAPTER TWENTY-SIX

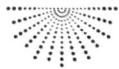

T he room fell silent again after Dominic left. Alex moved to the chair near the fire, exhausted and close to tears. She hated crying, because it made her feel as though her parents were right. In fact, when she thought about it, the only time she had cried since that awful day, was the afternoon Jake rescued her when she was lost on the moor.

"I'm so sorry you had to go through all that, love," Jake said, after giving Alex a few moments to compose herself.

"Thank you. Oddly, I don't feel as upset as I expected. Perhaps seeing a counsellor isn't the worst idea." She offered him a weary smile. A completely random thought came to her. "Bugger, I've been appallingly rude. I forgot to ask. Where are you staying?"

"At the hotel near the airport."

"Oh, no, that's half an hour away. Please, you must stay here, there are plenty of spare rooms... or perhaps..." she stopped. *Was she ready?*

"Perhaps what...?" Jake guessed what it was she had almost offered. What to others might seem a small gesture, to him was far more. It was hope, forgiveness, trust, and love.

His dream of a future together, no longer quite so improbable.

Alex twisted her fingers together and a pink tinge washed up her cheeks, but she held his gaze. "Perhaps you could sleep in my room." She said, shyly.

"I can't think of anything I'd like more," he replied with a warm smile.

"You might have to fight Bruno, but it's a large bed, so the three of us should be okay." Going off into a fit of giggles when Jake's eyebrows arched into his hairline.

"Bruno?" Trying to sound casual as he wondered who the heck this 'Bruno' was and why he was sharing Alex's bed.

"Oh, your face," wicked laughter spilt out, "stop panicking, Jake! Bruno is a dog… a very old, and sadly neglected dog. I'm hoping Reuben might allow him to join your pack. Mrs Nelson tells me he sleeps on my bed every night and has since I last saw him six years ago. Bless his paws. I cannot in all conscience leave him here.

"I've asked Mr Tomlinson — the lawyer — to ensure any deal includes the husbandry of all the animals on the property. Bruno is the only pet dog left. There are three gun dogs, but as steward, Dominic looks after them, so they'll be fine."

Jake, chuckled, *seriously he should have worked* **that** *one out — talk about paranoid.* "I'm sure Reuben will be more than happy to have Bruno live with us. All he wanted was for you to come home with me and made it very clear I had no business showing my face again unless you were with me. I don't suppose an extra dog will fuss him in the slightest."

"That is such a lovely word. Home. It's so strange, I lived here, on and off, for twenty-two years and it was never home, yet Moorview was, almost from the moment I stepped across the threshold." Alex stood up, stretching taut muscles. "What time is it? It feels like hours since I got up this morning."

Jake glanced at his watch. "Just coming up on four, and Moorview will always be home for you."

Alex smiled, and reaching for his hand pulled him out of the chair.

"Kiss me," she entreated.

He readily obliged.

❦

The ensuing days were hectic and, surprisingly for Alex, sadder than she anticipated. Her intention, when she left Moorview, was to sign away the house and get through the funeral. She never expected the rush of memories and emotions, which had taunted her from the moment she drove up to the magnificent wooden doors.

Dominic, Jake, and she, checked the inventory thoroughly, ensuring every item of worth was detailed. A Mallory built Lanchester Hall four hundred years ago, and the collections had been accumulating since that time.

Some, deemed too valuable to be left to the tender mercies of whoever took over the estate, Alex arranged to be donated to local museums or art galleries. A select few ended up in London. Mr Tomlinson was having his people do the same with any artefacts in the other properties.

Alex took pains to detail the likely change of circumstances to every member of staff. From those within the main house, to the stewards, the blacksmith, the carpenters, the tenant farmers — any and all, in whatever capacity they were employed.

As with many stately homes, the Mallorys had employed generations of families for decades if not longer, and the majority had an inkling as to why Alex no longer lived there. Most were unsurprised at her decision to divest herself of the Hall.

The funeral, held in Durham Cathedral, was attended by hundreds, as was the wake afterwards at the Hall. Members of the aristocracy, not to mention friends and business colleagues, from all over the world made the journey to farewell Lord and Lady Lanchester.

Most were still coming to terms with their untimely deaths, as well as the astonishing revelation, they had a daughter. By the end of the day, Alex was fed up of hearing how marvellous her parents had been.

How kind, what generous benefactors to this, that, or the other charity. How supportive they had been of so and so's business ventures, that the capital they invested made the difference between success and failure. She wanted to scream and rail at the iniquity of it.

The more people talked to her, the more Alex realised she had never known her parents at all, not even a little bit. The couple the guests raved about were complete strangers. She controlled her temper, as a lady of her station ought, and politely agreed.

Her face ached from all the smiling. Her hand bruised from being so rigorously shaken. The charade was made tolerable because of Jake's unfailing support and his hand in hers, as well as the added incentive of a *very* large whisky at the end of the day.

Finally, it was over. It was almost midnight. The last of the mourners had left moments previously, whisked away into the frigid night in their chauffeur driven Mercedes. Alex stood on the wide stone steps and lifted her eyes to the sky. It was a perfect winter's night.

Cloudless, inky blue sky, glistening with its veil of stars…

the chill making it seem as though they were close enough to be plucked from the heavens. She drew a cleansing breath, the keen air clearing her muggy head.

"Sometimes I am in awe of nature," she murmured. "It's so dark, but look at all the shades of white," flinging her hand towards the grounds, blanketed in deep snow. "The sky laden with stars, the frosty air. There's something magical about nights like this."

Jake wrapped her to him, her back to his chest, his chin resting on her head. "Me too, that's one of the great things about living in the countryside. Nothing to detract from the beauty of the night sky. I love being out on the moors, when the sky morphs from blue to that incredible pinkish-purple, and the first star winks into existence. I often stand and watch as the sky darkens, and the rest of the stars slowly appear. It's quite the sight."

Alex twisted in his arms, "Wow how poetic, and there was I thinking you were one of those fuddy-duddy, unimaginative engineers." A sassy grin accompanied her comment.

"Fuddy duddy? Fuddy du— why, you little minx." Trying to hold her against him, with one hand he started tickling her, but she wriggled out of his grasp.

Growling in frustration, he moved towards her. Guessing his intent, Alex squealed, hurtling down the steps and along the pathway until she rounded the end of the house.

Quickening her pace, hearing Jake pounding behind her, Alex reached the lawns and, bending while she ran, grabbed a handful of snow, quickly balling it up. Throwing it without any real aim, she hit Jake bang slap in the middle his chest, the snow mushrooming over his dark green jumper.

"Oh, it's like that is it?"

Alex tried to dodge, seeing Jake seizing his own handful. His aim was far more precise, causing her to yelp in shock when icy slush ran down her neck.

"Unimaginative huh? We'll see about that." He chased her down — and it was on in earnest.

The sounds of laughter and muffled thuds filled the quiet air, as snowballs arced, most missing but some finding their targets. Despite the cold, cheeks soon became flushed, and little puffs of white clouds hung around the couple as they tried to catch their breath.

The exhilaration of the game helped vent some of the tension the day had wrought, and for a few moments every-thing else faded into insignificance. It was just the two of them, protected by the night.

Jake claimed victory, tackling Alex when she tried to throw one more snowball, both of them tumbling onto the thick whiteness. Laughing. Alex tried to slither free, but Jake had her this time.

Her lips curved into a cheeky smile and he was about to tickle her mercilessly when something held him motionless.

Ignoring the fact neither were dressed for a romp in the snow, Jake stared at Alex, lying under him, on a bed of sparkling white crystals, and his amusement faded.

Under the pale light of the moon, her hair resembled rivulets of dark caramel against the snow. A rosy glow brushed pale cheeks, and her eyes shone like polished ebony. She bewitched him. There was no other word to describe how she had ensnared him, and he never wanted to be released from her spell.

"Jake...?" Puzzled at his abrupt change in demeanour, Alex lifted herself up on one elbow, tilting her head to read his expression. "What's wrong?"

"Absolutely nothing. For the first time in my life, every-thing is right."

She frowned, bewildered, but he didn't elaborate, merely bent his lips to hers and kissed her until the cold was no longer a problem. Minutes ticked by, passion rising in direct proportion to how quickly the air temperature was dropping.

"Dammit, Alex, what am I thinking? You'll catch your death," Jake's voice was raw when he broke their kiss. She smiled and brushed her lips to his.

"Oh, I don't know... I am beeyootifully warm," she winked, impishly.

Jake chuckled. "Nevertheless, it's freezing out here. I think we'd better get inside where, I believe you will find, whisky awaits." He kissed her cold nose and hauled her upright, brushing off the snow clinging to her clothes. They hurried indoors and into the library, Mr Nelson following on their heels carrying a tray on which stood two steaming hot chocolates, two large whiskies and a plate of sandwiches.

Thanking the genial butler, the pair fell on the sandwiches, unexpectedly hungry. Alex hadn't eaten a proper meal since breakfast, only nibbling at the delicious fare provided at the wake, and devoured her portion with more gusto than finesse.

"Lordy, I could eat them all over again," she sighed, leaning back in her chair, licking a blob of pickle from her little finger.

"I'm sure Mattie would rustle some more up if you like." Jake remarked.

She shook her head. "Much as I think I could, it's nearly one in the morning, and I won't sleep if my stomach is full." She took a large gulp of whisky, hiccuping as the spirit burned its way down.

"Well, I can think of an easy way to burn a few calories if that's the only thing stopping you." Waggling his eyebrows comically, drawing a tired laugh from Alex.

"Oh, you can, can you?"

He nodded.

"Hmm... not sure I'm all that interested in what you have

to offer." She waved her now empty whisky tumbler, artlessly, watching him through half-closed lids. On top of a very long day and insufficient food, the alcohol went straight to her head and she could feel herself sliding down the chair.

"Sadly for me, I think sleep is all you're good for tonight. Come on." He took her hand and pulled her out of the chair.

"Oh, so after all your fine talk, you don't want me, now?" Alex pouted dramatically. Jake bit down on bark of laughter as he led her up the stairs to her bedroom, where Bruno was already comfortably ensconced in the middle of the bed.

"Oh well, doesn't look like there's room for me anyway. It's fine, I know my place." Amused at the scene.

Alex caught his hand thinking he was leaving. "Don't go," she pleaded, exhaustion making her sway on her feet. He caught her to him, pressing a kiss to her forehead.

"I'm only going to the bathroom, love. I'll be back in two ticks." Good as his word, Jake was back in minutes, only to find Alex splayed across the bed like a starfish, Bruno curled into her side.

He managed to remove most of her clothes, and then chivvied the aged dog across, until he could slide Alex and himself under the sheets. Drawing her against him and grinning at her gentle snores, Jake shut his eyes, joining her in slumber almost instantly.

The house slept.

CHAPTER TWENTY-SEVEN

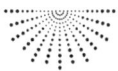

Four days later, a car pulled up in front of a rambling cottage. The door was yanked open revealing a very tall gentleman, who rushed to the car, dragging its occupant into his arms for a very satisfying kiss.

"Welcome home," Jake said after several moments of dizzying silence.

"I take it you missed me," Alex observed, flushing bright red at this overt demonstration of his feelings.

"More than you will ever know," came the considered reply.

"Maybe I should go away more often then, if that's what I'm to expect on my return," she countered, pertly.

"Don't you dare." He grinned, lifting her case from the boot. Taking her hand, he led her into the familiar warmth of Moorview.

"Oh, it is so good to be home," she murmured, prompting Jake to give her another searing kiss. "Why, good sir, you will be my undoing." Alex fanned her face, imitating the female characters from one of her favourite period TV shows.

"Get used to it, my lady," Jake bent at the waist in a sweeping bow, not noticing her smile slipping.

Leaving her case in the hallway, Jake ushered Alex into the kitchen. Reuben was standing by the stove, stirring something, which smelt heavenly.

The dogs spotted her, catapulting themselves off their respective beds and bouncing around as though she'd been gone for months instead of the eight days it had been. Her employer turned at the din, his face crinkling in a bright smile.

"Alex! Glad you're home. We've missed you haven't we, gang?" He banged the spoon on the rim of the pan, and making sure it was balanced, enfolded her in a welcoming hug.

"Hi, Reuben," she replied shyly, returning the gesture.

"All good?" he asked.

She nodded. "I think so. I'm a bit tired, but I suppose that's to be expected. I *am* ready to get back to work. I'm hankering to lose myself in ancient history for a while."

Reuben heard an odd note in Alex's voice, and glanced at Jake, eyebrow raised. His son shook his head, and mouthed 'later,' with which his father had to be satisfied for now.

"Not tonight, work can wait until tomorrow. Tonight, is for relaxing and chatting, over a hot meal, a large glass of red wine, and maybe a really bad movie. He grinned at Alex who smiled back in delight.

"Sounds perfect. I'll just freshen up if you don't mind."

The two men nodded.

Alex picked up her suitcase and made her way along the winding passage to her room. Once there, she sank onto her bed and stared out onto the garden. It was late afternoon, the light was almost gone, and the snow lay as thickly here, as it had in Northumberland, bringing to mind the last few days.

She felt antsy and out of sorts, which was irritating,

because she had was so looking forward to coming home, to seeing Jake, and getting back to the work she loved. It seemed her previous life wasn't ready to let her go.

Curiously, it had been more unsettling than she expected, packing her meagre belongings and saying goodbye to everyone. She handled that on her own. Jake left the Hall two days ago — engineering commitments calling.

Even Bruno left her, travelling to Moorview with Jake — for whom the dog had developed a slavish affection. Jake had argued it would be better for Bruno to travel with him and get settled with the other dogs. It would save Alex the extra worry of organising the elderly dog, on top of everything else she needed to finalise.

࿐

During one of her numerous telephone conversations with Mr Tomlinson, the solicitor confirmed that one of the prospective recipients had made the effort to forward their plans for the future of Lanchester Hall.

Their scheme would see the estate continue almost as it had done for centuries. They would open it, and the grounds, to visitors but hoped to convert much of the remaining areas into a training facility for those skills typically required on a large estate but rapidly dying out.

Historic professions such as stonemasons, blacksmiths, carpenters, thatchers, weavers and millers. Restoration of stained glass, antique windows and doors, or ornamental plaster and light fixtures. Techniques for seasonal and traditional horticulture, and animal husbandry, handed down from father to son until a generation decides they are no longer interested, and the knowledge is lost.

Such trades have lost popularity in recent years, yet their techniques continue to be in high demand. Centuries old properties will always require ongoing preservation, and many landlords are beginning to discover the benefits of less intensive farming methods.

It would be place where those already in training could attend for a given period; a place to hone their skills. Somewhere universities and colleges, offering courses in such subjects, would be able to send their students for valid work experience.

Not just in a workshop on campus, where no one is affected if you make a mistake, but on a vast property, where everyone has to pull their weight. Where errors are not so easily ignored, because they tend to have a ripple effect across the estate as a whole — in exactly the same way as would happen in real life.

In this way, the trust would be able to maintain Lanchester Hall as a working estate, with all the current staff keeping their jobs. They also offered Alex a position on their board, something she had vacillated over but, in the end, graciously accepted, inordinately glad she would get some say in the way her old home was administered.

Now it was just a matter of time. Nothing moved quickly when the legal profession was involved, and, in truth, Alex was relieved she wasn't responsible for the negotiations regarding the remaining properties. This one on its own had been exhausting enough, and she wanted to get back to normal. If that was even possible, now she was a countess — the very idea still making her giggle, uncontrollably.

Mr Tomlinson assured her it shouldn't change her life if she didn't want it to, but she feared it already had.

*

Sighing wearily, naval gazing wasn't getting her anywhere, Alex stripped off and trudged into the bathroom, standing for longer than necessary under the stinging jets of the shower.

Half an hour later, she was back in the kitchen, feeling much better, and was soon drawn into the usual banter that was the nightly ritual in the Faulkner household. They did watch an old B movie, falling into their habit of trying to guess what else the actors appeared in, and mocking the terrible acting.

By nine o clock, Alex was falling asleep, and excused herself

"Goodnight all. I'll be up for a walk in the morning... if that's okay?" she hesitated, unexpectedly unsure of her position in this house, even though she had only been away a little over a week.

Reuben grinned at her over his cup of tea. "It's more than okay, Alex and as long as it's not knee deep in snow they'll be chuffed to bits. They've missed out on so many walks while you've been away. It's not just me who's glad your home."

"Thank you," she whispered and left the room. Bruno following, a silent shadow in her wake.

❦

"What's going on in her head?" Reuben asked, after several minutes of quiet.

Jake shrugged at a loss. "I have no clue, Dad. Like I said when I got home, once we got past Diana's interference, last week was amazing. I expect it's because everything has been pretty overwhelming. She had a lot to deal with after I left, but Dominic is eminently capable, and once the convoluted process of donating the property is complete, it's out of her hands. Mind, I do believe they've asked her to join the board."

"Maybe all she needs is a good night's sleep and a return

to mundane routine. We'd best keep an eye on her. She's been busy, which could well delay any reaction to the huge change she's faced with. Has she had any more flashbacks?" Jake had told Reuben about Alex's childhood, and being locked up in the shed.

"No, but she agreed counselling might help. Okay, I know it's early, but I'm going to turn in too. I've missed her…"

Reuben raised his palm. "Stop! I don't need to hear it. That comes under 'too much information,' Jake. Just go. I'll see you in the morning."

Jake chuckled, patted the dogs and went to see whether Alex was still awake.

She was. Lying in bed reading, she turned when he pushed open the door, and her face lit up.

"Are you sleeping here?"

"If you'll have me."

"Please. I don't sleep properly unless you—" she clamped her mouth shut before finishing the sentence, but it wasn't hard to work it out.

"I'm glad to hear it."

She held his gaze, her eyes tired, and a little sad.

"What's going on Alex? What have I missed?"

"Nothing."

"Don't give me that. You are far too quiet, lost almost and I don't like it. Where's my firebrand?"

CHAPTER TWENTY-EIGHT

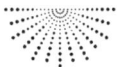

Alex stared at Jake. She needed to be honest. He had been incredibly understanding about what she had withheld and why. Since moving here, since meeting Jake, the tight control she had exerted over her emotions for all those years was slackening.

She knew some of her spontaneity had returned, but it would be a long haul. Was Jake up for that? Did he really want to be with someone who struggled to let anyone in, to open her heart? Then there was the whole being rich thing.

To be fair, she didn't think Jake was that shallow, but adjusting to your... *what was she anyway? His girlfriend? No, she was too old to be referred to as a girlfriend. Significant other? She hated that term. So, what was she? His mistress... ugh.*

Anyway, whatever she was to him, to have her go from relying on a monthly pay packet, to a member of the titled nobility and astonishingly wealthy — overnight, couldn't be easy. Even as the thought ran through her head, it sounded irrational, but she wanted to hear it from him. She blew a sigh, and realised Jake was still standing by the bed,

Shuffling over, Alex patted the space beside her. "Sorry, I was thinking. Sit with me?"

"Ahhh… which explains all that steam coming out of your ears," he teased. Alex giggled, as Jake kicked off his shoes and slid onto the bed. Hooking his arm around her shoulders, he buried his face in her hair, and kissed her just above her ear.

Alex felt the inevitable frisson trickle down her back and nestled against him.

Jake, I…" she paused, searching for the right words. Nope, she didn't have them. She'd have to wing it. "There's no easy way to say this…" she felt him tense, "…no…" anticipating his train of thought, "…that's not where I'm going with this."

He didn't relax but did begin to glide his fingers up and down her arm.

"Is my having a pot of money, going to be an issue?"

Whatever Jake thought she was going to say, this wasn't it. He burst out laughing, more from relief than anything else.

"What the dickens gave you that idea?" he said, twisting his body until he faced her.

"Well, doesn't it bother you? I haven't been very up front, have I? I hid the fact I'm, I was, the daughter of an earl, but before I have the guts to tell you about it, bang — I'm the countess with all that entails? Then there's the fact I'm clearly emotionally stunted. Do you really want to take on all my crappy baggage? In my head I'm plain old me, but I worry it might get in the way?"

"How could it… wait… did you say, 'emotionally stunted' and 'plain old me'? Alexandra Mallory, there is nothing stunted or plain old about you. How much more convincing do you need? Geez your parents did a real number on you didn't they?"

Alex flushed, but didn't reply, just watched him warily.

"Right let's clear this up, once and for all. First, I love you.

B, okay, it may take time for you to become who you used to be, but you are definitely not stunted..." he kissed her, a gentle finger coming to rest momentarily on the pulse fluttering in her throat. He felt her heart rate quicken, and heard the low moan wrenched from her throat.

Lifting his head, he grinned, "...see!" Third, I couldn't give a flying f—" he tempered his phrase, "two hoots, whether you're as rich as Croesus or poor as a church mouse. I might not be rolling in dough, but I am more than comfortable, with no need to get hung up on the fact you can afford first class flights, if you so choose. And fin—"

He didn't get any further. Alex launched herself at him, planting a fierce kiss on his lips, making his head spin, frantic fingers flying over his body.

Jake groaned at the sensations she was inducing, and with no desire to fight them, succumbed. Clothes flew in all directions, while hands tormented, and mouths seduced. Their coming together was frenzied, the fraught intensity of the preceding weeks coalescing into a blaze of passion.

As the night wore on, sleep banished for the time being, they talked, and Alex finally unburdened the remainder of what was bothering her. Minor things she had kept bottled up, concerned she sounded like a pathetic loser.

Most stemmed from her child and early adulthood, but one or two circled their relationship and her belief, not helped by Diana's comments, she wasn't clever enough or pretty enough or witty enough, to keep any man interested, let alone someone as drop dead gorgeous as Jake.

"Love, I doubt there is anything I can say to persuade you of your worth, it has to come from within yourself." Jake pointed out. "You have to trust that what we share is real and enduring. I had no intention of getting married or even becoming involved with anyone to the exclusion of everything and everyone else, and I know I behaved like a tosser when I saw you with Dad the day you were leaving for Northumberland, but you're not the only one with fears."

Alex pulled away to read his face.

"Fears? You have fears?" She was astonished. It never occurred to her Jake might be in a similar boat. It was quite comforting to know she wasn't the only one freaking out over this whole falling in love thing.

"Of course, I do… you women don't have a monopoly on these things, we just don't talk about it. I had Diana." He felt Alex stiffen, but simply kissed her brow, and carried on. "Diana was safe, easy and reliable. Nothing would be ruffled with Diana. She is poised, elegant and refined.

"Everything I'm not, in fact," Alex huffed.

"Yes, everything you're not," he agreed. She glared at him, unwittingly proving his point

"See, Diana would never get riled, it would involve frown lines and that would never do. My life would have been smooth, and calm had I stayed with her, had I never met you. But I *did* meet you, and you turned my nicely ordered life upside down. Life with you will be tempestuous, challenging, and unpredictable. With Diana, I wasn't bothered if I didn't see her for days on end. With you, I can barely last half an hour without kissing you. These last couple of days were torture. Dad was ready to kick me out."

He grinned in recollection of Reuben's frustration with his son's ornery behaviour when Alex wasn't around. "I need to hear your voice, touch your skin, feel your lips, and hold you in my arms, every day and hope to do so for the rest of my life."

Alex heard the 'will be' and the 'rest of my life' more than she heard his explanation.

"Say that again?" she asked, very quietly.

"What all of it?"

"No, the bit about 'will be' and 'rest of your life'."

"That's all you heard?" Amusement twitching at his lips.

"Well what do you expect?" she said plaintively. "You can't say things like that to a woman and not expect her to fixate."

"Alexandra Mallory. All at once it's you, it's you for evermore."

Was he joking around?

"Jake Faulkner, that's a line from a musical. Seriously? You are reduced to quoting from musicals now?" Her eyebrows arched in astonishment. He hated her musicals.

"Yes, I know it is, but the day of the storm when you were in my arms, it ran through my head and refuses to bugger off. Suddenly it was you. You were the one I didn't even know I wanted, and I want to spend the rest of my life proving how much I love you."

He took a breath and cupped her face in his hands.

"I want you, Alex. I want to marry you, if you think you could put up with me."

Alex's eyes widened, her mouth dropping open in shock. This was it, the proposal she hoped for, wished for, desired more than anything. The dream she had buried, presuming it improbable, unsure whether he was ready, whether he would ever be ready for that level of commitment. After what Jake had told her about his mother and Tricia, she was determined he would never think she was trying to trap him into marriage.

Staring at him, Alex let her gaze travel over his angular features, shadowed in the dim light from her bedside lamp. His beautiful grey eyes, a little wary, framed by long dark lashes. *Why did men always have amazing eyelashes? It really wasn't fair*. His black hair tousled from their earlier lovemaking. His sensuous lips that could weave the most seductive magic. She knew whatever happened, there would never be anyone else for her.

This was it.

"Hmmm… I suppose we might muddle along quite nicely, as long as you promise never, ever to whinge about my taste in music," she said, her tones deliberately casual, in stark contrast with her heart, which was racing like a freight train.

"Is that a yes?"

Alex could hear uncertainty in Jake's voice. She couldn't believe he imagined she might turn him down. Smoothing cool fingers up his jaw and into his hair, she brought his face down to hers, murmuring quietly, but clearly.

"*Of course*, it's a yes." She held his gaze, molten chocolate on smoky grey.

A shudder ran through him and she heard him exhale a ragged breath.

She heard him whisper 'I love you', then their lips met. For a very long time, nothing else mattered, as Jake sealed his proposal in a most effective manner.

❦

Alex was soon swallowed back into the familiar life of Moorview as though she had never been away. The snow began to melt, and she was able to get out onto the moors again regularly, with the dogs.

Bruno found his place among the crazy pack, as though he'd always been part of the family. He was slower than the other four and didn't always go for a second walk, preferring the warmth of the fire, but what he lacked in energy, he made up for in enthusiasm.

. . .

Reuben, thrilled Jake had proposed, rushed out in the snow to buy champagne to celebrate their engagement, declaring he knew they were meant for each other, and was glad his son had finally seen sense.

His delight was both heart-warming and amusing, and Alex hoped, even after Jake and she were married, that they would stay at Moorview. It might seem peculiar to others, but she could not imagine living anywhere else. The house was easily big enough to afford a newly married couple some privacy.

Alex arranged to speak to a counsellor, and had already attended a couple of sessions, surprised at how helpful they were. She was learning not to suppress things that bothered her although found it a challenge to relax her tight discipline, honed to perfection over twenty years.

Jake began to work from home and was in discussions with two other engineers about starting their own consultancy. Initially, it would probably involve a lot travel, but once everything was set up, the only trips would be occasional site visits. Alex was relieved.

That Jake still worked, albeit from a distance for the most part, in the same office as the woman with whom he shared an intimate past rankled. Especially, bearing in mind Diana had tried to split them up. Despite Jake's assurances, Alex was not convinced Diana had accepted her relationship with Jake was over.

Reuben's book was coming together quickly. The first draft was only weeks away from completion. There was still plenty of work to be done, but he and Alex were excited at their progress.

🐝

Christmas came and went, almost without notice. Reuben and Jake preferred quiet reflection to wild celebrations, and Reuben didn't think the latter would be appropriate, regardless, owing to Alex's recent loss.

For as long as Alex could remember, Christmas equated to loneliness. When she lived at home, her parents were rarely in attendance, preferring to holiday somewhere Alex wasn't welcome, their daughter left to the tender mercies of a nanny or the domestic staff. Even gifts, purchased by one of their minions, were few and far between.

As a child, it had been upsetting, but throwing a tantrum had no effect, and Alex quickly learnt to regard Christmas the same as any other day. Latterly, when everyone assumed she went home to enjoy the holiday with her family, all Alex did was treat herself to a night in a hotel and didn't enlighten them.

This year was the first time she had any reason to get into the spirit of the season, and she went all out. She helped to decorate the house within in an inch of its life — even the dogs didn't escape and suffered tinsel collars — not very graciously.

She relished the festive air in the local towns and the thrill of choosing gifts, which she wrapped in gaudy paper, placing them under the extravagantly large tree Reuben insisted on buying. The house smelt of pine and cinnamon and cloves, an assortment of festive foods appearing at random intervals.

The trio attended midnight mass together on Christmas Eve. The service, a mixture of reverence and joy, reduced

Alex to tears, as did members of the congregation who wished her a Happy Christmas as they left. Their sentiments making her feel welcome and a part of their community.

※

Once the New Year turned, Reuben and Alex were back to the grindstone. The first draft of the book was almost finished, and it was time to check and double-check all the sources and references. Then there were the endless meetings with the publisher, the editor, illustrators, photographers, and formatters.

Alex was relieved she wasn't responsible for any final decisions, there were way too many variables, but she was learning so much about the world of academic publications, and it fascinated her. There was still three months left of her contract and having seen Reuben's timeline, she anticipated at least another six months beyond that.

Only one tiny, weeny, minuscule thing marred Alex's happiness. Yes, Jake had proposed but he hadn't given her a ring, and they hadn't set a wedding date. In fact, since telling Reuben, they hadn't discussed any specifics at all, although when Jake talked about the future, he always said 'we.' It gnawed at the edge of her consciousness, but she had no intention of quizzing him about it and, as was typical, she bottled it up.

What Alex didn't know, was that Jake had a plan. He thought it brilliant and fool proof. When the weather eased, he wanted to take Alex to Fountains Abbey, and give her the ring he had purchased a matter of days after he found her huddled against a bush, in the middle of a raging storm on the moor.

The day, which seemed a catalyst for what was to follow, good and bad. He wanted it to be a grand gesture, an unequivocal indication of how much he loved her, and Fountains Abbey offered the ideal backdrop.

Unfortunately, before he had the chance, fate deemed it necessary to intervene one last time, threatening to derail his infallible plan.

CHAPTER TWENTY-NINE

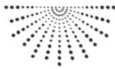

By early January, the snow had melted enough to allow normal business to resume and Jake was away for a few days, attending meetings in Nottingham. Alex missed him but, if she was honest, she was so busy, she scarcely had time to register his absence, except at night.

Mid-morning, the second Tuesday of the month. Alex and Reuben were standing at his desk, discussing the merits of a particular image, while sipping good strong coffee, when there was a loud rapping at the door.

Reuben glanced at his watch. "Wonder who that could be? Are you expecting anyone?"

Alex shook her head. "Nope, I don't know anyone," she chuckled.

Placing his coffee on the table, Reuben strolled along to answer the knock. Alex heard a muted conversation, then the door to the office banged open, and a very tall, dramatically beautiful woman all but fell into the room. Alex gaped at the new arrival whom she supposed was one of Reuben's academic colleagues and, slightly concerned the woman was unwell, approached her.

The woman brushed away her hand. "You! You! Why couldn't you just leave us alone?" she hissed, wild eyed. Her shining blonde hair was unravelling from its severe style. Her lips, a bright red slash across her unblemished complexion.

"I'm sorry, I have no idea who you are or what you're talking about," Alex replied, calmly, wondering where Reuben was. Was this crazy woman something to do with the publication of his book? A notion immediately banished at her next words.

"Everything was fine until *you* came along with your doe eyes and your curly hair. What the hell does he see in you? You are nothing, nobody, you have a pathetic job working for him…" scornfully flicking her hand in the direction of the hall, "…and you're not even pretty. I was exactly right for him. We share the same interests and we both love engineering. What the f—" she bit back the expletive settling for "bloody hell do you have that I don't? Why can't you accept it's me he loves, not you?"

The woman paused, spearing her fingers — the sculpted nails looking as though they'd been dipped in blood — through her hair, which gave up, spilling across her shoulders, in disarray.

Oh, yay, this must be Diana.

The tension mounted, as the two women stared at each other, one furious, one wary, then Reuben shot into the room.

"*Diana!* Really? What gives you the right to come back here? This isn't your home, and Jake is not your property, he never was. You just like to think you owned him."

Sneering, Diana turned on him. "Whatever you, and this bitch think, Jake wants me. Did you know he wasn't in Nottingham for the last two days? No, he's been with me in Whitby. Clearly you can't satisfy him." She spun back around, her eyes boring into Alex, who was fighting a desperate urge to laugh, which probably wasn't the best idea. Diana looked distinctly unhinged.

Diana ranted on and on until Alex decided enough was enough. She was not going justify her relationship with Jake to anyone; it was nobody else's business. She also acknowledged that although Diana did not deserve a second of her time, following her recent stunt, the woman might well be nursing a shattered ego, if not a bruised heart.

"Diana," she waited, but the woman continued to mutter. "Diana! I think you might let me speak." Diana stopped mid-sentence and glared down at Alex, who barely came up to her shoulders.

The contrast between the two was acutely evident. Alex, small, with dark blonde curly hair, and soft brown eyes, wearing faded jeans, and a cowl necked jumper, faced Diana. Tall and coolly beautiful, Diana with her straight blonde hair — no longer confined in its elegant chignon — blue eyes, flawless make up, wearing a lady's power suit, and a pair of kick-ass heels, that Alex would fall off soon as look at.

The epitome of sophistication, in fact!

For a split second, Alex allowed her insecurities to overcome her heart. This woman was far more suited to Jake than she could ever hope to be. She, Alex, didn't understand his world — the world of engineering, the massively complex projects, the deadlines and all the pressures associated therewith. What did they have in common?

Before habitual lack of confidence in herself and faith in

her relationship with Jake took hold, memories of all those days of chatter and laughter and fun flooded in. The times they ended up talking until dawn, about anything and everything. Heated debates about all manner of subjects, from politics to the economy to their vastly differing taste in movies and music — although they did both enjoy classical music. Their shared love of history, of Moorview, of this idyllic countryside.

Simultaneously, it dawned on her, she wasn't actually a nobody. She belonged to a world Diana might well crave to be part of, and another bout of irreverent laughter threatened.

Alex sucked in a steadying breath. "Right, Diana, you and I need to talk. It's okay, Reuben..." whose expression was thunderous at Diana's high-handed attitude. "Please, might you be so kind as to make a coffee? Diana, would you like one?"

The older woman nodded absently, Alex winked at Reuben, who threw up his hands in resignation, and stalked off.

Drawing Diana over to the desk, Alex indicated one of the chairs. The woman sat down, fury bristling off her. Without warning, the fight went out of her, and she seemed to deflate.

"Oh God, look at me, I'm the pathetic one. Can't handle being dumped. Seriously, I thought I had it all. Good-looking boyfriend, great job, a fabulous apartment in London, and a house up here in this godforsaken part of the world. I hate it here, you know. I hate the weather and the people and that horrible accent," she shuddered delicately.

"Having Jake made it worthwhile. Yes, okay, I admit it, I was never head over heels in love with him. It's clear he didn't love me, like he obviously loves you, but we had so much in common. We had fun, we enjoyed each other's company, the sex was great. Now what am I supposed to do?"

Her litany of woes finished on a plaintive wail. Alex, resolutely ignoring the remark about great sex… that fell under TMI… although Diana *was* correct, was torn between falling about laughing or pulling the other woman into a hug. She restrained herself from doing either.

"Diana, come on get a grip, look at you, you're a stunner. You've gotta realise, if Jake was besotted with you, he wouldn't have noticed me. There'll be an amazing guy out there, just waiting for you to walk into his line of sight. If you hate it up here, why stay? Ask to be transferred back to London. I'm sure anyone with your expertise would be welcome there. Have you thought about working overseas? What about Engineers Without Borders? Or there's Australia, Dubai, the States. It's a big old world out there — do you know how many sexy cowboys there are?"

Alex rested her hand on Diana's, her emotions sympathetic rather than antagonistic. This woman, who had all but wrecked her relationship with Jake, was hurting. Okay, Diana hadn't handled it well, and was probably, hopefully, mortified by her behaviour, but who was to say she wouldn't have felt the need to lash out had the tables been turned.

The door swung open, and Reuben came in, carrying a tray with three steaming coffees and a plate of biscuits.

"Here," Alex handed Diana one of the mugs, "coffee always helps. It's your life, but maybe on the drive back to Whitby, have a think about those other options. I understand female engineers are in high demand… I bet you could land a job pretty much anywhere."

Diana smiled rather tremulously, and Alex could see the effort her next words cost.

"Thank you. I doubt I'd be as understanding as you've been. I am sorry, truly. It was just that everything was ticking along nicely, then all of a sudden it was as though the rug had been yanked out from under me, and I couldn't keep my feet."

Alex chuckled and said, with a touch of irony. "I know exactly what you mean."

Diana had the grace to blush. Swallowing a large gulp of coffee, she heaved a huge sigh. "I know, I've been a total bitch. I'd have slapped your face if you'd spoken to me like that."

"Oh, believe me, I was sorely tempted... it was that or fall about laughing. You looked like an avenging angel whirling in the way you did. I know you were mad, but it was pretty funny."

The two women looked at each other, and for no reason either could come up with, burst into laughter. Their mirth banishing any lingering tension.

Baffled at their behaviour, Reuben gaped and shook his head over the vagaries of women, but decided it was prudent not to comment. He didn't have much time for Diana, but if she and Alex had settled their differences, who was he to question it? It would make everyone's life a whole lot easier.

Half an hour or so later, Diana took her leave, thanking both Reuben and Alex for their understanding.

"I get it, trust me. Until I met Jake, I assumed I was on the shelf. Things have a strange way of working themselves out, and I wish you the best of luck in whatever you decide to do; but don't sit about waiting for things to happen — go, grab 'em!"

At the front door, Alex followed her earlier instinct and pulled Diana into a hug. She could afford to be generous now; after all, she *had* kinda won. She got her man. A smile playing about her lips as an image of Jake swam through her head.

They watched Diana drive away.

⚬

Reuben turned to Alex, a quizzical expression on his face. "Wanna tell me the heck that was all about?"

Alex grinned, and as they went back to work, told him what Diana said. "I actually felt sorry for her. I mean look at her, she's gorgeous, sophisticated, elegant. I still struggle to believe Jake chose me over her…"

"You aren't still questioning how Jake feels about you?" Reuben interrupted.

Alex shook her head. "No, of course not, but I can see where she's coming from. Jake is drop dead gorgeous, and Diana has everything going for her. Then there's me, I'm just average and it's hard for women to accept what attracts men to us, as individuals I mean.

"You would automatically assume tall, dark, and hand-some men would fall in love with tall, beautiful women, not short, fair-haired mousey women." Her tone indicated she was stating the facts as she saw them, not asking to be contradicted.

"I am endlessly amazed Jake loves me." She shrugged, nonchalantly. Her attention was caught by the pile of notes on her desk, and once immersed in history, all but forgot their conversation.

Reuben, however, didn't forget, making a mental note to mention to Jake he might like to make their engagement offi-cial sooner rather than later.

CHAPTER THIRTY

The following afternoon, Alex decided to take the dogs for a long walk. Reuben and she had worked late into the previous night, leaving her feeling decidedly muggy. Selecting a playlist from the app on her phone, she stuffed her earbuds in, smiling when her favourite music filled her head.

It was a cold, yet sunny winter's day and although pockets of deep snow clung to sheltered spots, it had all but melted everywhere else, revealing extensive swathes of bare moor.

The dogs were ecstatic, lolloping alongside her, leads stretched to maximum. Bruno stayed close to Alex, he rarely left her side, either at home or on these walks. Alex loved his company, glad she could offer the faithful hound some comfort in his elder years.

Coming upon a chunk of rock jutting out of the earth, she sat down. Angling her body backwards to let the sun warm her face, Alex contemplated her life and the events of the past twelve months.

This time last year she was working at a mundane job in Chichester, never expecting for a single moment that within three months everything would change. Being granted the boon of working for Reuben, meeting Jake, visiting Rome, the loss of her parents and everything between. For the first time in longer than she could remember, Alex realised she was happy.

An unusual emotion, happiness.

Until recently, she would have been aghast had anyone suggested she wasn't happy. Watching the dogs messing about in front of her — scrabbling in the undergrowth and rolling in the prickly moss, their antics making her chuckle — Alex acknowledged much of her previous supposed contentment was an illusion. A façade she had created to keep anyone from getting too close. If you appeared cheerful and light-hearted, no one asked questions or pried too deeply.

Together, Jake and Reuben had broken through her barriers. Each in their own way making her feel appreciated, and loved, and part of something enduring.

Grinning, Alex shook off her introspection, untangling the several leads and corralling the dogs. "Come on you lot, less of this nonsense, let's go." The six tramped for another mile or so, then she turned for home.

Alex had reached the edge of the moor, so close to the house she could see the smoke curling up from the chimneys, when something made her turn.

The air was cooling rapidly and, aware she should probably hurry indoors, the scene in front of her held her captive. The sun was dipping beyond the horizon, the last rays shooting up through a crystal-clear sky, their amber glow painting the wild emptiness of the landscape in warm bronze and faded gold.

Enthralled, she watched Venus, the evening star, appear, and was reminded of the night at Lanchester Hall. Slowly, slowly, the sky changed from blue to soft pink, darkening into the most incredible shade of purple in the far distance.

At that moment, the song, the line from which Jake had quoted, started playing through her earbuds, and she blinked away sudden tears. This was the most astonishing display of nature's art and she desperately wished for Jake to be there to share it with her.

Unbeknownst to Alex, Jake had arrived home a day earlier than expected.

Reuben updated his son on the previous day's events., concluding with, "If you give a flying fig about Alex, why isn't she wearing your ring yet?"

Unaccustomed to this type of discussion, Jake's cheeks reddened. "I want it to be unforgettable, Dad. I've got it all planned out. When the weather's better, I'm going to take her over to Fountains. We can have a lovely walk and I can propose again, this time with the ring, in front of the Abbey.

Reuben arched an eyebrow. "Do you really think the place matters? Alex needs to know you're committed to her to the exclusion of all others. Whenever you do it, it will be unfor-gettable. You should go and meet her as she comes down the hill. It looks like the sort of evening when magic happens."

Jake gaped, nonplussed by his father's whimsical turn of phrase. Reuben shrugged, blaming Alex for making him sit through Disney movies and old Hollywood musicals. Jake chuckled, but when he glanced out of the window at the changing light, he decided his father's suggestion might not be the worst idea.

Digging out a thick jacket, he collected a small, dark green velvet box from the drawer next to his bed. Calling to Reuben that he'd be back shortly, Jake hurried into the cool of the evening.

Turning onto the moor path, he saw a familiar silhouette, a motionless figure surrounded by a pack of impatient dogs. They were prancing around, but she didn't seem aware of their presence.

Alex was facing the sunset, so absorbed by the view she didn't hear his approach. That and, the fact she probably had her earbuds in, confirmed when he heard the muted sound floating around her head as he closed the gap. He saw a single tear roll down her cheek and felt his heart clench.

The dogs spotted him, spoiling any chance he had of surprising her. Alex twisted to see what they were straining towards. Her face, albeit slightly shadowed, lit up.

"Jake," she breathed, and yanking out her earbuds, flung herself into his arms. He crushed her to him, kissing her as though it was the first time; heady, intoxicating and achingly sweet. By the time he lifted his head, both were trembling.

He cupped her face, kissed her nose, then slipped his hand into his pocket and knelt on one knee. Alex, assuming he needed to tie one of his shoelaces, was about to step away, but he grasped her hand. She looked down at him in confusion.

"Alex, I know I already asked you once, and I know you said yes, but I wanted the grand gesture, the perfect setting and I had it all planned. A day out, a picnic and maybe a walk, then with a flourish, I would produce a ring. Turns out, anywhere you are is perfect, and I can't wait any longer. Alexandra Mallory, with five canine witnesses and under a starry sky, almost as beautiful as you, would you do me the greatest honour and marry me?"

Alex stood motionless, gawking. *So poised Alex, so poised.* She tried to speak, but nothing came out. The dogs jiffled about, bored with all this romantic nonsense — it was dinnertime what were these humans messing about at? They tugged on their leashes, but Alex didn't, couldn't, move.

Jake opened the dark green velvet box, in which nestled a sparkling gemstone. As the fading light caught it, the colour of the stone seemed mercurial. Was it green or was it red? Any other time, Alex might have stopped to think about it, but Jake was lifting out the ring, his fingers hovering over hers.

"Alex? Please will you put me out of my misery?" His expression, tortured.

Her lips twitched upwards, as a joyous laugh rippled over them.

"YES!" She shouted her acceptance, falling onto her knees next to him as he slid the cool metal over the third finger of her left hand.

She raised her hand, palm out, tilting it this way and that, admiring the simple yet exquisite cut of the ring. She was to discover later the style was apparently called pavé halo with a twisted shank, right then. All she knew was it took her breath away.

"It's an alexandrite," Jake explained. "It mostly looks like an emerald during the day and a ruby at night and is considered rare and valuable…" his voice lowered to a murmur, "… just like you."

"Jake this is the most beautiful ring I've ever seen, and it fits, how on earth did you manage that?"

He laughed, relief making him a little giddy, "I've had it since before you went to Rome. I spotted it in a tiny jeweller's in York, about a week after I first kissed you. I guessed the size, so that was sheer dumb luck."

"There's nothing dumb about it!" She sucked in another breath, the chill air forming little puffs of white gossamer around them.

"Oh my God, Jake, you really want to marry me? I know you asked when we were at the Hall, but I thought... maybe you'd decided..." She trailed off, willing him to tell her she was all he would ever want from now until he drew his last breath. *Yeah, okay, that was a bit possessive, but dammit, she deserved it.*

"Alexandra Mallory, believe me when I say I love you beyond measure. I cannot wait to have you as my wife, to share the rest of my life with you. The ups, the downs, the laughter, and the tears, even your execrable taste in movies and musicals. Any man who deliberately chooses to put up with that must really love you."

He grazed her lips with his, sparking inevitable heat. "Come on, time to go home, these dogs are driving me nuts and I think we deserve at the very least, a glass of Champagne before I whisk you away for a more intimate celebration." The desire in his eyes unmistakable.

"Wait," Alex stopped him as he stood, pulling her to her feet, ready to walk the last few yards to Moorview.

"Jake Faulkner, for the longest time, I didn't think I had the capacity to love someone so unconditionally, okay, to love someone at all. Such emotions were frowned upon and I learned to bury them, I thought beyond recall. Almost from the first time we touched, you somehow broke through, and shattered the ice around my heart. You taught me how to feel again, and the day I realised I loved you was one of the most freeing days of my life.

"I love you more than I ever dreamed it would be possible to love another, and to be lucky enough to have that love returned is a gift I do not take for granted. I promise to love you through the ups and the downs, the laughter, and the tears and that I'll only make you suffer through one or two musicals a week."

Her words were poetic and maybe a little formal, but this last made Jake chuckle, lightening the mood, as she stood on tiptoe to kiss him.

They gathered the dogs and, as darkness enveloped the moor, Jake and Alex went home.

EPILOGUE

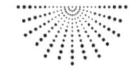

A YEAR LATER

The sky was the most intense cerulean blue, and the air, sharp. A hard frost dusting the spectacular landscape in shimmering white powder, the wintry sun not warm enough to banish the chill. Dressed for the weather, in jeans, chunky jumper, boots, jacket, scarf and gloves, Alexandra Faulkner was gazing in awe at the view from where she stood high above the main path.

She was at Fountains Abbey and had decided to follow the High Ridge track up to Anne Boleyn's seat, or its more popular moniker Surprise View. It was aptly named. Below her, Half Moon Lake, fed by the River Skell as it snaked its way through to the Studley Royal Water Gardens, was like a mirror. The reflections so clear it seemed there was a whole other world just below its glassy surface.

Around the edges, dark-green pine trees softened the stark skeletal shapes of those trees lying dormant, and underneath, scatterings of nodding snowdrops braved the cold, the promise of an early spring.

Alex sucked in a breath. It was so beautiful. It was a shame Jake couldn't be there too, he would love this. Using her phone, she took several photos, pinging a couple to Jake, showing him what he was missing. The light, the colours, the magic this place always wove around her, seemed heightened, as though nature had laid it on, especially for her.

Today was her first wedding anniversary, and she was on her own.

❦

The last year had flown by, what with preparing Reuben's book for publication — released four months previously — and all the promotion surrounding it, they had been frantically busy.

The book had been critically acclaimed and Reuben, in high demand to share his research, was about to embark on a series of guest lectures at major international universities. It was very exciting.

Their research had turned up a few other intriguing threads, which Reuben was inspired to trace, and a new book was in the offing. Although, financially, Alex didn't need to work, ever again, she loved research; ecstatic that Reuben wanted her to continue as his assistant.

Jake's new consultancy was flourishing — an increasing client list and steady influx of contracts, justifying his decision. Thankfully, he rarely travelled now, often working from home, allowing them to spend more time together than most working couples, of which they both took full advantage.

All property and other matters pertaining to the Mallory's estate had been finalised, to everyone's satisfaction and Lanchester Hall, for both tourist and student, was proving popular.

❦

Alex sighed, it wasn't Jake's fault he couldn't be with her, it was a Wednesday, and he was at work. At least, he was in the same county. They planned to go to the local pub for dinner that evening and, later… well later would take care of itself! An impish smile lifting the corner of her mouth.

Rather than have a pity party at being all alone, Alex chose to treat herself to a day out. Fountains Abbey was now her favourite place to visit, she and Jake renewing their National Trust memberships, so they could go whenever they pleased… which was often. As always, Alex never had any qualms about coming on her own if Jake was unavailable.

Snapping a few more photos, Alex slid her phone back into her pocket and made her way down the winding track to the bottom of the hill. Coming out onto De Grey's walk, she paused to watch the river tumbling over the low waterfall, and then continued on to the abbey.

She meandered around the site. There was barely a handful of other visitors on so cold a day, but Alex preferred it this way, nothing to mar the serenity. By mid-afternoon, a stiff breeze began whistling through the nooks and crannies, and Alex deemed it time to head back, before traffic clogged up the roads. She wanted to be home in time to take a hot shower, and pamper herself a little, before the evening.

Hurrying out of the undercroft, aiming for the shorter route back to the car park at Studley Royal, she slammed into a solid object.

"Ooof," she grunted, her feet sliding out from under her on the frosty ground. A hand grabbed her elbow preventing her from falling.

"Lordy, I'm so sorry, I wasn't concentrating on where I was going. Can't think how I didn't see you there." Lifting her head to thank the person who had prevented her from making a complete idiot of herself, her gaze collided with a pair of wonderfully familiar grey eyes.

It was Jake.

Her mouth dropped open in astonishment.

What was he doing here? He was supposed to be at work.

"How on earth…?" She stared at him, a wide grin curving her lips.

"Happy Anniversary, love. Knew I'd find you here."

His smile made her heart thud.

Gathering his wife against him, Jake bent his head, and kissed her until neither was aware of the icy breeze. Feeling Alex shiver, Jake broke their kiss and slung one arm around her shoulders, anchoring her to his side. "Brrrr… it's chilly. I can feel a blazing fire and a hot chocolate calling my name."

"How come you're not at work? Not that I'm complaining, by the way," Alex slipped her arm around his waist as they walked briskly along the path.

"Told them I had more important things to do. They took the mickey for a bit until I reminded them who pays their wages. That shut 'em up, and here I am.

"How did you know I'd be here?"

"You sent me the pic from Surprise View… plus where else would you go on a day like today? Come on, we need to get a move on, or we'll be late."

"It's only the pub, it's not like they don't know us there," Alex puffed, increasing her pace to keep up with Jake's long legs. "Wait up, remember I'm not as tall as you."

"We're not going to the pub. I've got something way better planned."

She stared at him, questioningly, as he slowed to match her shorter stride, noticing his suspiciously bland expression. "Jake?"

"Nope not telling, it's a surprise."

Giving up for now, she quickened her pace, a thrill of anticipation rippling through her.

"Where's your car?" she asked, glancing around, unable to see his dark grey Aston when they reached the car park. Jake grinned as he took the keys to her trusty VW and ushered her around to the passenger side.

"I got a taxi."

Alex gaped. "Bloody hell, Jake that must have cost a fortune."

He shrugged, nonchalantly, "Don't stress, sit back and relax." Soon they were motoring through Ripon, but instead of turning towards Moorview, he took the other road towards York.

"Pleeeeeease, where are we going?" she pleaded, making her eyes as wide as possible and pouting, hoping she looked winsome rather than ridiculous. Jake chuckled, but was not to be swayed, chatting about this and that, until he drew up in a car park at the rear of a small boutique hotel in the centre of the city.

Removing two bags from the boot, he took Alex's hand and led her inside, collecting a key from reception. Clearly this had been set up in advance.

"Please tell me," she implored, as they stepped out of the lift on the fourth floor.

"Still no." He opened the door to a luxurious suite. A king-sized bed stood against one wall and opposite the door, floor to ceiling windows offered a panoramic view over the city, the majestic cathedral towering overhead.

"Wow, this is something else, Jake. A night in a hotel, how exciting." Alex went to the window and stood against the frame, twitching the curtains as she admired the view.

"I have your stuff here. I wasn't sure what you'd want to wear so I brought a couple of choices."

Intrigued, Alex crossed to the overnight case he was

pointing at and unzipped it. She pulled out a forest green woollen dress, a pair of dark grey trousers, and a deep blood red, cowl neck jumper. Underneath these she found her wedge-heeled boots, and a selection of underthings, along with her toiletries.

"You did all this?" Staggered he had been able to find everything she would need.

He nodded. "Hope I remembered everything." He glanced at his watch. "Now go on, you've got half an hour."

Alex kissed him, and dashing into the bathroom, showered and dressed in record time. Twenty minutes later she was ready, opting for the trousers and jumper, arguing they were more comfortable. Shrugging into warm coats, they went down to the lobby and then out on to the street.

The evening was frigid and there was a sour smell to the air, heralding snow. They resumed their earlier conversation, while they walked along, brushing past dozens of people wending their way home after the long workday.

Jake stopped in front of a theatre. Alex waited, unsure why, assuming they were heading to a restaurant, until she spotted the billboard advertising the show.

It was a musical.

It was Guys and Dolls.

"Jake you didn't?" she breathed, beaming an astounded smile at him. "You would sit through this for me?"

"*With* you, sweetheart, and of course I would. It's our anniversary and one of the lines in one of one of the songs is very special." He produced tickets for box seats and handed them to the usher.

From the moment the show began, Alex was riveted. She had never seen this musical, despite loving the songs from it. Jake was content to sit back and watch her reactions. Myriad emotions flickered across her face as the story unfolded, and she silently mouthed the words to every song.

After three standing ovations, the cast came back onto the stage. The actor who played Sky Masterson grabbed a microphone, begging the indulgence of the audience for a few more moments.

Everyone sat down, and the theatre fell quiet.

"Among us tonight we have a very special couple. It is their first wedding anniversary and we are honoured to say a line from one of our songs has personal meaning for them. Without further ado…" he swung his arm, and the cast stepped forward.

Stunned, and more than a little embarrassed, Alex twisted in her seat to raise a quizzical eyebrow at her husband, who grinned and took her hand, kissing her palm. Facing the stage once more, Alex remained transfixed as Sky and Sarah sang the poignant words, the chorus joining in half-way through.

Swept up in the moment, tears poured down her face and she gripped Jake's hand like a lifeline. When the last note died away, the auditorium erupted with cheers and clapping.

Sky ran off the stage and along to their box, handing Alex a huge bouquet of fragrant, pastel hued peace roses. "Congratulations," he murmured kissing her cheek.

This set the audience off again and it was several minutes before everyone calmed down.

Her cheeks glowing, Alex rose to her feet, and in a very wobbly voice, thanked them for such an extraordinary gesture, blowing all those on stage a kiss, and dipping her head to everyone else. Then she sank down onto her seat, face aflame.

"Jake, I cannot believe you did this! Why... how... did you...?" At a loss, she shifted in her seat until she was facing him. Deliberately reaching for his left hand, with her left hand, she entwined their fingers together, until their wedding rings touched, and held his gaze, her smile dazzling. Desire smouldered between them.

"This song says it all and it's true. It *is* you for evermore. I love you, Alexandra Faulkner. Every day we are together is a gift, but today it is especially so, and I wanted to celebrate in a memorable way."

"Well you certainly did that. I won't be forgetting tonight in a hurry." She winked, and a wicked gleam glinted in her eyes. "I love you too, Jake Faulkner, now what do you say we return to that gorgeous hotel and make a few more memories?" Trailing her fingers up his leg, delighting that his breath hitched.

"Why, Mrs Faulkner, are you seducing me?" He rasped.

"Why, Mr Faulkner, I do believe I am. Any objections?"

"Not a single one!" Jake picked up the bouquet and, tucking her against him, hurried to join the rest of the throng heading for the exit.

Outside, snow was falling; delicate flakes muffling the chatter of those spilling into the night. The echoes of a haunting refrain drifting after them, Jake and Alex walked from the theatre and into the rest of their lives. Their hearts safe. The score known.

❧

EXCERPT FROM COBWEB DREAMS

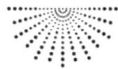

C hloe ate her picnic in splendid seclusion, perched on a rock, resting against her backpack. Happy in her own company, she whiled away a good couple of hours, content to do nothing but stare at the scenery, and maybe doze a little.

Eventually, collecting her stuff and making sure she left nothing behind, Chloe set off back. She didn't hurry, there was nothing wasting, just her and the evening. While ambling along, she pondered dinner. There was a new Italian restaurant close by, and you were always guaranteed a good feed at the Salen Hotel, or she could have beans on toast at the cottage. No decision made, she noticed she was almost at the pull-in where she left Bessie — her car.

Loath to leave yet, she strolled down to the water's edge, and stretched her back — unused muscles already beginning to tighten. A multitude of pebbles, flattened smooth by the constant ebb and flow of the water tumbling them together, crunched underfoot and, suddenly, Chloe had an urge to skim them, a favourite pastime.

Intent on improving her skill, it took her several minutes to register a mewling cry. Presuming it to be a late-born lamb calling for its ewe, she ignored it, exchanging the pebble she was holding for her camera, to take her millionth photo of yet another exquisitely formed purple thistle, which caught her eye.

The crying did not abate, in fact, it seemed to become more frantic. Dropping her camera into her backpack, which she slung over her shoulders, Chloe headed in the direction of the sound.

Backtracking a little way, she soon spotted the cause of the plaintive wail; a lamb, apparently stuck in a boggy bit of ground. It wasn't sinking, but it was definitely panicking, and its mother was standing to one side, her head swinging back and forth in distress. At least, Chloe assumed it was distress.

Glancing along the road, there was not a soul around; not a farmer, a walker or even a passing car, and she knew sheep were apt to wander a fair way from their home farm.

Well, she couldn't leave it, who knew when or, more likely, *if* the farmer would happen by. Thankful she was wearing fast drying, three-quarter, hiking pants, Chloe rolled them up as far as possible, removed her walking shoes, and socks, placed her backpack on the mossy ground, then gingerly slid down to the same level as the two sheep.

Cautiously inching closer, Chloe talked soothingly to the lamb hoping to calm its fear, while at the same time telling herself it was a good job none of her colleagues could see her, this would give them a good laugh. Quiet, mousey, staid Chloe up to her armpits in muck trying to rescue a lamb.

Mud squelched around her toes and crawled up her

calves; she *really* hoped nothing wriggled around her ankles, there would definitely be screaming if that happened. Reaching the lamb, she stroked its woolly head, shuffling until she could get a purchase on its body. Wrapping her arms around its midriff, Chloe pulled — nothing. She tried again, tried several times — nothing, absolutely nothing.

Dammit, the creature was stuck fast.

Taking a breather, she pondered her options. The afternoon was almost over, the summer evenings were long, but the air would cool down fairly quickly and Chloe had no intention of leaving the lamb stuck in a bog all night.

She could try to flag down a car or drive to the nearest house and hope it was the farm to which the lamb belonged, or she could persevere. While she didn't think the lamb would get sucked under — she had not sunk any further than her knees — she was concerned it was vulnerable to birds of prey, or foxes — unsure whether there were any of the latter roaming around on Mull.

Gritting her teeth, she tried one more time and, at last, was rewarded by a squelching sound as the bog began to relinquish its hapless victim.

Beads of sweat formed on her brow, as she heaved and pulled. Inch by painful inch the lamb came unstuck, then, without warning, and accompanied by a sort of loud sucking gulp, the lamb was free.

The suddenness sent Chloe sprawling, and the lamb rolled on top of her. With a 'baaaaa' the creature shook itself, and gambolled over to its relieved mother, the pair trotting off along the grass, without so much as a backwards glance.

Chloe was covered from head to toe in smelly mud. There was no way she could get in the car like that. Shivering a little in the breeze, she glanced at the loch. The sun was still on it, and although she knew it would be icy cold, it was better than getting mud on the car seat.

Decision made, she padded across to the shore, and hurriedly stripped down to her lacy underwear. Trying not to yell with shock when the chill water met her overheated skin, she braved the loch and without pausing to think — for to do so would be to retreat — dived under.

※

A sleek grey car rounded a curve in the road, the driver's eye, catching sight of a head bobbing at the edge of the loch. Thinking it was a seal, he pulled over to watch for a moment, before grabbing his camera to capture the perfect shot of the marine creature in the late afternoon sunlight.

He was startled when the seal stood up and started to wade out of the water. Lowering his camera and shaking his head, sure he was imagining things, the man peered at the figure. It was a woman. A tall, shapely woman, long fair hair streaming across her shoulders, water running down her body in rivulets.

He was mesmerised.

Dominic Winters was a reluctant visitor to Mull. His family owned a holiday house on the island, one they rented out, and, because he happened to be in Oban on business, his mother asked him to check on it.

There was someone booked to rent it at the end of July and, despite an eminently professional letting agent handling it, Mrs Winters had a bee in her bonnet. Dominic grudgingly agreed; it was easier than dealing with her complaints if he ignored her.

Arriving on the island that morning, he checked into the Isle of Mull Hotel at Craignure, then decided to take a drive around the island. It was a beautiful day; he might as well enjoy his stay. Tomorrow, he would inspect the house; there was time enough to organise any required repairs.

He took the long way around, passed Duart castle, skirting Loch Spelve and all the way down to Ffionphort. Parking up, Dominic strolled down to the narrow strait separating Mull from Iona, and sitting on a convenient rock, lunched on a doorstop of a beef sandwich and a cup of piping hot coffee.

Under the bright, late spring sunshine and cloudless azure sky, the water between the two islands was turquoise, glimmering in the light breeze. Seagulls wheeled and turned; their keening cry the only sound to shatter the peace. Surprisingly, on so glorious a day, there were few visitors. Dominic, not one for crowds, preferred it this way, and relaxed with his coffee.

Dawdling back along quiet roads, he turned left at the head of Loch Beg, taking the route which loosely circled the lower western slopes of Ben More — the highest peak on Mull — and on towards Gribun Rocks.

By now it was late afternoon, the roads remained empty, and Dominic indulged his passion for photography by stopping here and there to take pictures of the endless views. He was enjoying himself. To have no real responsibilities, even for a brief while, was liberating — a feeling somewhat alien to him.

It was as Dominic cruised along the edge of Loch Na Keal, in the shadow of Gribun, that he spotted what he assumed to be a seal. His mistake had him squinting in disbelief, when a woman rose out of the loch. Refusing to heed the stories nudging at his brain about selkies, however insistent they were, Dominic lowered his camera a couple of inches and stared unashamedly.

ABOUT THE AUTHOR

Rosie Chapel lives in Perth, Australia with her hubby and three furkids. When not writing, she loves catching up with friends, burying herself in a book (or three), discovering the wonders of Western Australia, or — and the best — a quiet evening at home with her husband, enjoying a glass of wine and a movie.

Website: www.rosiechapel.com

OTHER BOOKS BY ROSIE CHAPEL

Historical Fiction

The Hannah's Heirloom Sequence

The Pomegranate Tree - Book One

Echoes of Stone and Fire - Book Two

Embers of Destiny - Book Three

Etched in Starlight - Prequel

Hannah's Heirloom Trilogy - Compilation – e-book only

Prelude to Fate

Regency Romances

The Linen and Lace Series

Once Upon An Earl - Book One

To Unlock Her Heart - Book Two

Love on a Winter's Tide - Book Three

A Love Unquenchable - Book Four

A Hidden Rose - Book Five

The Daffodil Garden

The Unconventional Duchess

His Fiery Hoyden

A Regency Duet

A Regency Christmas Double

Fate is Curious

A Christmas Prayer with Ashlee Shades

The Lady's Wager

Winning Emma

Fairy Tale Romance

Chasing Bluebells

Contemporary Romances

Of Ruins and Romance

All At Once It's You

Cobweb Dreams

Just One Step

His Heart's Second Sigh

HISTORICAL FICTION

The Pomegranate Tree

Hannah's Heirloom - Book One

Hoping to trace the origins of an ancient ruby clasp, a gift from her long dead grandmother, Hannah Wilson travels to the fortress of Masada with her best friend, Max. Strange dreams concerning a rebel ambush begin to haunt Hannah and following a tragic accident, she slips into the world of Ancient Masada.

A woman out of time, Hannah must rely on her instincts and her knowledge of what will befall this citadel to survive. Will she escape, or is she doomed to die along with hundreds of others as Masada falls – and what does any of this have to do with an ancient ruby clasp?

Echoes of Stone and Fire

Hannah's Heirloom - Book Two

Pompeii - a vibrant city lost in time following the AD79 eruption of Vesuvius. Now rediscovered, archaeologists yearn for an opportunity to uncover the town's past. Some things, however, are best left alone - revealing the secrets hidden beneath the stones could prove perilous. Hannah and Max are brought to Pompeii by a surprise invitation to join an excavation team who are trying to uncover the city's long history.

After entering an excavated house that bears a Hebrew inscription, Hannah's two worlds collide, and she falls back through time to ancient Pompeii. A place where her ancestor is a physician to gladiators engaged in mortal combat, where riotous mobs run amok and where a ghost from the past returns to haunt her.

Will Hannah and her loved ones manage to escape the devastation she knows is coming, before the town is engulfed in volcanic ash?

Will she ever find her way back to Max the love of her life, waiting not so patiently millennia away? Or will echoes be all that remain?

Embers of Destiny

Hannah's Heirloom - Book Three

AD80 - Hannah and Maxentius must embark on a new journey to Northern Britannia. This harsh frontier is far from the comforts of Rome and danger lurks where least expected; a garrison of soldiers, some unhappy with their isolated posting; local tribes, outwardly accepting of their Roman occupier, but who may still resent the seizure of their lands.

Millennia away, Hannah Vallier finds a familiar item while working in a museum near Hadrian's Wall. It is the pomegranate; carved by Maxentius on Masada. Before Hannah can discuss it with Max, disaster strikes! Believing her husband has been killed, Hannah retreats into the past, her soul melding with that of her ancestor, but with little idea of what they could face. Is the risk from the conquered tribes, or much closer to home?

As rebellion threatens to shatter a fragile peace, Hannah's heart whispers that just maybe Max isn't dead and that he is calling her home. Can she trust her heart, or will she remain caught out of time, her destiny floating away like embers on a breeze?

Etched in Starlight

Hannah's Heirloom - Prequel

Maxentius - a Roman soldier fresh from the battlefields of Armenia, arrives to take command of the military outpost of Masada, Herod's isolated citadel in the Judaean desert. A seemingly mundane posting after years of warfare, Maxentius finds it more challenging to maintain a focused garrison than to face the wrath of the Parthians across a disputed frontier.

Hannah - a young Hebrew physician spends her days dealing with injuries from street brawls, deprivation, disease and loss. As her beloved Jerusalem plunges into chaos; her brother — who belongs to a band of rebels determined to drive out their Roman occupiers — tells her of their plans to storm a desert fortress and steal the weapons stored there, persuading his reluctant sister to go with him.

Masada - following the ambush, Hannah finds and treats three badly wounded Roman soldiers. In the aftermath and against impossible odds, Hannah and Maxentius realise that they are more than healer and captive, their fate already etched in starlight.

Prelude to Fate

For Lucia, staring into the jaws of an horrific death, escape seems impossible.

Rufius Atellus, a veteran Roman soldier, is appalled when he recognises one of the victims about to be executed. Surely this is a ghastly mistake?

A ferocious she-wolf, anticipating a tasty meal, suddenly finds herself under a human's control.

In an unexpected twist, and as danger threatens, the lives of all three become inextricably entwined.

Was it chance brought them together in that theatre of bloodshed, or simply a prelude to fate?

Once Upon An Earl

Linen and Lace - Book One

When Fate saw fit to intervene in the life of Giles Trevallier, the very respectable Earl of Winchester, by dropping a female — soaked to the skin and with no memory of who she is or how she came to be there — literally at his feet, no one could have predicted the outcome.

While uncovering her identity, Giles realises he is falling hopelessly in love with his mystery guest, who unbeknownst to him, is succumbing to similar emotions; but, when the heart is involved, a thoughtless word or gesture can thwart even Fate's best-laid plans.

Faced with misunderstandings, whispers of scandal, secret documents and foreign agents, their chance at a happy ever after seems elusive, but fairy tales often happen when least expected, and love — however inconvenient — usually finds a way to conquer all.

To Unlock Her Heart

Linen and Lace - Book Two

Abused by a duke, and shunned by Society, relief seems at hand when Grace Aldeburgh is bequeathed a house in a small village, far from malicious gossips.

Once there, a tentative friendship blooms between Grace and Theo Elliott, the local doctor, who has already resolved to be the man to unlock her heart.

Just when happiness appears to be within her grasp, her erstwhile tormentor once again stalks Grace. After a failed kidnap attempt, the duke's quest culminates in an acrimonious confrontation, and the reason for his venal pursuit becomes agonisingly clear.

Love on a Winter's Tide

Linen and Lace - Book Three

Every day, Helena disappears into a world few acknowledge, helping the poor, downtrodden, and abused. A husband is the last thing she can be bothered with.

Busy managing his shipping line, Hugh Drummond sees no need for a wife, whose only joy is dancing and frivolity. If — and it was a huge if — he ever married, it would be to a woman as capable as he, not some giddy society Miss.

Then, Hugh meets Helena and despite their resolve, fate, it seems, has other ideas. As their attraction deepens however, treachery threatens to tear them apart. Will they uncover the perpetrator in time, or will their love be swept away, lost forever on a winter's tide?

A Love Unquenchable

Linen and Lace - Book Four

Jessica Drummond, a bright and cheerful young woman, rarely gives romance, let alone love, a thought. Long hours working in her brother's shipping office affords little chance of her ever meeting an eligible bachelor.

Duncan Barrington, veteran of the Napoleonic Wars, believes himself wounded in both body and soul. He has no intention of inflicting his demons on anyone, certainly not a beautiful and, in his opinion, irresponsible city lady.

One cold and snowy morning, the plight of a bedraggled puppy throws Jessica and Duncan together and, as a spark of something indefinable yet wholly unquenchable begins to burn, it is unclear who rescued whom.

A Hidden Rose

Linen and Lace - Book Five

After witnessing his mother's grief at the loss of his father, Nick Drummond resolved never to cause someone he loved such distress. Even the happiness of his siblings would not sway him – until he met Rose.

Rose Archer was almost content assisting her doctor father in a tiny fishing village in the north of Yorkshire. To experience the world beyond, a tantalising dream – until she met Nick.

Unexpectedly, the impossible becomes possible, and the renounced – desired above all things, but the shipwreck that brought them together, may yet tear them apart. Will Nick learn to trust his heart, or will his love for Rose remain forever hidden

The Daffodil Garden

Horrifically scarred during the war, William Harcourt - Marquis of Blackthorne - prefers to spend his days in the quiet of his daffodil garden; plants do not pity, turn away, or judge.

Lucy Truscott, whose life is far removed from that of the *ton*, has no idea that by saving the life of a young woman, to whom she bears an uncanny resemblance, her own will be placed in mortal danger.

A chance encounter leads to something more. William begins to trust that Lucy sees the man beneath the scars, while Lucy is persuaded that love might actually transcend status.

Unfortunately, before their courtship has really begun, someone has every intention of ending it - permanently.

The Unconventional Duchess

Refusing to suffer the humiliation of her husband flaunting his mistress at Society events, the newly married Duchess of

Wallingstead, Ella Lennox, takes control of her life. She leaves London for the family's country seat in remote Yorkshire.

A woman alone, Ella spends the next four years turning a cold, grim house into a home, and transforming the fortunes of the estate. Not afraid of hard work, she soon earns the respect of those around her with her determination and unconventional attitude.

Out of the blue, the duke arrives. Resigned to another arduous visit, Ella is stunned when it seems he is attempting to court her.

Impossible!

Could her dream of a happy marriage be about to come true?

Everything hangs on a snowstorm, a herd of cows and an uninvited guest!

His Fiery Hoyden

A Novella

Livvy has no respect for the nobility; they let her down when she most needed them. Why should she accede to their demands now?

Philip, Lord Harrington, is stunned to discover the young heir to the dukedom lives a stone's throw away in a ramshackle cottage, and resolves to restore the child to his birthright.

They meet in a clash of wills, but just when it seems Livvy might surrender, the victory Philip desires, may not taste all that sweet.

A Regency Duet

Luck be a Pirate

Luck wasn't something retired pirate Kennet Alexson believed in – good or bad. However, even he had to concede that landing a job at

Trentams shipyard, and meeting Lynette Collins, was more than coincidence.

Fortune it seemed, was smiling on him for once.

As Kennet adjusts to life on dry land, his friendship with Lynette deepens into something far more enduring, and what once seemed elusive now becomes possible.

Unfortunately, fate has other plans, and Kennet's good luck is about to run out.

The Highwayman's Kiss

Surrendered Hearts – Book One

Nothing exciting had ever happened to Juliette St Clair. Her days were spent assisting her father or calling on friends, wandering art galleries, taking constitutionals or, and more preferably, escaping into her books. Her evenings her evenings — an endless round of balls, where she preferred to remain invisible.

Until the day she was robbed by a highwayman.

A Regency Christmas Double

Heart Rescued

Four years since Jasper lost the woman he was hoping to marry. Four years since he closed his heart and withdrew from Society. He has no idea his reclusive existence is about to be shattered.

Enter his sister's best friend, Harriet, a flame haired beauty, who needs his help.

Reluctantly he agrees and as they spend time together, it is clear their feelings run deep. Although Harriet affects Jasper in a way no woman ever has, he believes her to be out of his league ~ but it's Christmas and she might just be the one to melt his frozen heart

Catch a Snowflake

Romance often blossoms in the most unlikely of places - but in a ward full of wounded soldiers - surely not?

When Lucas Withers comes face to face with Jemima Parsons - a young woman who blames him for her brother's injury - falling in love is the last thing on their minds. What neither of them anticipated, was the magic of snowflakes.

❦

Fate is Curious

A Novella

Happily, ever after? No such thing! Bereft, following her beloved husband's sudden death, Lady Charlotte Sherbrooke has lost her belief in such romantic nonsense.

Successful shipping merchant, Zacharie Romain, is no stranger to loss; his business can be hazardous. Moreover, his wife died in childbirth and even though it happened a decade ago, he has no mind to expose himself to such sorrow again.

They meet in less than joyful circumstances but, as the year turns and grief diminishes, the woes of a small boy become the catalyst for something wholly unexpected. Can Charlotte and Zacharie trust what Fate has in store or will past heartbreak prevent them from taking a chance on love?

❦

A Christmas Prayer

with Ashlee Shades

A Short Story

An entreaty from a frightened child.

Orphaned and only nine, Caroline Thorne has to grow up before her time. She is doing everything she can to keep what is left of her family together and out of the workhouse but is terrified her prayers are not being heard. Or maybe they are...

A petition from a woman desperate for a family.

A chance meeting with three orphaned siblings, tugs at Elizabeth Barrington's heart strings. Thus far, she and her husband have not been blessed with children and, as Christmas approaches, a plan begins to form - one which might just be the answer to her prayers.

Two Christmas prayers, as different as they are the same.

Will they hear and, more importantly, heed the answer?

The Lady's Wager

Surrendered Hearts- Book Two

A Novelette

Ged Mowbray will do anything to avoid being married off to the suitable prospects his parents insist on parading in front of him.

Melissa Bouchard is under no illusion her sizeable dowry is the attraction to suitors, not her.

An overheard conversation leads to an offer too good to refuse, but what happens when a lady's wager, becomes a gamble on the happily ever after, you did not even realise you wanted?

Winning Emma

Surrendered Hearts - Book Three

A Novelette

Randolph Craythorpe — earl, covert operative, and occasional highwayman — believed his dalliance with Lady Felicity Hartwich would lead to marriage. It did, but not to him! The arrival of an unwelcome guest, however, provides the perfect opportunity to indulge in a little retaliation.

Emma Newbury accompanies her cousin, Lady Charity Anscombe, to London for the Christmas season. Once there, she comes face to face with the three men who witnessed the humiliating aftermath of her father's disgrace — one of whom, to her irritation, has taken up residence in her dreams.

Their infrequent encounters only serve to confuse but, while winter tightens its grip on the city, what was inconceivable becomes the one thing for which they both yearn, yet bound by Society's rules, cannot admit.

As the snow falls, Randolph begins to understand that to win Emma, he will have to surrender.

FAIRY TALE ROMANCE

Chasing Bluebells

A Novella

Once upon a time, somewhere in France, there was a man whose reckless obsession led him down a dark path. One which, ultimately, cost him his life.

That ought to have been the end of it. Regrettably, as is so often the case, those who least deserve it, suffer for the actions of others.

A decade after being sent away, Sebastien Daviau returns to the little village where everything began, hoping to lay the ghosts of his childhood to rest, studiously ignoring the possibility, he might run into Charlotte de Montbeliard.

As luck would have it, Charlotte is the one who runs into him... well his horse. Although the encounter leaves a lasting impression, neither recognises the other.

A name revealed causes a freak accident, catapulting Sebastien's past into his present, and bringing him face to face with a man whose reputation would intimidate the most ardent of suitors.

Can whatever is blossoming between Charlotte and Sebastien survive the challenge imposed, or is their happily ever after about to fade as quickly as the bluebells they loved to chase?

❧

CONTEMPORARY ROMANCE

Of Ruins and Romance

Kassandra Winters has intrigued Gabriel St Germain since he accidentally knocked her flying outside her university professor's office. Her face haunts his dreams, yet he never expected to see her again. So, he is surprised when she appears, as though destined to do so, in the middle of a ruin, and he concocts a plan to win her heart.

Gabriel's old-fashioned courtship touches something deep inside Kassie and, although struggling to believe someone as handsome as Gabriel could possibly be interested in her, she soon realises she has fallen irrevocably in love with him. However, just as Kassie shares everything of herself with Gabriel, her world comes crashing down.

Can their romance survive or will it fall in ruins, like the relics of antiquity that brought them together.

All At Once It's You

When Alex arrives in the small village of Rosedale Abbey, to take up a position as a research assistant for a renowned archaeologist, the last thing she is looking for, or expects to find, is love.

Jake was perfectly happy with the status quo. When it came to relationships, he didn't do committed or long term. He called the shots, and if his current flame didn't like it, she knew what to do. A philosophy, which served him well - until he met Alex.

Romance blooms, but even as the untamed wilderness of the North Yorkshire moors weaves its spell, a long-buried secret might yet jeopardise their happily ever after.

Cobweb Dreams

A Novella

A holiday on the Scottish isle of Mull was just the break Chloe Shepherd needed, an escape from her boring office job and her complete lack of anything resembling a social life. Romance, it seems, isn't on the cards and, although Chloe dreams of finding her soulmate she is beginning to believe love is like cobwebs — spun overnight, only to vanish in the early morning breeze.

Under sufferance, Dominic Winters makes a flying visit to Mull to check on a rental property owned by his family. He hasn't got time for this — so indulging in a holiday fling is the last thing on his mind.

A lamb stuck in a bog proves a most unexpected matchmaker and, while Mull weaves its magic, Chloe wonders whether those fragile cobwebs might be far more stubborn than she thought.

&

Just One Step

A Short Story

In the aftermath of an horrific car accident, Daisy Forrester travels to Italy - hoping, so far from her memories, she might begin to heal.

Archaeologist, and single father, Adam Willoughby is too busy looking after his young daughter to give romance let alone love, a thought.

Neither expects a chance encounter in an ancient ruin to be anything more, but sometimes, that's all it takes.

&

His Heart's Second Sigh

A Novella

Reuben Faulkner and Paige Latimer are two happily single people, who have no desire to upset the status quo.

Unexpectedly, they are thrown together, only to discover both want far more than a casual friendship.

Just when things take an interesting turn, Reuben's past catches up with them, and threatens to derail their blossoming romance before it has chance to start.